War of the Squirrels

A Laugh-out-loud Cozy Mystery

Kirsten Weiss

misterio press

Special Offer!

THANK YOU FOR BUYING *War of the Squirrels!* I have a free gift if you'd like to read more funny small-town mystery! You can download *Fortune Favors the Grave*, a novella in my Tea and Tarot series, FREE right here —> Get the Book.

Will Abigail become a hostage to fortune?
    Independent Abigail Beanblossom finally has the tearoom of her dreams, even if it is chock full of eccentric Tarot readers. But when her Tarot reading business partner, Hyperion Night, becomes embroiled in a rival's murder, Abigail discovers that true partnership is about more than profit and loss.

Fortune Favors the Grave is a Tea and Tarot novella exclusive to Raven(ous) Society Members. Join the society and escape into this hilarious caper today.

About War of the Squirrels

HELICOPTER PARENTS, SUSPICIOUS SQUIRRELS... and murder.

All Susan wants is to get through this visit from her controlling parents without tumbling down a black hole of despair. But galactic forces are colliding at her whimsical B&B, Wits' End, and her parents have plans of their own.

When two men die on the same day, both mysterious deaths are tied to her mom and dad. Meanwhile, a squirrel scofflaw is riling up the tiny mountain town of Doyle, and Susan's the only person who can stop the madness. If Susan and friends can't put these crimes to rest fast, her carefully organized life may come crashing to earth.

This fast-paced and funny mystery is book four in the Wits' End series. Packed with quirky characters, small town charm, and murder, it's perfect for fans of Jana Deleon, Tricia O'Malley, and Charlaine Harris.

Get cozy and start this hilarious whodunit today!

Contents

Copyright

The publisher does not have any control over and does not assume any responsibility for author or third-party websites and their content.

misterio press / paperback edition February, 2021

ISBN-13: 9781944767648

CHAPTER ONE

IF THERE'S ANYTHING WORSE than walking in on your parents in the throes of disposing of a body, I don't want to know what it is.

But I'm getting ahead of myself.

Earlier that day, unaware of the disaster unfolding, I bent my head toward my reception desk and pretended this was a normal day.

"Susan," Arsen said gently.

I drew careful diagonal lines through the completed tasks in my planner.

"Susan," my boyfriend said again. "Now you're starting to freak me out."

At my feet, Bailey woofed in agreement. The aging beagle sat on my sneaker to punctuate his argument.

I set down ruler and pencil and straightened in the creaky swivel chair. "What am I supposed to do? My two ex-jailers are arriving any minute. They're going to be watching me like hawks. Any signs of weakness, and..."

He sat on the desk and grasped my shoulder. "First, you're not weak. Second, you're not a teenager anymore. You're an adult. There's nothing they can do if you don't let them." He smiled, his hazel eyes crinkling.

Normally, crinkling hazel eyes would make me melt. This is especially true when they're accompanied by an easygoing personality, square jaw, and killer smile.

But not today.

Arsen thought my parents were simply controlling. And they were definitely that. But there was a lot more to my parents than met the eye. If he knew the truth...

I swallowed. One or both of us might wind up in jail. The US government is particular about breaches of national security.

Car tires crunched in the gravel driveway. My head snapped toward the door, and oh, God, was there something wrong with the Wits' End A/C? Because the room suddenly felt really warm, and I couldn't afford another repair bill.

Arsen stood and smiled down at me from his six-feet-plus height. His muscular form showed off his golf shirt with the logo for his newish security company. "Now let's say hello to your parents."

"And give up my tactical advantage?" I gripped the edges of the battered wooden desk. The reception area was my space. And the desk provided a solid barrier to hide behind. True, the rows of alien bobbleheads on the nearby shelves didn't exactly scream *authority figure lives here.* But from the right angle, this desk could stop a bullet.

"These aren't war maneuvers," he said.

"Yes, Arsen. Yes. They are."

He rubbed his chin. "I could divert them with my airplane barf bag collection."

"Don't you dare." If my parents had bothered to collect any, they'd probably be able to beat him. They'd put on some serious miles over the course of their careers. I hesitated. "But... if you told them you used to be a Navy—"

"No," he said flatly. "I'm not going to use that to impress them or anyone else."

I sighed. "I guess that's fair." He'd only told me about his time in the military recently. The rest of Doyle thought he'd spent his time away as a dive instructor at various exotic resorts. I was still a little irked I'd fallen for his fib. But he had the right to his secrets.

I certainly had my own skeletons in the closet.

Arsen sketched a lazy salute. "Then I'll man my station and execute the plan."

Outside, two car doors slammed.

I grabbed my pencil and clutched it like a weapon. "That might not even be my parents. It could be another guest. I wouldn't go running outside to greet a random guest. It would look desperate."

His tanned forehead creased. "Do you have any other guests checking in today?"

The porch's first screen door screeched on its hinges.

"I don't know," I said, biting my lip. "Let me just check my planner." I flipped it open to the calendar section.

The interior screen door opened, and my father walked in. Sparse and unassuming, his gray eyes blinked like an owl's behind his thick glasses.

He looked around the foyer, at the faux Persian carpet, at the colored light through the stained-glass transom falling across its fading shag, at the green-carpeted steps leading upstairs.

"This old place hasn't changed a bit," he said. "Hello, Susan."

I rose, gripping my pencil. "Hi, Dad."

My mother strode into the foyer. Her dowdy green skirt and oversized blouse made her appear well-padded rather than well-muscled. But I knew better.

Her nose wrinkled. "I thought you would have made *some* improvements. That ridiculous UFO is still in the roof. How do your neighbors stand it?"

Bailey shrank behind the desk and pressed against my ankle.

"Hi, Mom," I said. "And we *are* a UFO-themed B&B."

Arsen stepped forward, hand outstretched. "Hi, Mr.—"

"Do you have any neighbors who drive a blue Honda Civic?" my mother asked. She rattled off a license plate number.

"No," I said. "Why?"

Arsen and my father shook hands.

"There was one abandoned by the roadside not far from here," she said. "I thought they might have had car trouble."

"They probably stopped to hike," Arsen said. "Hello again, Mrs. Witsend."

My mother's eyes narrowed. "So. You and Susan are still seeing each other, I take it?"

"Yep." He grinned. "Susan can't get enough of me."

My face warmed with embarrassed pleasure.

"Can I help with your things?" Arsen continued.

"They're in the Audi," my father said. "And yes, you can give me a hand. I think my wife packed lead bars in her suitcase. You know women." He chortled and walked outside.

Arsen followed, and the screen door banged shut behind him.

Pointing at my mother, I walked around the desk. "You don't really care if someone abandoned their car."

"Of course not," she said. "But I'm certain we were being followed by one."

I stiffened. "Followed to Doyle? By a blue Civic? Why would anyone follow you... here?"

She rolled her eyes. "If I knew that, I wouldn't be asking about the car, would I?"

"But—"

"Smile and keep up appearances, Susan. Everything is fine." She sauntered out the front door.

My jaw tightened. *Fine?* How could she…? I breathed deep and forced a smile. And kept up appearances.

I walked onto the porch and stopped beside my mother at the top of the steps.

Morning sun shot streamers across the eastern mountaintops, still gilded by snow though it was June. Roses danced along the picket fence. A Sierra breeze scented with pine fluttered their blossoms.

"Careful with that blue one." She pointed at Arsen, hefting a blue suitcase onto his shoulder.

"Why?" I tried to joke. "Is it going to explode?"

She shot me an annoyed look. "You know we don't work with explosives," she whispered. "Not unless we have to. And certainly not while on vacation. Thank you, Arnold," she said more loudly.

"Arsen," I gritted out. "You know his name is Arsen."

"Sorry," she trilled. "*Arsen.*"

"No worries," Arsen said, striding toward us.

A pine branch at the end of the drive drooped, and a squirrel hopped from it onto the picket fence. The branch snapped upward, swaying.

A mighty howl sounded from inside the B&B.

"What on earth?" My mother began to turn.

A blur of brown and fawn barreled between her legs.

My breath caught. "Bailey, no!" I shouted.

My mother stumbled, teetering on the edge of the porch step.

Arsen dropped the suitcase and bolted forward, his arms extended to catch her.

My mother pivoted like a ballerina, then straightened. Unruffled, she smoothed her skirt. "I asked you to be careful with that suitcase."

Arsen stopped beside the bottom step. "Sorry, I thought... Are you okay?"

"Of course I'm okay." She scowled at Bailey, barking frantically at the squirrel. It raced back and forth on the fence, taunting, out of the beagle's reach. "Maybe you should show us to our room, Susan?"

"Oh. Right." Returning inside, I grabbed the key card I'd prepared. I handed her the thin piece of plastic. "You're in room five, upstairs."

"*All* the guest rooms are upstairs," she said. "Telling me ours is upstairs is redundant, don't you think?"

"Right. Sorry. I'm so used to my spiel to new guests—"

"And where is my niece?"

"Dixie?"

"I only have the one," she said.

"Right. She's uh, not here." *Lucky Dixie.* My cousin had gone into hiding when she'd realized today really was the day my parents arrived. Dixie had a strong sense of self-preservation.

"How typical." My mother sniffed and marched up the narrow stairs.

Looking contrite, Arsen walked in with her suitcase on his shoulder. "Room five?"

I scurried around the desk and brushed bits of gravel off the suitcase. "Go on up," I muttered, "if you dare."

He nodded and carried the suitcase upstairs.

Puffing, my father staggered in a minute later, dragging a yellow suitcase behind him. "I don't suppose this old Victorian had elevators installed since I was last here?"

I shook my head. He was laying the frail-old-man schtick on a little thick, especially since Arsen was upstairs and out of sight.

"All right then." He huffed up the steps.

I forced my hands to unclench. I could do this. It was only a week, and my parents were on *my* territory.

But a cold shadow touched my shoulder blade, and I shivered, shrugging it off. I wasn't going to fulfill my parents' expectations and have an anxiety attack. Not now. *One step at a time.*

I studied my planner. Next on my agenda was writing this week's B&B blog. I could have put it off, but I'd been careful to book my afternoon with excuses to evade my parents.

Arsen jogged downstairs. "Your dad wasn't kidding about that suitcase. What did your mother pack?"

"Armaments, most likely," I said, glum.

He laughed. "Sure." Arsen checked his massive dive watch. "Hey, I've got to meet a new client downtown, and I was hoping to get in a bike ride. Your parents said they were up for a night hike. That work for you?"

I checked my planner. "My evening's free." I'd planned that too, because I couldn't avoid my parents forever. Though maybe a smarter play would have been to pack it full of activity.

"Awesome." He bent and kissed me, then kissed me again, longer and slower. He smelled of soap and pure Arsen. And despite the horror of my parents' arrival, my insides warmed.

"You've got this," he said. "I'll see you tonight."

"Bye." I watched him leave, then glanced at the ceiling. My stomach rolled. Why was—? I shook my head.

No, I did *not* want to know why my mother's suitcase was so heavy. They were on vacation. She could pack what she wanted.

I got to blogging.

My parents trooped downstairs. They grabbed a map of Doyle from the rack by the door and informed me they were going shopping.

"What are you doing?" my mother asked.

"Blogging." Feigning regret, I pointed at my planner. "Got to get it done today."

She shook her head and walked outside.

"People still blog?" my father asked and followed her.

I slumped in my chair. It squeaked rudely.

I'd done it. I'd gotten through my first encounter with my parents since Gran's funeral. They hadn't bossed me around, and no one was dead.

I could get through the week. Of course I could get through the week. I was a Witsend, and Witsends are made of stern stuff.

Feeling cheerier, I outlined my blog. I drafted my blog. I wrote and rewrote my blog. And when it was done, I found the perfect photo to go with it and posted my blog.

Done.

I checked my planner. Next up, housekeeping. I frowned. Dixie still hadn't made an appearance, which meant I'd have to do her share as well. Honestly, my cousin would have to face my mother at some point.

I vacuumed and dusted and scrubbed. While I was cleaning the windowsills in the octagonal breakfast room, my parents returned.

I stuck my head into the foyer, but they were already halfway up the steps to the second floor.

And since discretion really *is* the better part of valor, I edged backward into the breakfast room and finished up.

Silently cursing the absent Dixie, I bumped the heavy vacuum cleaner up the stairs. It was nearly five. The cleaning was taking me twice as long as it should have without Dixie's help. Though in fairness, I *had* spent a lot of time on that blog.

I vacuumed the long, green hallway and dusted the UFO photos lining its walls. Retrieving the cleaning bucket and supplies from the upstairs closet, I started toward the end of the hall.

Bailey's collar jingled behind me, and I turned. The beagle huffed upstairs and sniffed the bucket.

"Thanks for making the trek. I could use some company." I bent and ruffled the dog's fur.

I tackled the rooms at the end of the hall, knocking on doors and working my way forward.

At room seven, I paused to shift the bucket to my other hand. The room was empty, so I opened the door without knocking and stepped inside.

My father clung to the lower part of a man's black-clad leg, shoe pressed to my father's ear. The rest of the dead man—and he *was* dead, he had to be dead—dangled out the open window.

The man's Hawaiian shirt rucked down, exposing a Kydex holster between his pants and his skin.

CHAPTER TWO

As if my fingers were far, far away, I felt my hands loosen. I dimly heard my cleaning bucket of brushes and other supplies thud to the carpet in room seven.

Bailey howled and raced from the room, his ears flapping. And who could blame him? The room itself seemed to revolt at the scene. Even the faked pie-tin UFO photo hung at an awkward angle above the rumpled bed.

Early evening shadows knifed across my mother's sensible shoes. She sat in a vintage wing chair in one corner of the room. "Shut the door," she commanded and removed the clip from a Russian pistol.

Automatically, I obeyed.

Mouth slack, I backed against the door. "You... That's..." My breath came in quick gasps. Dots swam in front of my eyes. This wasn't my first body in the B&B. But...

The leg slipped in my father's grip, the shoe inching closer to his shoulder.

Briefly, I wondered if this was what lost time felt like, this sense of being out of phase, outside ordinary reality. Unthinking, I groped for my day planner. But of course it wasn't there. I didn't carry it around when I cleaned.

Should I?

No, that was nonsense. My head cleared. *Of course.* I was finally having that psychotic break.

Warm relief flooded my veins. I'd been bound to crack up at some point. The sheriff had once warned me I was delusional. I didn't think I was, but wasn't denial a sign of insanity?

My mother set down the gun. Her expression pinched. "Hank, it's happening again. Help her."

He let go of the leg. The body thudded unpleasantly onto the shingled overhang, outside.

In three steps my father was at my side. He seized me hard by the elbow, and sat me on the bed. My father grasped the back of my neck and bent me forward in an iron grip. "Head between your knees, Susan."

I didn't struggle. There wasn't a whole lot of point. "My planner," I gasped, staring between my flats at the throw rug.

"No," my father said, "it *wasn't* in the plans."

I groaned. "This wasn't how your visit was supposed to go."

"I know," my mother said. "You made your expectations crystal clear. How did you put it? We weren't supposed to treat you as a child anymore, but as an adult? Well, this is our adult world. Congratulations, you're in it."

My father released me, and I sat up.

"That wasn't what I meant." I wasn't a spy. This had never been my life. I'd *never* wanted this.

My mother laid the gun on the desk and propped her head on her fist. "That's life."

"It's not—" I pointed to the window. "He's dead." My hands bunched in the fabric of my navy capris. "You killed a man. In my B&B!"

"Not a man, an assassin," my mother corrected.

"Why is there a dead assassin in my B&B?" I asked.

"Now, now, don't dwell." She glanced at my father. "She always was a dweller, wasn't she, Hank? That's why you have those anxiety attacks, Susan."

His brow wrinkled. "You *can* get a bit obsessive, Sue."

"There's a dead body in my B&B," I whined and hated myself for it. But under the circumstances, who could blame me? My gaze darted toward the closed door.

My father glanced at the window. "Technically, he's no longer *in* your B&B."

The emerald curtains waved a mournful farewell.

"And don't whine." My mother examined her nails.

"He's *dead*," I said.

"It was self-defense," my father said.

"He wasn't a very nice man," my mother said.

"And he didn't give us much of a choice," my father agreed.

"He was Russian," my mother said.

I gripped my knees tighter. "What does that have to do with anything?"

"I believe his accent was Crimean," my father corrected.

I gaped. "A Crimean assassin?" That sort of explained the empty holster and the Russian gun. But... *here?* "In Doyle?"

My father knelt in front of me, adjusted his glasses, and gazed into my eyes. "Are you feeling better, darling?"

"I told you she shouldn't have moved to such a small town," my mother said. "Doyle's done nothing for her mental health."

"A body in my B&B is doing nothing for my mental health," I snapped.

"What about Doctor Feinberg?" my mother asked. "She's done excellent work with anxiety disorders."

Hunching, I rubbed my upper arms, chilled. "There's nothing disordered about feeling anxious after someone's been killed in your home."

"Doctor Feinberg only works with agency employees," my father said to her.

"Why?" I asked more loudly. "Why kill him?" My parents' "business" had always taken them overseas. They weren't *allowed* to work stateside. I think it's unconstitutional.

"I told you," my father said patiently. "It was self-defense."

"But why did you have to defend against anything *here*?" Wits' End, my UFO-themed B&B, was in a small town in the Sierra foothills. What did we have to do with assassins?

My father grimaced and glanced at my mother. "That's an excellent question."

"One someone will answer to," my mother said, grim.

"But—"

My mother stood. "Now straighten your hair, put on a smile, and go outside and pretend everything's just fine, because it is." She handed my father a business card. "Take a look at this."

"But—"

My father steered me out the door. "Do as we tell you. There's a good girl."

"But—"

"No buts," he said. "This is dangerous knowledge, Susan. It's up to you to keep this secret and everyone safe. National security, you understand. You've done it in the past. You can do it again." He handed me my cleaning bucket and shut the door in my face.

My legs trembled. A chill touched my left shoulder. Fists clenched, I closed my eyes, willing the shadow away. But the shadow—my anxiety—was always nearby, always waiting to drag me down. And this... this...

And why did my mother have a business card for the Historic Doyle Hotel, my B&B's archrival? Could she have taken it off the assassin's body? It made sense. Even assassins had to spend the night somewhere, and the Historic Doyle Hotel had once hosted the outlaw Black Bart.

"I am calm and in control," I muttered, though I patently wasn't. My heart was racing. My head felt floaty. My breath came too fast.

Why now? Why me?

Spy parents aren't as fun and exciting as they might sound. As soon as I'd been born, I'd become part of their cover. And to keep control of their cover, they'd meticulously controlled *me*.

Now, as an adult, I understood they'd been trying to protect me. But the rational mind and the emotional mind don't always see eye to eye.

A whimper sounded in the hallway, and for a moment I thought it had come from me. Then I looked down.

The beagle stared up at me from the green carpeting, his doggy eyes wide with worry.

"It's fine." My voice came out somewhere between a whisper and a gulp. "I'm sure the action was completely legal." My parents had always been scrupulous about legalities. After all, they'd sworn an oath. "Everything's fine."

"What's fine?" a masculine voice boomed from behind me.

I yelped, jumped, and turned to face Arsen in an ungainly pirouette. "What are you doing here?"

"Whoa," Arsen said. "I didn't mean to startle you. I was just looking for your parents." He stared pointedly down at my cleaning bucket. "We were supposed to go on a night hike, remember? I thought we could grab dinner first."

He'd changed into a fresh shirt and pair of khakis. The ends of his whiskey-colored hair were damp, so I guessed he'd gone for his bike ride and showered before returning. How had time passed so quickly?

"Everything's fine," I blurted, too loud.

His bronzed brow creased. "I know. I mean, I guess I'm a little early, but—"

"My parents can't come."

He grinned. "Just you and me then? Even better. No offense to your parents."

Something thumped inside room seven, and I stiffened.

"Is someone in there?" Arsen pointed his thumb at the door.

"No. That's why I just cleaned it. A new guest is coming in tomorrow, and I wanted to give it an extra freshening."

"I thought I heard—"

"Sorry, tight schedule." I turned and bustled to the stairs, hoping Arsen would follow. Thankfully, he did.

"Is everything okay?" He picked up Bailey, who has trouble going down steps.

"Everything's fine."

"Yeah, but you don't seem fine. You seem stressed. Is it your parents?" he said in a low voice. "Look, I don't care if they like me or not, or want to spend time with me or not. Your parents don't scare me."

They should. Though Arsen was an ex-Navy SEAL, I really didn't want to see the man I loved pitted against my parents. That would be awkward. "Everything's fine."

He set Bailey on the foyer's faux-Persian rug and touched my arm. "Now I know something's wrong. That's the third time you've told me *everything's fine.* Is this more of your positive self-talk?"

"No, I just..."

Arsen cocked his head.

"You're right," I said. "It's my parents."

"I knew it."

"I wish they hadn't come," I said fervently.

He rested his strong hands on my shoulders. "You've got this. You're a grown woman with a successful business."

"Not that successful," I muttered. I still wasn't sure how I'd pay for the new roof the B&B needed.

"The point is, you can do what you want. They can't control you anymore."

"Right." I nodded like a bobble head. "Right. I've got this. And I need to prep for tomorrow's breakfast."

Meal prep actually *wasn't* on the schedule. I'd planned on doing the prep work after our hike. But cooking soothed me, and if I didn't keep busy with something, I'd break and tell Arsen about the body on the roof.

And knowledge was dangerous. A lead weight pressed on my lungs, and I hugged my arms.

I hurried to the kitchen. Bailey and Arsen followed at a more leisurely stroll.

Bailey trotted to his bed beneath the kitchen table. The beagle turned three times and collapsed into the aqua cushion.

I beelined for the fridge and pulled out ingredients for tomorrow's breakfast enchilada casserole. *Normal, normal, normal. Everything's normal.*

Something scraped above us. I looked up, a carton of eggs in my hands. Bailey lifted his head.

"So what are your parents up to?" Arsen sat at the table and stretched out his legs.

"Oh. Ah. You know." Warmth flushed my cheeks.

Arsen pinked a little too. "Don't tell me you walked in on them?"

"It was awful," I whisper-croaked.

He grimaced. "I can imagine."

Wait. He could? Slowly, comprehension dawned. He thought they'd been... My face flamed hotter. I set down the eggs and pulled two from the carton.

Outside, there was a soft thump.

I sucked in a breath and imagined the body falling onto my grandmother's rose bushes. My fist clenched, crushing the egg. Yellow goo spattered across the front of my blouse, the butcher block counter, the white subway tile backsplash.

Bailey leapt to his feet and howled.

Arsen stood, panther-fast, and whipped a dish towel from the modern oven. "Whoa there. Careful." He handed me the towel, and I blotted at the mess.

Bailey raced through the doggy door and onto the porch.

"Your parents really have got you tense." Gently, he massaged my shoulders.

I leaned against him, my muscles loosening at his touch.

A feeling of safety and wholeness flooded my chest. This was going to be okay. My parents were professionals. The government would send a cleanup team. Everything would be perfect again by morning. Everything really would be fine.

Outside, Bailey bayed, a cry that raised the hair on my arms.

"Something's wrong." Arsen made a move toward the kitchen door.

"No, wait." I grabbed his wrist, missed, and caught his hand instead. He'd see the corpse. My parents couldn't have possibly moved it by now. "It's only another squirrel."

"What's with Bailey and the squirrels? They never bothered him before."

"I've got no idea. He used to like squirrels. Maybe it's like an allergy that develops later in life?"

He rubbed the back of his neck. "I know this dog psychologist—"

Bailey loosed another Hound of the Baskerville's cry.

"It sounds like he's hurt." Arsen stepped toward the kitchen door.

Bailey's head shot through the doggy door, his shoulder jamming against its edge. The beagle wriggled through and bolted between Arsen's legs.

"There he is." I trotted across the kitchen. "Bailey's fine."

The beagle raced across the linoleum floor and through the open door to my private parlor.

"See?" I said. "Everything's fine."

My hands shook a little as I finished prepping the casserole. Hoping Arsen hadn't noticed how uneven my enchiladas were, I covered the dish in aluminum foil and stuck it in the refrigerator.

The foyer door opened. I hop-stepped backward, banging the refrigerator door shut with my hip.

Sheriff McCourt, her blond curls quivering beneath her wide-brimmed hat, strode inside. "Good. You're here." The sleeves of her uniform shirt were rolled to her elbows, all business.

"Hey, Sheriff." Arsen waved, nonchalant.

She nodded to him. "Are your parents in, Susan?"

"My parents?" A bead of sweat trickled down my forehead. "Why do you ask?"

She fixed me with a steely gaze. "I'm here about a murder."

CHAPTER THREE

I COLLAPSED AGAINST THE counter. "Murder?" I squeaked. "What would my parents know about murder?"

Oh my God. The window. My new neighbor must have seen them dump the body and reported it. The room seven window was right in her cabin's line of sight.

"They were seen arguing with the victim earlier today," Sheriff McCourt said. She laid her hat on the kitchen table and ruffled her Shirley-Temple curls.

I studied the kitchen's linoleum floor. My parents had been arguing with the assassin? In front of witnesses? How could they have made such an amateurish mistake?

"Who was the victim?" Arsen asked.

The sheriff turned to me. "And I want to make this clear. I do not—I repeat, *do not*—require your assistance in any way. Aside from getting your parents down here so I can question them."

"Question them?" I plucked a dish towel from the counter and wrung it between my hands. This was awful. Terrible. Really, *really* bad.

"Talk to them," she amended.

A metallic creak sounded outside my kitchen window.

The sheriff turned to the porch door and frowned.

"It's okay," Arsen said. "I'll go upstairs and knock on your parents' door."

"No," I said. "I'll—"

He stood and patted my shoulder. "You've been traumatized enough." He strode out the door into the foyer area.

"Traumatized?" the sheriff asked.

"I, uh, walked in on them."

The sheriff flinched. "Ouch."

"You have no idea." I cleared my throat. "So this, um, murder. I suppose someone called to report a missing person?" And *not* that they'd seen a body fly out my upstairs window. Because if my neighbor was a witness—

"He's not missing. He's dead. Why do you think I got here so fast?"

I blinked. "You mean, you've seen the body?"

"Of course I've seen the body."

My thoughts jumbled. The sheriff had come through from the front, not the side yard, where the body had landed. Something wasn't right. "Who did you say was killed?"

She braced her hands on her utility belt. There was enough equipment weighing her slim hips to form a blackhole. "I didn't," she said.

Hope rose in my chest. "No, but seriously. Who was it?" I knew she'd tell me eventually. The sheriff liked to pretend I was a nuisance, but she'd brought me in to assist on lots of cases.

In our last, I'd had one of those dark-night-of-the-soul moments people talk about. I'd been certain I'd imagined our friendship, and she didn't want my help at all. But then she'd asked me to step in to quell a UFO panic.

She'd needed me. Of course she had, and she still did. This was a small town, but people could be wary of the law. Lips were looser around innocent innkeepers.

Sheriff McCourt sighed. "Mr. Van Der Woodsen."

"You mean the old guy up on the hill?" I asked. That couldn't have been the body in room seven. My father would have had a much easier time lifting him through the window.

"Yes," she said dryly. "The old guy up on the hill."

My face heated. Van Der Woodsen was much more than an old guy. He was a famous writer of spy thrillers.

My parents hated them.

"And you have the body?" I asked.

"Of course I have the body. Why wouldn't I have the body?"

"No reason." Relief oozed through my bones, and I dropped into a chair beside the kitchen table. My parents weren't wanted for the body in my garden.

At least, I assumed it was somewhere in my garden. My grip tightened on the dishtowel. Where *was* the body?

My breath caught. Unless they'd killed *two* people in Doyle. But old Mr. Van Der Woodsen couldn't have been a foreign spy or assassin. So why *had* they been arguing with him?

Could he have been a Nazi war criminal in disguise? He might have been old enough, but only if he'd been in the Hitler Youth. Did Nazi hunters go after ex Hitler Youth?

The sheriff snapped her fingers. "Earth to Susan."

"What?"

"I asked when your parents returned to the B&B this afternoon."

Uh, oh. Was I their alibi? I licked my lips. "I don't exactly know."

Her blue eyes narrowed. She folded her arms and leaned against the butcherblock counter. "You keep the most detailed planner of anyone in Doyle, and probably all of California."

I reached for my planner on the kitchen table and pulled it closer. "I plan *my* life, not other people's." That would just be rude. "I was cleaning, but the cleaning had run late because Dixie's not here—"

"Where's Dixie?"

"No idea." But knowing my cousin, she was up to no good. I drummed my fingers on the table. "The point is, I'm not sure exactly what time they got back. Before five though." I opened the leather-bound planner and flipped to a note page. "All right. Let's construct a timeline. When was the body discovered?"

"Three—" The sheriff shook her head and straightened off the counter. "We're not collaborating. Unless you can tell me when your parents returned to the B&B, or have any intel on who's been posting those squirrel flyers around town, I don't want to hear it."

A yowl erupted from my parlor, and I winced.

"Squirrel flyers?" I whispered, so Bailey wouldn't overhear.

"It's more UFO baloney."

"Alien squirrels?" I asked, puzzled, and sat back in my chair. What did squirrels have to do with UFOs?

"Never mind. And why are you whispering?"

"Bailey has excellent hearing. What do UFOs have to do with squirrels?"

"*Flyers* about squirrels, alien squirrels. It's ridiculous. There's no such thing as aliens, much less alien squirrels. But I've had six complaints about those flyers today."

Bailey pushed through the parlor door and growled at the sheriff. His dislike of squirrels was recent, his dislike of uniforms long-standing.

I scooped the beagle into my lap before he could make more trouble. "I don't get it. Why are people complaining about a flyer?"

"They're illegally posted." She shook her head in disgust, her curls swaying. "And a few people are worried about possible squirrel influence."

"Influ—?"

Bailey barked furiously and scrabbled toward her. I tightened my grip.

"What does that even mean?" I asked.

"Hell if I know. But this town is crawling with squirrels."

Bailey barked some more, and I shushed him.

"I just don't want another panic," the sheriff shouted over his barks.

"Maybe I can help. UFOs *are* my specialty. I mean, how many people have one in their roof? Well, it's a fake UFO, but you know what I mean. If there's talk about alien you-know-whats—"

"I'll call the Forest Service. Squirrels are plague carriers. People should be more worried about disease, but—"

My parents breezed into the kitchen, Arsen trailing behind them, and Bailey fell silent.

"Sheriff," my father said heartily. "Arsen told us you have some questions?"

Sheriff McCourt stood and shook hands with my parents. "Let's start with something easy. What brought you to Doyle?"

"Susan's birthday's coming up." My father beamed at me. "We wouldn't miss that."

The sheriff grunted. "You were seen arguing with Mr. Salvatore Van Der Woodsen early this afternoon."

"At the spice store," my father agreed. "Yes."

"What time was this?" she asked.

"Around one I'd say, wouldn't you agree, Pansy?" he asked.

Interesting. If the body had been discovered at three something, Van Der Woodsen must have been killed between one and the time of discovery. Though the sheriff had never finished saying exactly what time the body had been found.

"Yes," my mother said. "We walked there after lunch. I bought one of those salt cutting boards."

"It weighs a ton." My dad laughed. "You could club someone to death with the thing."

I winced. This was *not* the time for jokes about murder.

"Can you tell me what the argument was about?" the sheriff asked.

"Mr. Van Der Woodsen was a horrible, rude man," my mother said hotly. "And his books are atrocious."

"Oh?" the sheriff asked.

"Everyone thinks spies are flashy martini-swilling sex machines," she said. "But it's complete balderdash. Spies have to look like ordinary people to blend in. His books are garbage."

"And all those explosions and gun fights and car chases," my father said. "Complete nonsense. Most spy work is simply talking to people and trying to turn them. Anyone who's been to that spy museum in DC would know that."

"And that's why you argued?" the sheriff asked. "Over a book?"

"I thought our literary critiques were fairly civilized until he struck my wife in the ankle with his cane," my father said. "I may not be the perfect husband, but one doesn't let that sort of thing go."

The sheriff blinked. "He hit you?"

My mother stuck out her ankle and tilted it this way and that, showing off a slim red mark. "It stung like nobody's business."

"And Mr. Witsend, you then...?" the sheriff raised her brows.

"Told him that if he didn't leave immediately, I'd take that cane and shove it right up his—"

"An anatomical impossibility," my mother said quickly. "But it was merely a colorful way to make a point."

The sheriff arched a brow. "The point being...?"

"Don't hit my wife," my father growled.

"And then?" the sheriff asked.

"And then he left," my father said.

"What was Mr. Van Der Woodsen doing in the spice shop?" I asked.

Everyone turned to stare at me.

I coughed, tingling sweeping up the back of my neck. "Well, doesn't he have that butler to do his shopping?"

"They have excellent balsamic vinegars and dry rubs," my father said.

"Yes," I said, "but—"

"Don't mind Susan," my mother said. "She's always been inquisitive, but sometimes she doesn't know when to stop."

I clamped my mouth shut, heat flushing my chest and neck. It was one thing for them to boss me around. It was another thing for them to do it in front of my friends.

"I think Susan goes exactly as far as she needs to," Arsen said mildly, and I shot him a grateful look.

"And what time did you return to Wits' End?" the sheriff asked my parents.

"Oh," my mother said, "I think it was around two, wasn't it Susan?"

"I'm not sure," I said. But I thought it had been later than two. Why were they lying?

"But you were right there," she said.

I folded my arms, my jaw jutting forward. "I was cleaning. I wasn't paying attention to the time."

"Really?" My father rubbed his chin. "I suppose you were rather involved in your work when we walked in."

But what was I doing? I couldn't let the sheriff think they had no alibi. Then she'd just nose around more. "Oh," I said, "you know, I think you're right. Maybe it was around two o'clock."

The sheriff raised a brow. "Really?"

"Yes," I said, "definitely."

Arsen frowned.

"And where were you for the rest of the afternoon?" the sheriff asked them.

"Here, in the B&B," my mother said.

"I'm afraid we've got no alibi, if that's what you're angling for," my father said gaily. "We can only alibi each other, and since we're married, I suppose that's not much good."

The sheriff slipped her notebook into a holder on her belt. "What do you two do for a living? Susan never said."

"We're forensic accountants," my mother said.

Emphasis on forensic. I glanced toward the white ceiling.

"For a private firm," my father said.

"Fascinating." The sheriff returned her broad-brimmed hat to her head. "Well, thank you both. If I have more questions, I know where to find you."

I saw Sheriff McCourt to the front door.

She paused, one hand on the screen door. "Just because I questioned your parents, doesn't give you the right to interfere with my investigation."

"Of course not." I *never* interfered.

I assisted.

Her cornflower eyes narrowed. "And in case that wasn't clear enough, stay out of my investigation. You're not a detective."

"I don't think who is or isn't a detective is really the issue here." Not when there was a dead assassin at Wits' End.

But if an assassin *had* come to Doyle... What did that mean? Had the man only been here because of my parents? Or was there something more going on?

"What's that supposed to mean?" the sheriff asked, her voice sharp as a chef's knife.

"Nothing. I'm not a detective." This was so bogus. *Interference in an investigation* was just a way to keep intelligent civilians from cracking cases. It's a union thing.

But solving murders is a simple matter of gathering evidence and recording it diligently. I'd already proven myself on that count several times over.

The sheriff grunted and strode down the porch steps to her SUV at the end of my driveway.

I hurried back to the kitchen.

"Never a dull moment," Arsen said, "eh?"

"Not in the life of a forensic accountant," my mother said. "You wouldn't believe the scandals we've uncovered. But we're sorry we had to miss our night hike."

Arsen checked his watch. "It's only six thirty. We can go hiking now or grab a bite to eat first."

"Thank you," my father said. "But I think we've had enough drama for one day."

Arsen nodded. "Gotcha. You never know what you might encounter at night in the Sierras. I've got some paperwork to do anyway." He kissed my cheek. "Walk me out?"

"What? Oh. Right." I followed him to the door.

He pulled me close and kissed me more deeply, his muscular arms firm about my waist. "You could ditch your parents and let me take you to dinner."

Tempting, but I'd never be able to relax with a corpse on the premises. "I'd better stay in."

"Gotcha. You three could probably use some alone time. And Susan, you're going to get through this."

"Sure. Right. Of course I will."

His brow furrowed, but he smiled and shook his head. "I wish you'd tell me what you're thinking."

"That's easy. I wish my parents had never come to Doyle."

"But they have, and we're still standing." He brushed his thumb across my cheek. "Though I don't think the sheriff bought your story."

"Bought what story?"

"About seeing your parents come in at two," he said.

I opened my mouth, closed it. Oh. Damn. It had been a clumsy save, but I'd had to back up my parents, even if it did make me look guilty.

"You didn't need to cover for them," Arsen continued. "I'm sure the sheriff was only here to get a timeline on Van Der Woodsen. McCourt can't really think they're suspects."

"Maybe she should," I muttered.

"What?"

"You're right. The sheriff knows what she's doing." Which under the circumstances, was mildly terrifying.

He kissed me again. "I'll see you tomorrow."

I walked onto the front porch and watched him back down the driveway in his Jeep Commander. The huge car swiveled onto the court, and he turned on his headlights, then drove down the road.

I raced back to the kitchen. My parents were making themselves at home with my grandmother's coffeemaker. Their heads were bent together, and they spoke in low, intense tones.

"Why did you tell the sheriff you got back at two?" I asked. "You got back at least at three."

"We were busy doing something the sheriff doesn't need to know about," she said.

"What—?" I shook my head. *Never mind.* They'd never tell me anyway. "What did you do with the body?" I hissed.

"Don't worry." My father turned from the counter, a mug in his hand. "It's in a safe place until it can be removed."

"Removed by whom?"

"That's really none of your affair," my mother said.

What? It was totally my affair. "It's my B&B!"

"Tell us about this sheriff," my father said. "You two seem to have more than a casual relationship."

"She's a friend. And don't worry. Sheriff McCourt is smart and thorough. She'll figure out what happened to Mr. Van Der Woodsen."

No matter what else you could say about the sheriff, you couldn't say she was bad at her job. I was lucky we were friends.

My parents shared a worried look. I'd seen them worried so rarely, it took me a moment to identify the expression on their faces.

"What?" I asked. "What's wrong?"

"I'm afraid a smart and thorough sheriff doesn't work in our favor," my father said.

"Why not? You didn't kill Mr. Van Der Woodsen." I bit my bottom lip. Though they'd *really* disliked his books. "Did you?"

"Of course not," my mother said. "How could you even think such a thing?"

I braced my fists on my hips. "I don't know. Maybe because I'd just seen you disposing of a body?"

"The problem," my father said, "is that after we returned to Wits' End, we were rather busy taking care of the man in your garden—"

"You killed him in my garden?"

My mother rolled her eyes. "Why on earth would we kill him in your garden, then drag him upstairs? Use your head, Susan. He attacked us outside our room. We moved him into that vacant room—"

"Why?"

"For privacy." She smoothed her baggy blouse. "We expected you or Arsen might knock on our door and annoy us. The Russian assassin—"

"Crimean," my father said.

She glowered at him. "Is in your garden *now.*"

"You didn't dig up the roses, did you? Those were Gran's roses."

Unimportant. Unimportant!

"And we can't have an efficient sheriff poking around." My father brandished the mug.

"She'll need to be taken care of," my mother said quietly.

I felt the blood drain from my face. *Taken care of?* "You can't kill the sheriff!"

CHAPTER FOUR

By DEFINITION, YOU JUST can't trust spies.

Realistically, my parents couldn't kill a U.S. law enforcement officer. It would be, a) immoral, and b) a lot of trouble. Also, they'd promised me they wouldn't. But that wasn't worth much. (See above regarding not being able to trust spies.)

I leaned against the counter and looked toward the kitchen window. The curtains above the sink fluttered in the warm morning breeze.

There was a lot I didn't know about how my parents operated. Growing up, they'd kept me as protected from their work as they could, and I'd let them.

I was starting to regret that.

I regretted a lot.

Their version of protection had involved controlling every step I made, critiquing every piece of clothing I wore, and vetting every friend like they were White House interns.

I inhaled the familiar breakfast smells wafting from the oven. They reminded me of Gran. Everything about the B&B did, and at the thought of her, sorrow weighted my heart. Summers with my grandmother had been my only freedom. If she hadn't left me Wits' End after she'd passed on, I don't know if I'd ever have broken loose of my parents.

I returned to Arsen, seated at my kitchen table. He frowned over his computer tablet.

I sat and watched him nervously. This wasn't the sort of thing you kept from your boyfriend. But it wasn't the sort of thing you told a civilian either, and he was a civilian now.

I blew out my breath. My parents worked for the good guys. I'd *seen* them get official help in the past when things had gone wrong. But why hadn't that official help come swooping in now, when there was a body somewhere at my B&B?

And why had an assassin come to Doyle in the first place? A heaviness settled in my stomach. My parents had claimed not to know why they'd been targeted. But could I believe them?

And could the assassin be connected to Van Der Woodsen's death? I didn't see how. My parents had returned home after three, and then been attacked. So the assassin... could have killed Mr. Van Der Woodsen.

And two violent deaths in one day in one small town seemed... strange.

Determined, I opened my planner. The sheriff might not want my help, but she needed it. The best way to keep my parents off Sheriff McCourt's back was to prove the sheriff was no threat.

And to do *that*, I had to solve the murder of Mr. Van Der Woodsen. Once the murder was solved, she'd have no reason to look twice at my parents.

I made columns with suspects across the top of the page and MEANS, MOTIVE, and OPPORTUNITY down the side.

"What are you working on?" Arsen looked up from his tablet, Bailey asleep and drooling on his hiking boot.

"Mr. Van Der Woodsen died sometime between one and three-something yesterday. I need to figure out where all the suspects were at the time."

"Why? Are you still worried about your parents? They can't be serious suspects, unless you know something I don't?"

"I don't know any reason why the sheriff would think they were serious suspects. But I also don't understand why my parents were the first people the sheriff grilled."

"You don't know they were the first people."

"Sheriff McCourt got here awfully fast."

He grimaced. "Who've you got as suspects?"

"Van Der Woodsen's son and daughter. They must inherit. So I suppose their spouses are suspects too, since they'd also benefit."

"They're not going to like us poking around," he said mildly.

He'd said *us*, not *you*, and I smiled, my insides warming. "Who else might be a suspect? Could the butler have possibly done it?"

"I don't think Franklin was technically a butler," Arsen said.

I put him on my list. "We need to talk to him."

"Susan," he said.

I looked up.

"This list is about more than the Van Der Woodsen murder," he said. "Isn't it?"

"Who else's murder would I be investigating?" I asked, shrill. Arsen wasn't stupid. At some point, he'd figure out the truth. I just hadn't thought he'd get to that point so fast.

"Of course you're looking at who killed Van Der Woodsen," he said. "But it hasn't been that long since you've become independent of your parents. It seems like they still haven't gotten the message you make your own decisions now."

Muscles loosening, I drew a timeline across the top of the page and wrote, *spice shop*, 1:00. "But I'm over thirty, and I do make my own decisions. And I've decided to help solve this murder as quickly as possible. The logical place to start is by making a timeline of the victim's final day."

"The sheriff's got to be doing the same thing."

"But does she have my highlighting system?" I edged each suspect's column in a different color.

"It just seems," Arsen said, "that your lists and schedules are a sort of coping mechanism. To take back control."

"And they work brilliantly. If it's in my planner, I have to do it." It was almost like magic.

I added to my calendar: *take condolence casserole to Maive Van Der Woodsen.*

Arsen checked his dive watch. "I've got a meeting with a new client this morning."

"That's okay. I can take the casserole to Maive on my own." I didn't really know her that well, but it was a small town, and condolences must be paid.

He took my hand between his, calloused from a life outdoors. "Susan, you're going to get through this."

"Of course I will." After all, this wasn't my first rodeo. I knew how to turn my planner into a murder book.

The oven timer beeped, and he released my hand.

I rose and turned off the oven. While I got started on the bacon and the spiral galaxy pancakes, Arsen poured pitchers of juice.

I added a bit of chili powder to the pancake's chocolate swirl mix. I prided myself on our breakfasts. The pancakes' flavor profile needed to "fit" with the enchilada casserole.

As I whisked the chocolate and chili, I covertly watched Arsen's sure, economical movements, the play of his muscles against the back of his golf shirt. I never expected him to help me prep breakfasts, but it was wonderful that he did. He wasn't just my boyfriend. He was also my best friend, and love for him bubbled in my chest.

I finished cooking the breakfast. In the octagonal dining room, I set hot food into chafing dishes. Laying out bread beside the toaster, I studied the empty table with its white cloth.

Blue curtains billowed at the windows, cracked open to let the warm, Sierra air inside.

"Good morning, Susan."

I started.

One of my new guests, a cheerful brunette in her forties, wandered into the breakfast room.

"Hi, Layla. Did you sleep well?"

"Like a hibernating bear." She smiled and lowered her voice. "Hey, I wanted to talk to you about something, if you don't mind."

"Sure. What's up?"

She glanced around the room. "There's something very wrong in this B&B."

I stiffened, my blood turning to ice. Oh, no. She'd seen my parents disposing of the body. "Oh?"

"I've been studying the UFO photos on your walls. There's nothing from the last invasion."

I relaxed slightly, and adjusted the roses in their vase on the table. "Wait. Last invasion?" When had the first invasion happened? Layla was mixed up about something.

"The one last year."

My hand spasmed, and a thorn pricked my thumb. "Ow." I shook my hand, as if I could toss the pain away. Last year, Doyle had been seized by a UFO panic that had sent our town hall up in flames. But the UFO obsessed had convinced themselves there'd been a *real* invasion.

"Are you okay?" she asked.

"Fine. The UFO photos. Right. I just haven't gotten around to framing any photos from that incident."

Her eyes narrowed. "But it's an important part of the Doyle story."

"Ye-es," I said. It had also been awful. Arsen had been part of the volunteer fire department fighting the flames at town hall. I'd found out weeks after the fact he'd nearly been crushed by a falling beam while rescuing a clerk from the building.

"You must have some pictures of your own from that day," she insisted.

"Unfortunately, I was so busy trying to... Well. I didn't take any photos. All I have are copies of other people's pictures from online. But I will hang some soon."

I knew I sounded defensive. I guess I *was* defensive. But the panic was more than an embarrassment. People had gotten hurt. Town hall was still under reconstruction and would be for a long time. And Doyle hadn't yet recovered in other, more important ways.

Some townspeople still hadn't forgiven each other about accusations of alien influence. I guess once you accuse someone of not being completely human, it's hard to go back.

Layla frowned. "Where were you when everything was going down?"

"I was here," I said, "at the B&B and in downtown Doyle."

"Did you see..." She leaned closer. "...any visitors?"

It would be easy to laugh at UFO conspiracy theorists. It would be easy to get uncomfortable and angry about their views on the panic. But these were my guests, my bread and butter. They were curious, and they didn't mean any harm.

So I shook my head. "Only the usual tourists. But it was pretty chaotic."

"I can imagine." She studied me for a long moment. "I'm glad you weren't hurt."

Layla ambled to the long table and loaded pancakes onto her plate.

I backed from the room, and a young couple walked past me.

"Even a blind squirrel finds a nut every now and then," the male half of the couple said and laughed.

"No, that's not fair," his girlfriend said rapidly. "I think we can figure this out. After all, we're trained in UFO investigation. Why not this mystery?"

They disappeared into the breakfast room.

This *mystery? Trained in investigation?* What were they...? My breath sped. I didn't know what mystery they were interested in, but I knew all too well how easy it was to solve a crime.

My B&B was packed to the rafters with conspiracy theorists. They lived to examine evidence and search out oddities.

This could be a problem.

Because what were the odds someone *wouldn't* suss out there was a corpse on the grounds? Wits' End was the absolutely *worst* place for my parents to hide a dead assassin.

I gulped. What if one of my guests unearthed the body?

Where *was* the body? I needed to know.

I hurried into the kitchen.

Bailey lifted his head from his dog bed.

"Bailey, come." I opened the door to the side porch.

Obligingly, he stood, yawned, and shook himself, collar jingling. The beagle trotted past me and stopped at the top of the porch steps. He looked over his shoulder at me, his expression plaintive.

"There are only three steps," I grumbled. But I picked him up and carried him onto the lawn. After all, I needed a favor.

I knelt beside him. "I know you're not a hunting dog, but do you smell anything, um, dead?"

The beagle cocked his head.

Dumb question. Half the time Bailey couldn't find his own food bowl.

I stood. "Let's look together."

We walked to the rose bushes beneath room seven. Several branches of the President Lincoln rose had snapped and hung at depressing angles. Curling leaves lay scattered beneath its base.

Pained at the damage, I grimaced. "Sorry, Gran," I whispered. President Lincoln had been one of Gran's favorites. I hoped it would survive.

I studied the ground. Two faint tracks, like drag marks, led across the grass toward the gazebo.

Feeling slightly sick, I followed their trail.

The marks faded in the thick lawn, but I plodded onward to the gazebo. Since there was obviously no body on its low, white benches, I walked past its steps, past the UFO fountain.

I stopped short. The fountain trickled merrily. At the rear of the gazebo, one of the sections of lattice at its base was askew.

I knelt and studied the section more closely. It looked like someone had just leaned the loose section of lattice against the gazebo. The section's corners, where nails had been, were splintered, as if pried free. Four nails lay in the soft earth. I pocketed them.

Bailey sniffed at the lattice, and suddenly, I knew.

Dizzy, I braced one hand on the hard earth. *The body was under the gazebo.* This was the perfect place to hide a corpse... If all you cared about was ease of disposal.

My parents hadn't considered all the guests who came here for selfies or to relax. This was so typical of them, I fumed.

But more importantly, why was the body still here? My parents' "company" should have removed it by—

"What are you doing?"

I yelped, wobbled, and fell on my butt.

My cousin Dixie, arms akimbo, stared down at me. She wore her usual summer attire—olive shorts and a black tank top. Her hair color changed with the seasons. Today, the tips of her dark, shoulder-length hair were dyed pink.

I stumbled to my feet. "You're here early," I said. Dixie never woke up before nine.

"I was up. I was bored. What are you doing?"

Oh no, oh no, oh no. Dixie was the biggest conspiracy theorist of them all. She had a police scanner and some sort of crazy radio setup in her trailer to scan the skies.

I swallowed. "Nothing."

"Why were you staring at the gazebo?"

"I just..."

"Just what? You looked freaked out. Are your parents freaking you out?"

Bailey whined and dug at the earth beside the lattice.

"No," I said. "Well, yes. A little." And the best defense was a hot offense. "I noticed you got out of Dodge when they showed up. Where were you yesterday?"

"Around." She examined her chipped nails. "It's not like I was avoiding them or anything. I'm not the one who acts like they're a couple of ax murderers."

A bead of sweat trickled down my brow and into my eye, stinging. I blinked rapidly. It would be a miracle if I got through my parents' visit without developing a tic.

"Look," she continued. "You're an adult. Why don't you do what I do, which is whatever I want?"

"That's good advice," I said in a strangled voice. "Except I have a B&B to run. There are chores. Schedules—"

"So what's with the gazebo?"

"The gazebo?" I parroted. "This gazebo?"

"You've only got one."

I clawed a hand through my hair. I had to get my cousin away from here. But if I acted like I *wanted* her gone, she'd only try to figure out why.

Rational arguments wouldn't work. Appealing to her better nature...? I wasn't sure my cousin had one. And I couldn't frighten her off. The only thing that scared Dixie was... work.

She picked at a scab on her elbow. "What's—?"

"The gazebo needs work," I blurted.

Dixie edged backward. "It looks fine to me."

"It hasn't been painted in ages," I said, working up some enthusiasm.

She jammed her hands in the pockets of her shorts. "Gran had it painted the summer before she died."

"But in the mountains, things weather faster. Yes, it definitely needs painting. Could you...?"

Dixie turned on her heel and hurried toward the Victorian.

My shoulders sagged. Good thing I was a quick thinker. Dixie wouldn't go within a hundred yards of the gazebo now.

But a body in the gazebo? How could my parents be so thoughtless?

Bailey dug more vigorously, and the lattice wobbled.

"Bailey, get away from there."

The beagle paused, cocked his head, and resumed digging.

I'm in control. My mouth pinched. *Ha.* I wasn't even in control of my own dog.

CHAPTER FIVE

THERE WAS NO WAY I was going to excavate beneath my gazebo. Digging up bodies is for grave robbers and weirdos. Plus, there had to be a ton of spiders under there.

Instead, dragging a reluctant Bailey, I returned to the kitchen, and I consulted my planner.

Breakfast casserole to Maive was next on my agenda. I grabbed a cheesy potato casserole from my freezer. Since I like to plan ahead, I always keep a few on hand for emergencies. I taped re-heating instructions to its foil.

Bailey slunk toward the doggy door.

"Oh, no you don't." I clipped a leash to the dog. I couldn't leave an innocent beagle to possibly dig up a dead body. I had to keep Bailey close until the body was gone for good.

Looking mutinous, he sat on the linoleum and scratched behind a floppy ear.

I loaded the dog into my Crosstrek, and we drove into Doyle. As we cruised down Main Street, I scanned tree trunks and buildings for squirrel flyers. But the lamp posts and utility poles were flyer free.

Turning off Main Street, I drove up a wooded hill to Maive Van Der Woodsen's luxury condo complex.

I parked and stared sadly at what had once been a farm. The condominiums *were* nice. Finely manicured lawns. Low, stone walls.

Peaked rooflines. But the buildings looked like they belonged in Vail or Aspen, not funny little Goldrush-era Doyle.

Yet here they were. I'd heard that most of the condos were being rented to wealthy vacationers. But a few people lived in them permanently. People with money, like Maive.

Bailey nosed my arm, and I scratched his head.

The condos were beautiful, but they were also change. And who likes that?

Letting Bailey out of the Crosstrek, I looped his leash around my wrist. We walked up the paving stone path to the glass front doors.

They opened automatically before me, and I strode inside the foyer. A burnished, curving security desk stood parallel to a stone wall.

A well-dressed man and woman in their thirties sat in soft-looking leather chairs. They spoke in muted tones, their backs to me.

The uniformed guard behind the high desk looked up and smiled. "Can I help you?"

"Bernie?" I asked, casserole chilling my hands. "What are you doing here?" Bernie was an ersatz handyman. I'd used him on occasion to fix things around Wits' End.

He grinned crookedly. "Hey, Susan. I got a new gig." Bernie bent closer and lowered his voice. "Second day on the job."

"Congratulations then."

He shrugged. "Thanks. It's not the most exciting work, but the pay's good."

And jobs were hard to come by in tiny Doyle. I shouldn't be so negative about the new condos. Growth meant more employment. I just really hated change. "I'm here to see Maive Van Der Woodsen."

He grimaced. "Is she expecting you?"

"No." I raised my casserole. "I'm here to pay my condolences."

"I'll call up and see if she's available."

I nodded, sunk. Maive and I didn't know each other well. She'd no reason to let me inside.

At least I could re-freeze the casserole.

He grimaced and hung up. "She's not answering."

I lowered my head. Well, what had I expected? A detective's life is filled with potholes and misdirection.

"Not answering?" The man rose from the leather chair and turned to his companion. "I hope your husband hasn't killed her," he said with a wry smile. He wore a tweed jacket with arm patches, and looked like a sexy college professor.

The woman leaned forward, twisting her body. "Or vice versa." Her near-black hair was perfection, her skin smooth, her muscles taut. She probably had a personal trainer, and yes, I was jealous. I got most of my exercise pushing a vacuum.

"Maive gives as good as she gets," she continued. She glanced at me, her brown eyes wide and serious. "You're that innkeeper, aren't you?"

"Susan Witsend," I said.

"I thought so. She's friends with Arsen," the woman said to the man.

He brightened. Or maybe that was the effect of the chandelier, shimmering off the golden streaks in his brown hair. "Arsen? How's that lunatic doing?"

I adjusted the casserole in my arms. "Good."

Bailey sat heavily on my foot.

"Still jumping off buildings?" he asked.

I sucked in my cheeks. "What?"

The two laughed.

"Sorry." The man's face contorted. "The family's had a shock—but I guess you know about that." He nodded toward the casserole.

"For some reason, things that shouldn't be funny seem hysterical. I can't stop laughing at inappropriate moments, or faking laughter during appropriate ones."

"No," I said quickly. "I understand. It's like the stress demands a release, and you just need to laugh, even if it's not right."

"Besides," the man continued. "I don't suppose there are any roofs high enough in Doyle to make it worthwhile."

"What?" I asked.

"Jumping off roofs," he said. "Did Arsen tell you about the time he got caught rappelling up the biology building? They were convinced he was trying to steal a test. His scores were way too good, but I really think he just did it because he could."

"No," I said distantly. "He hadn't told me about that." I knew Arsen had gone to some fancy boarding school, but he'd said nothing about his hijinks there.

The man walked toward me, his hand extended. "I'm Jacob, Jacob Parker." He motioned toward the woman. "And this is Lupita."

"Van Der Woodsen," she said.

Malcolm's wife. "Nice to meet you." I shifted the casserole to one hip and shook his hand.

A corner of her mouth crooked upward. "I'm sure it is. What's that you've got?"

"A, um, casserole for Maive." Which was starting to seem very down market. "And for you, I guess," I said reluctantly, knowing what would come next.

Jacob extended his arms. "I can take it up."

Lupita checked her exercise watch. "We have to see the newspaper office about that obituary, remember?"

"I'll take the casserole with us and bring it back," he said.

"It should stay frozen," I said. I suppose I *could* question Jacob and Lupita here, but it wasn't part of my plan. Plus, Bernie was watching. Interrogating suspects in front of witnesses didn't seem very professional.

"Oh, Bennie," Lupita said, "let her up. Maive adores home cooking and gets it so seldom. I'm sure she's just away from her phone."

"He's Bernie," I said, because I knew he wouldn't correct them, and then they'd be calling him Bennie forever. "Not Bennie."

"Sorry," she said.

"I'm really not supposed to let people up without permission," Bernie said.

"You have my permission, Bernie," Jacob said. "I live there too. You can look up the name. Jacob Parker and Maive Van Der Woodsen, unit 306."

The doorman colored. "Yes, Sir. Sorry, I—"

"You're new," Jacob said. "It's fine. No one expects you to have all the tenants memorized."

I hesitated, shuffling my feet. "Well, thank you," I said.

"Any friend of Arsen's," Jacob said.

I walked toward the stairs. Bailey tugged me toward the elevator.

"You and Arsen helped solve a murder once, didn't you?" Lupita asked.

I pulled again on Bailey's leash. The beagle sat on the tile floor, a stubborn glint in his toffee-colored eyes.

"If you can put my father-in-law's death to bed," Lupita said, "you'd be doing us a favor."

James nudged her. "You're too much. She doesn't mean it," he said to me.

"Actually," she said slowly. "I do."

"Then I'll try." Giving up on the idea of getting in my ten-thousand steps for the day, I walked to the elevator and stabbed the button with my finger.

"If this is the start of a new trend, I don't like it," I said to Bailey when the doors had closed. "You can still go *up* the stairs, you know."

Bailey whuffed.

The doors slid open. We walked down a hallway with a gleaming wood floor and what looked like original modern art on the walls. It was a far cry from my B&B, but I catered to a different type of guests.

I raised my hand to knock on the door of 204.

"You hated him," Maive's voice floated through the closed door. "All you ever cared about was his money."

There was a faint, caustic masculine laugh. "You're one to talk. You've never worked a day in your life."

"That's not true."

"Your feng shui?" His words dripped acid. "Have you had a single client?"

"I've had plenty of clients."

"Paying clients?"

Silence followed.

I leaned closer. Eavesdropping is a low and dirty habit...unless you're an experienced investigator. Then it's just good sense.

"Don't play the martyr with me," he said. "You need the old man's money as badly as I do. If you're ever going to become a—"

Their voices dropped, too low for me to hear, which was really inconvenient. So, I rang the bell.

After a moment, Maive answered the door, and I tried not to stare. Her left eye was green and the right eye brownish. The effect was startling and beautiful every time I saw it. Which hadn't been often.

She frowned at me. "Yes?"

"Hi." I glanced away from her eyes to a sculpture of a donut and then back again. Did she remember who I was? "I just wanted to tell you how sorry—"

"Who is it?" Her brother, Malcolm, appeared behind her and rubbed his palm up one of his sideburns. He had the same eye condition as his sister. But in Malcolm the colors were reversed—a green right eye and brownish left eye. The siblings looked like fairy twins, lovely and terrible.

"It's..." Her gaze narrowed. "Susan, right?"

"Susan Witsend," I said. "From Wits' End."

Maive's freckled face cleared. "The girl dating Arsen. Right."

"Every day's a holiday, Arsen Holiday?" Malcolm smiled, stepping closer, and I inhaled the scent of his cologne. I didn't know what it was, but it smelled good. And expensive.

"He must have told you we went to boarding school together," he continued. "The trouble he got into made the rest of us look like saints. Arsen saved my hide on more than one occasion, I'll tell you."

"That's Arsen," I said. "Always thinking of others." Except for me, I guess, because he'd never mentioned going to boarding school with the Van Der Woodsens. But in fairness, why would he? He didn't talk much about boarding school at all. He hadn't liked it.

Jacob gave one of those half-laughs, one that said he either didn't mean it or couldn't muster up the energy for real laughter.

"I'm so sorry for your loss," I said. "I wanted to give you both my condolences, and a breakfast casserole. The baking instructions are on the foil." I lifted it slightly. The hallway lights cast a golden, romantic glow on its aluminum foil.

"Casserole?" Malcolm's nose wrinkled.

"Don't be gauche," his sister said to him. "You know mid-century modern cooking is *in* right now. Thank you, Susan." She took the casserole dish. "It's very thoughtful."

"Your father was a wonderful writer," I said.

"He'd agree," Maive said. "And he would have been delighted by his mode of death. Famous spy novelist murdered—I can see the headlines now." Her mouth spasmed. "Actually, I have seen them."

"When was the last time you saw your father?" I asked. Ugh. That hadn't exactly been subtle.

"Not for ages," she said. "Why?"

Because I was on a mission to clear my parents' name before the sheriff got into massive trouble. "No reason. I'm just making small talk. Badly, it seems. Is there anything I can do to help?"

"Can you have that butler arrested?" Maive asked.

"The butler?" I said, taken aback.

"Oh," Malcolm said, "he definitely did it."

"I, uh—"

Maive laughed. "Don't worry, I know you can't do anything about murder. Thanks again for the casserole. Give our best to Arsen."

She shut the door.

"Every day's a holiday..." Her snort drifted through the closed door.

I looked down at Bailey.

He shook his head, and his collar jangled.

"I'm not sure what to make of that either," I whispered, since the door wasn't as solid as it looked.

I returned to the foyer. Jacob and Lupita had vanished.

Lacking more suspects to interrogate, I drove toward home. My thoughts tumbled uncomfortably over each other.

I knew Arsen had had an entire life away from Doyle and beyond my experience. But that fact had never made me feel like an outsider before now.

I shook myself. It wasn't as if Arsen had lied to me about knowing the Van Der Woodsens. So he'd made some snooty friends in boarding school? That didn't change who Arsen was today.

I pulled into the gravel drive.

Bailey bounded from the car and raced across the lawn. He disappeared around the corner of the Victorian, toward the gazebo.

My heart seized. *Not the body.* I hurried after him.

Bailey raced to his favorite spot beneath a spirit house, and I relaxed. Arsen had sent my grandmother the tiny house back from Thailand, when he'd supposedly been away at the circus. The raised structure perched between two rose bushes, at the edge of the lawn.

Bailey rolled in the dirt, then stretched out and closed his eyes.

At least I didn't have to worry about the beagle's corpse-detecting skills. Relieved, I walked toward the side porch.

My parents' voices drifted through the open kitchen window.

"...no good," my mother was saying. "We'll have to silence..." Her voice dropped.

I bolted up the steps and into the kitchen. The screen door banged behind me, and they looked up from the small table.

"Who are you going to silence?" I demanded. "You can't silence anyone."

"You overheard that?" my father asked.

"She's always had excellent hearing," my mother said proudly. "But darling, that blouse."

"Forget about—" I looked down at my shirt. "What's wrong with my blouse?"

"That pattern, all those tiny flowers. It's not right for you."

"I like this blouse," I said.

"And your hair," she continued, "it's getting so shaggy. When's the last time you've had it cut?"

How long *had* it been? I'd been keeping my blond hair in a ponytail, which was neat enough. "I don't know, I—"

"She needs to go to a real salon," my mother said. "I can't imagine there's a worthwhile stylist in a small town like Doyle."

I reached up to smooth my hair. It *had* looked a little frazzled compared to Maive and Lupita's.

I stopped my hand above my head and dropped it to my side. No. My parents were doing it again, bossing me. But I was in control of my life and my hair and whatever shirt I decided to wear. I opened my mouth to argue.

"And capris?" my mother said. "They're so dated. And you didn't even iron them."

Enough was enough. I raised my chin. "Well, you won't have to look at them after you leave."

"About that." My father shifted. "I'm afraid we can't leave until we get our little problem cleared up."

I gaped. "Problem?" A dead body beneath my gazebo was more than a little problem. "Don't tell me the *problem* hasn't been removed yet?"

"Not that problem. The sheriff." My mother scowled. "She interviewed us again. We're going to have to do something about her."

"No," I said. "No. Don't do anything. Leave the sheriff alone."

"It's not that simple," my father said gently.

"I think it is," I said, panic raising my tone.

"You're getting anxious again, Susan." My mother stood and paced toward me. "You know how you get when you're anxious."

"I'm not anxious. I have to help Dixie clean the rooms." Chest heaving, I bolted from the kitchen and to the reception desk. I turned, watching the swinging kitchen door, but my parents didn't follow.

Which meant they were probably plotting against me. Not that I'm paranoid or anything. But when it came to my parents—

"Hey, Susan," Arsen said.

I squeaked and whipped my head toward the front door.

"You okay?" Arsen strode across the Persian rug and rubbed my shoulder. It felt really good.

"What are you doing here?" I asked.

"I thought we were going to lunch." His forehead wrinkled.

We were? How had I forgotten that? I pulled my day planner from my bag and flipped to today.

"Don't you believe me?" Arsen asked, wry.

"I do, I just…" There it was, in pencil on paper. Lunch with Arsen.

I slumped against the scarred wooden desk. I was on schedule. Everything was working out. Except for the part about hiding a dead body from Arsen. That wasn't working out at all.

That was also my parents' fault. I scowled.

"What's going on?" Arsen asked.

"I just got back from Maive Van Der Woodsen's place. Everyone was really nice, but I overheard her and her brother talking about how much they needed their inheritance. And then they accused the butler of killing their father. After I gave Maive the casserole. Did you know mid-century modern cooking is trendy?"

"Whoa. Malcolm was there?"

"Shouldn't he have been? He is her brother."

"No," Arsen said, "it's normal, I guess. Those two were always close. I just wish I'd been with you."

"Me too, but you had that meeting. And things have gotten worse. My parents…"

"What about them?"

I couldn't tell him about their vague threats toward Sheriff Mc-Court. "They're worried about the sheriff," I hedged. "She questioned them again."

"McCourt can't really suspect them."

"Maybe not, but I've got to solve this crime before my parents send me around the bend."

"The sheriff talked to them again?" He scrubbed a hand along his jaw. "That's weird."

"I know," I hissed. I glanced at the kitchen door.

"But I don't like you running off to interview suspects."

"Arsen," I said, affronted. "It's what I do."

"No," he said. "It's what *we* do."

"Oh. Oh."

He drew me close and kissed me. My knees trembled, and I looped one arm around his shoulder so I didn't fall. For a moment, the murder, the body, my parents, dropped away. I *knew* everything would work out.

A little breathless, he raised his head. "Now," he said, "let's talk about what's really going on."

Dread slowed my heartbeat. I stepped away and pressed my hands to my stomach. *He knows.* "Really going on?"

"And what you're keeping from me."

CHAPTER SIX

I'M JUST GOING TO say it. A boyfriend who notices your moods and subtle little emotional signals is irritating.

"I'm not keeping anything from you," I lied and gripped the edge of the reception desk behind me. "You know how much I love crime solving. And why wouldn't I like to see my parents on their way ASAP?"

Arsen cocked his head. His hazel eyes narrowed. "And those are the *only* reasons you're ignoring the sheriff's orders to stay out of this case?"

"Arsen. When have you ever listened to an authority figure?"

He grinned. "Never. But I'm not you."

"Besides, you know the sheriff doesn't mean it."

He canted his head. "Hm. Did something else happen between you and your parents?"

I swallowed. It wasn't that I didn't trust Arsen. I did. I wanted to tell him everything. But for over a decade, my parents had drilled me on the importance of silence.

And there were good reasons for that silence. And Arsen was ex-military. He could understand those reasons.

If I told him.

But how could I tell him? How could I tell him that I'd loved him since he'd flown over my head on his bicycle at ten years old? That I loved the sparks of controlled chaos he'd brought into my life?

The way he made me feel safe and wild and free all at the same time? That all I wanted was to be with him here, in Doyle, just the two of us in our own world, because my parents were killers.

My chest tightened. I had to. I owed Arsen the truth.

I drew a deep breath.

The front door opened, and Layla strode in with her husband, Fred. "Susan, have you seen the flyers? What's with the squirrels? Are we in danger?"

"From squirrels?" Arsen asked.

"Someone's claiming they're aliens," I explained, relieved at my reprieve.

Layla tucked her chin. "Really? I hadn't heard that. Fred?"

Her husband shook his balding head.

"That's... strange," she continued. "But I meant the bubonic plague flyers."

"Oh, those," Arsen said. "The Forest Service plasters those across the Sierras every year. I've never encountered an infected squirrel, but they're real. So don't feed the squirrels, and if you see any acting lethargic, steer clear."

"Lethargic squirrels?" Fred asked. "That *would* be weird."

The two ambled upstairs.

"Alien squirrels?" Layla's voice drifted down. "We have to get our hands on one of those flyers. What a great souvenir! And something else I saw... There's something strange..." Her voice faded.

I stiffened. *Strange*? She'd seen something strange? At Wits' End?

"Anyway," Arsen said. "Back to crime solving. Since you don't seem interested in lunch, want to interview some suspects?"

"Really?"

"Or we could go hiking—"

"Let's talk to the butler." I'd been on Arsen's hikes. They tended to be off-trail, up-hill and involve scrambling down loose scree. I only scrambled when circumstances were desperate.

We drove to Mr. Van Der Woodsen's faux-Tudor mansion, half hidden behind a high brick wall. Behind the iron gate, its gabled roofline blotted out the pines.

We parked on the street and walked down a long, gravel driveway to the arched front door.

Arsen rang the bell. A gong sounded inside the house.

"What's our excuse for being here?" he asked. "Condolences seem a little off, under the circumstances."

"We don't know that. The butler might be prostrate with grief."

Arsen snorted. "Franklin? Hardly."

I jammed my hands in my pockets. "You know him too?" It was like Arsen had this whole other secret life. And the thing was, he *had* had a secret life once. He'd lied to me for years about working at resorts when he'd really been in the military. Not that that still bothered me or anything.

He folded his bronzed arms. "A little. I've seen Franklin around Antoine's Bar."

"Doing what? Aside from the obvious, I mean."

"Keeping the bar entertained with stories of his employer. He's a good storyteller, and I admit I laughed at them, but I shouldn't have. He shouldn't have said anything." Arsen pressed the bell again.

"Because the stories should have been private, or because they were unkind?"

"A little of both. They were really gripes disguised as stories."

"I suppose it's natural to complain about your employer." I frowned, wondering what Dixie said about me. Scratch that. I didn't want to know.

"It may be natural, but not professional." He angled his head to the door, as if listening. "I don't hear anything."

"We can spend the wait time thinking up a new cover story," I said.

"I thought we were doing condolences."

"You said that seemed off."

"It does," he said, "but what are our options?"

"I can say I'm looking for a casserole dish Gran left here years ago."

"That would have to be some casserole dish."

I braced one shoulder against the cool brick wall. "I guess it *would* seem petty asking for it now. But it's the principle of the thing."

"Casserole dishes have principles?"

"Gran had some lovely dishes. They're vintage."

Arsen's brows lifted. He leaned sideways and peered through a narrow, paned window. "I don't see anyone. Let's try around back."

We took a flagstone path around the side of the house.

A lush, green lawn unfolded before us, leading to a swimming pool. At the edge of the lawn, ringing the blue water, were pineapples made of strips of dark metal. A man in swim trunks lay on a lounge chair and stared at the sky.

"Franklin," Arsen said grimly.

We walked toward the pool.

"Were his stories that bad?" I whispered. "You sound like you don't like him."

"I don't."

We walked to the lounge chair, Arsen casting a long shadow across the man.

Franklin didn't react, still as a corpse. A cigar, smoldering down to its end, dangled from his half-parted lips. Was he dead? I stepped backward and onto Arsen's foot.

Gently, Arsen shifted me off his hiking boot.

I dragged my hands down the thighs of my slacks. *Please, don't be dead.* I cleared my throat. "Hello?"

Franklin Asher didn't stir. His white Nehru shirt was open, exposing a smooth, still expanse of bronzed chest.

"Mr. Asher?" I tasted something sour. *Please, not another body.*

"Hey." Arsen lightly kicked the chair. "Wake up."

The body raised his sunglasses.

I jumped backward and gasped.

Franklin squinted at us. "Arsen? What are you doing here?"

Arsen grunted. "Condolences."

"Really?" The butler raised his eyebrows. "That's uncommonly decent of you."

"We're so sorry for your loss," I said. "I'm Susan. Susan Witsend."

"Oh, yeah. The woman with the crazy UFO B&B." Swinging his tanned legs off the lounge chair, he sat sideways on it. Franklin removed the cigar from his teeth and reached for a brandy decanter on a low, glass table. "Can I offer you a drink?"

"No thanks," Arsen said. "I'm more of a beer guy."

Franklin raised the crystal decanter to me, and I shook my head. Awake, Franklin had a man-of-the-world, Cary Grant look—smooth, dark hair, even features, and brilliant white teeth.

Franklin poured himself a generous measure and took a gulp. "I'm not usually a day drinker," he said. "But I'm in shock."

"I can see that." Arsen folded his arms.

"Were you the one who discovered the body?" I asked.

"I did. Poor Salvatore. Bashed in the head with a bottle of wine. A good one."

"How horrible," I said. "Then you must have been nearby when he was killed."

Franklin belched. "All I can think about is if I could have saved him."

"I'm sure you couldn't have stopped it," I said. "Er, where *were* you when he was killed?"

"I don't know exactly when it happened, so I couldn't say where I was. But I left him alive to do a bit of tree trimming out here." The butler motioned with his glass toward a greenhouse. A neatly stacked pile of tree limbs stood beside it. "Salvatore never skimped on equipment. His chainsaw is a thing of beauty."

"You were running a chainsaw?" No wonder he hadn't heard anything.

"Don't you have gardeners for that?" Arsen asked.

"We do," Franklin said, "but they come on Mondays, and Salvatore got a bee in his bonnet about that tree. So I took care of it. When I returned inside, I found Salvatore. Dead."

"What time was that?" I asked.

Arsen nudged my arm. And okay, maybe I wasn't being super subtle. But Franklin was answering.

"Around three-thirty," he said. "I found him in the parlor."

"And what time did you leave him to go to the greenhouse?" I asked.

"About three."

Ah, ha. Salvatore had been killed between three and three-thirty. I'd narrowed the time of death! Honestly, anyone can be a detective. It just takes persistence and organization.

"The wine bottle Salvatore was hit with," Arsen said. "Had it been opened?"

"It must have been." Franklin's brows drew downward. "The bottle didn't break, but there was wine splashed around. The cork must have been out. And why are you asking?"

"Were there wine glasses nearby?" I asked.

Asher tilted his head, frowning. "No," he said slowly. "There weren't."

So someone had removed them. "And you didn't see or hear anyone come in?" I asked.

He narrowed his coffee-colored eyes. "Malcolm and Maive had keys. I wouldn't have heard either of them enter the house."

"So you think one of his kids did it?" I asked.

"They're spoiled monsters. They want his money, and they assumed they'd inherit." He frowned, his Hollywood face creasing. "We all assumed they would. At least until the old man threatened to cut them off."

"He did?" I asked.

"He told Malcolm and Maive they were long past old enough to stand on their own. They weren't happy about it."

"I imagine not," Arsen muttered.

"But when was this?" I asked.

"A couple weeks ago. You *do* own that awful B&B, don't you?" Franklin asked. "You're not a reporter?"

"Of course I'm not," I said, indignant. "And Wits' End isn't awful. It's charming."

"Huh," Franklin said, swinging his feet onto the lounge chair. "I guess you are who you say you are. I heard you were nosy."

"Watch it," Arsen said sharply.

"In fairness," I said to him, "I am being nosy."

The butler stretched out on the chair and laced his hands behind his sleek head. "It's okay, I love telling a good story."

"Good," I said. "Did Salvatore have any other enemies?"

"Plenty." Franklin nodded. "Malcolm and Maive's so-called better halves were even more grasping when it came to the old man."

"Lupita and Jacob?" Arsen asked. "Why do you say that?"

"I've seen things," Franklin said cryptically.

Arsen's jaw hardened. "Huh."

"And then there's that hothead across the street."

"Hothead?" I asked.

"The neighbor reported us for leaving our garbage cans out overnight." Franklin chuckled.

I didn't think it was funny, but I smiled and nodded. Bears were attracted to garbage, and it wasn't healthy for them. It also wasn't healthy for bears to start seeing humans as a food source.

"You should have seen it when the town inspector showed up," he continued. "Mr. Van Der Woodsen ran him off the property. Then he interrogated the neighbors until he figured out who'd turned him in. Their shouting echoed down the street, and it was mostly on Mr. Van Der Woodsen's part. But that was the old man."

"Oh?" I asked. "He argued a lot?"

Franklin took another sip of the amber liquid. "The day he died, he got into it with a couple at the spice store."

I stiffened. *My parents.*

"You don't say?" Arsen asked innocently. "Were you there? You know who they were?"

"Yeah." He shrugged. "A couple of tourists. You know the look. They really hated his books—said his characters were derivative."

"Why was he at the spice store?" I asked.

"They had a new dry rub in. He wanted to check it out himself. Salvatore liked getting out of the house." He nodded toward the looming mansion. "It's a great place, but who wants to be inside it all the time?"

"Were there any other visitors to the house the day of Van Der Woodsen's death?" I asked.

Franklin grinned. "His daughter dropped by for money—again. The old man turned her down flat."

Maive had told me she hadn't seen her father in ages. I stared at Franklin. One of them was lying.

"How do you know?" Arsen asked him.

"I was listening at the door." He smiled. "It's part of the job. How else could I know when to bring in the drinks?"

"Did Maive let herself in with her key when she stopped by yesterday?" Arsen asked.

"I believe she did." Franklin rolled his shoulders, and his shirt opened wider.

We asked him a few more questions, I muttered more condolences, and we left him at the pool.

A tuneless whistle struck up behind us, and I glanced over my shoulder. Franklin lay in his lounge chair, his hands cradling his head, elbows out.

Arsen and I walked along the side of the brick mansion.

"It didn't take Franklin long to enjoy his employer's brandy and cigars." He gave a brief shake of his head.

"And do you believe that story about the chainsaw?"

"No," he said shortly. "Did you see his hands? Smooth as a model's."

"He could have worn gloves," I said, jogging to keep up with Arsen's long strides. "*The butler did it* may be a common saying, but it's not exactly evidence. We need to find out where everyone was yesterday afternoon between three and three-thirty."

We rounded the front corner of the house and stopped short.

Sheriff McCourt, arms crossed, glowered, blocking our way. "Or—and here's a crazy thought—you could stay out of my case."

CHAPTER SEVEN

Stay out of her *case? Oh, please.* The sheriff knew full well I was an integral part of this investigation. I shifted my weight on the thick lawn. "But sheriff—"

An alarming wave of red swept up her cherubic face. "I thought you were over this. This isn't a suggestion, Susan. It's an order. Stay out of my case, or I'll arrest you for interfering." Sweat stained the armpits of her uniform shirt.

"We're leaving now," Arsen said hastily.

"Wait for me at your car." She rounded the corner of the Tudor mansion and strode toward the pool.

I pressed my lips together and let Arsen lead me down the long driveway.

The sheriff had picked a bad time to play authority figure. She thought she was dealing with a normal murder, and okay, yes, maybe she was. But my parents had somehow gotten tangled up with it, and that made everything more dangerous.

Despite my earlier panic, I didn't believe they'd actually hurt the sheriff. But if their agency got involved, they could damage her career. The murder of Mr. Van Der Woodsen might even be buried if it meant preserving national secrets. And if I knew the sheriff, she wouldn't stand for that.

"You're awfully quiet." Arsen helped me into his Jeep, hot as a solar flare.

"I'm not stopping our investigation." How could I with the sheriff under threat?

He grinned. "Duh."

And that was one of the wonderful things about dating a devil-may-care man. I never had to worry about Arsen telling me to do the sensible thing. Though usually I did do the sensible thing. After all, I'm a reputable business owner and member of the community.

I opened the planner in my lap and noted down the highlights of our conversation with Franklin Asher. He'd not only given us some good intel, but he also made a great suspect.

I was editing my suspect table, when the sheriff rapped on the Jeep's hood. She leaned in my open window, her sleeves rolled to her elbows. I shut my planner.

"I'll escort you to Wits' End," she snapped.

That would throw off our interrogation schedule. I hated changing plans, but I forced a smile. I *could* shift around my B&B work with detecting. The unexpected was why I used pencil in my planner. "Sure."

My smile faded. Unless the sheriff was multitasking. Was she making sure I got home *and* using the opportunity to do some interrogating of her own? What if she wanted to talk to my parents again? My hands clenched on the planner's leather cover.

The sheriff nodded and walked to her SUV, parked behind us.

Arsen started the Jeep. "Don't worry. We'll get you back on schedule. You can move some stuff around, right?"

"Right." I dragged my hands through my hair. "I can be flexible."

One corner of his mouth lifted. He shifted the Jeep into drive.

We wound down the hill to the more modest section of town, and onward to Wits' End. My muscles unknotted at the sight of its vanilla-colored wood slats, its burnt-red and brown gingerbread trim. Rosebushes cascaded over the picket fence. The roof UFO glinted in the afternoon sunlight. *Home.*

Dixie leaned against the porch banister beneath a hanging fern, her arms crossed. Bailey sat at her feet.

I got out of the Jeep and pretended everything was normal. "Hi, Dixie. Any problems?"

Behind us, the sheriff's SUV crunched on my gravel driveway.

"Why would there be?" my cousin asked.

Arsen and I walked up the porch steps. The sheriff's car door slammed.

Dixie raised a brow. "Did *you* have any problems?"

"You know where Susan's parents are?" the sheriff asked from behind me.

My chest tightened. Sometimes I hate it when I'm right. She *had* come here because of my parents.

Dixie's absinthe eyes narrowed. "I might."

"Where?" the sheriff asked.

Tail thumping, the beagle growled at the sheriff. Bailey was clearly torn between his dislike of uniforms and pleasure at our return.

Dixie examined her nails. "Why do you want to know?"

"Where are they?" the sheriff snarled.

Dixie shrugged. "I saw them go into the garden."

My heartbeat pounded in my ears. The garden? Where they'd hidden the body? What if they were...?

No. They wouldn't. They couldn't. Surely their cleaning crew had removed the body by now. Maybe my parents were just enjoying the fresh air?

"Are you okay Susan?" Arsen touched my arm.

"I'm fine," I croaked.

The sheriff pushed back the brim of her hat. "You look sick."

"There has been a bug going around," I said faintly.

Dixie leapt backward. "Ew. Stay away from me." She pivoted and hurried into the Victorian, the doors banging behind her.

Bailey looked at the screen door, then at me.

"I'll find your parents," the sheriff said. "You stay here."

Sheriff McCourt jogged down the porch steps and strode around the corner of the Victorian. Rose blossoms rustled in her wake.

"Hurry," I told Arsen. I raced inside the B&B and to the kitchen.

"Susan?" Arsen called after me.

I peered through the window into the side yard and leaned against the counter for a better view. My hip knocked a spatula into the sink. There was no sign of my parents.

Bailey whuffed.

"Not now," I said. "This is important."

The sheriff strode past the porch and toward the gazebo.

The gazebo. I gripped the edge of the butcher block counter more tightly.

"Susan?" Arsen pushed open the kitchen door and walked inside. "What's—"

"This way." Jogging past him, I banged through the swinging door and into the foyer. I raced up the stairs, taking them two at a time.

Bailey whimpered at the bottom. Arsen scooped him up and charged after me, his booted feet loud on the old stairs.

I hurried down the green-carpeted hallway, lined with black-and-white UFO photos. At the end, I cracked open the door to the rear exterior stair landing.

The sheriff called a greeting, raising her hand.

I tracked her gaze.

My parents emerged from the garden shed. My father dusted off his hands. Even from this distance, I could see they were filthy.

Almost like they'd been burying a body.

I groaned.

Arsen rested his hand on my lower back. "So the sheriff's got more questions for your parents. It's no biggie."

It was if she figured out what they'd been doing in my garden shed.

"I don't think we need to spy on them," he continued.

My muscles twitched. "No, we don't. We need to interrupt them."

"Whoa. The sheriff said—"

I pushed open the rear door and trotted down the wooden stairs. "Mom! Dad! I told you that you didn't need to help with the gardening."

My mother, in a track suit, her hair tied in a neat bun, smiled. "But you know how your father feels about those roses your grandmother planted."

She turned to the sheriff. "No one can figure out the secret ingredient in her fertilizer. It keeps them blooming all year. We're thinking of getting it tested by a chemist."

That actually wasn't a bad idea. I'd make a note of it in my planner later.

"It looks like you've been exhuming a corpse," the sheriff said.

"That's more work than I care for on my vacation," my father said.

"Ha! Ha, ha!" I wrung my hands. "My father's always making bad jokes."

"I didn't think it was that bad," he said.

Sheriff McCourt glared at me. "I was hoping for a private conversation."

"I'll make tea," I said. "You can use my private sitting room."

"Have you got any more of those scones left?" my father asked. "I could kill for some carbs."

Another laugh, high-pitched and false, emerged from my throat. "Of course. Right this way." I pretended not to notice Arsen's frown.

We trooped around the side of the house, up the porch steps and into my kitchen.

I motioned toward the door to my private rooms. "You know where everything is."

My parents strolled into my sitting room.

The sheriff threw me a sharp look. She followed them and shut the door firmly behind her.

I put the kettle on the stove.

Arsen set Bailey on his bed beneath the kitchen table. "What's going on?" he asked quietly.

I pressed a finger to my lips and my ear to the door. "Eavesdropping," I whispered.

"...haven't I seen you two around Doyle before?" the sheriff was saying.

"I'm afraid we were estranged from my mother-in-law," my mother said. "It's our greatest regret that we didn't make things up before she passed."

Was that true? My parents had never said anything about regrets to me before.

The sheriff said something too low for me to hear. Since when had she developed a demure voice? It was almost as if she suspected I'd listen in or something.

Arsen arranged scones on a cake plate and handed it to me.

"Thanks." I kissed him quickly and bustled into the sitting room. In a fit of modernity, my gran had decorated it in slick, modern-Victorian black and white. A fluffy white throw rug lay before a coffee table. Plush black and white chairs sat opposite an ebony velvet couch.

My parents sat on the sofa. The sheriff was standing.

I set the cake plate on the black coffee table between them. "The tea's going to be a bit longer."

Sheriff McCourt glowered. "*Thank* you, Susan."

"No problem." I dropped onto an empty wingchair. "I heard the neighbor across the street complained that Mr. Van Der Woodsen was leaving his garbage cans out for the bears. It was quite the neighborhood drama."

Sheriff McCourt's eyes seemed to spark blue with annoyance. "I heard that too."

"When Van Der Woodsen found out," I said, "he confronted the neighbor."

"Goodness." My mother adjusted a velvet pillow behind her back. "Was it a violent confrontation? That Van Der Woodsen struck me as a very violent man. Writers. I suspect he spent too much time in a fantasy world of spies and guns."

"I don't believe in guns," my father said primly. He brushed a speck of dirt off his khaki slacks.

"Don't get me wrong," my mother said to the sheriff. "I enjoy a good book too. But we have to know the difference between reality and fantasy."

I nodded, then realized my mother was staring at me. Why was she staring at me? I knew the difference between reality and fantasy.

"Are you still wearing that?" my mother asked me.

I looked down at my capris and neat, lilac blouse. My neck tensed. "Why would I change? There's nothing wrong with what I'm wearing."

"Capris make your ankles look big." My mother raised her hands and let them drop helplessly to her lap. "There, I've said it."

I crossed my legs. "My ankles aren't big."

"I didn't say they were big. I said they *looked* big when you wear capris."

"No, they don't." I turned to Sheriff McCourt. "Sheriff? These don't make my ankles look big do they?"

The sheriff blinked, shook her head, and walked toward the kitchen door. She stopped, turned, and grabbed a scone off the cake plate.

Sheriff McCourt pushed through the door, narrowly avoiding Arsen coming through with the tea kettle.

He looked after the sheriff. "What happened?" Arsen asked.

"She had some more questions about our afternoon," my father said jovially. "Imagine, Pansy. We might be actual suspects in a murder investigation if we can't come up with a better alibi."

"So exciting," she agreed. "Think of the stories we'll have for our friends back home."

My hands turned clammy. My parents didn't have friends. They had colleagues and superiors. If they told any of them about the sheriff... "Tea?" I squeaked out.

"Lovely," my mother said. "Arsen, tell us more about your security company."

He set the kettle on the black coffee table, and I slipped one of Gran's doilies beneath it.

"I focus on consulting and equipment." He sat on the arm of my wingchair and rested one arm along its back. "Most security is based on procedures rather than gadgets. But there's something to be said for the gadgets."

"I'm surprised you've let Susan get away with all those bathroom mirrors," my father said.

"Mirrors?" Arsen asked.

"This is earthquake country," my father said. "Imagine those shattering on the guests when the big one hits."

"I can't *not* have mirrors in the bathrooms," I said, jerking down the cuff of my blouse, which *was* my color. "They're sort of expected. And you have a mirror in your bathroom at home."

"We don't rent out rooms," my mother said.

"The mirrors are safety glass," Arsen said. "It's a federal and state rule."

"How silly of us." My mother poured tea. "Of course it is. I know you wouldn't allow Susan to do anything stupid."

"It's not about allowing," Arsen said. "Susan doesn't need permission—"

"Okay, that was fun." I leapt to my feet. "Arsen, would you help me in the kitchen?"

He trailed after me.

Bailey raised his head from the dog bed. When no treats were forthcoming, he flopped back down.

"Susan, there's something I've got to say."

Worried, I turned to him. "My parents—"

"No," he said gently. "This is about *my* parents. I never knew them. I'd give anything to—" He looked at his hiking boots, and my chest tightened.

"You get it," he said, gruff. "If there's a way we can make things work with your parents, I'm all in."

I looked away, toward the window over the sink. I'd been so insensitive. Arsen had been raised by his aunts. My parents weren't perfect, but at least I'd had them. "Arsen—"

"Let me finish. You've been doing an awesome job standing up to your parents. But I'm not going to let them put our relationship in a box either."

I leaned my head against his broad chest. "And I love you for that." He was the best. He understood me. He supported me.

And I was lying.

"But?" he asked.

Tell him the truth. "But... But I don't know if their attitude is worth kicking up a fuss. Soon they'll leave, and everything will get back to normal." It wasn't what I'd meant to say or what I should have said, but how could I tell him they'd knocked off an assassin?

His arms came around me, and he kissed the top of my head. "Okay. I'll keep my mouth shut if that's what you want." His watch beeped, and he glanced at it. "Oh, damn."

"What's wrong?"

"I've got a client meeting. No worries. I'll cancel."

"No. I don't want my parents to mess up our schedules. I mean our lives. I mean—"

"I know what you mean." He ran a hand up my arm, and I shivered. "Are you sure you'll be okay?"

"Like you said, I've been doing okay standing up to them. Sort of."

"Not sort of. Totally."

"And I need to get in some more practice before they leave."

He grinned and kissed me again. "Go get 'em."

I walked him to the door, and watched his Jeep back from my driveway.

Then I hurried back to my sitting room. "What did the sheriff want?"

My mother looked up from the couch. "Just as we said. She wanted more information about our afternoon."

"Well, is it gone? The body, I mean."

"No." My father's brow wrinkled. "We haven't been able to get a disposal team out yet."

Are you kidding me? "You—when—he—why not?" I sputtered.

"Budget cuts," my mother said darkly from her perch on the ebony couch. "At least, that's what they *say.*"

"Why would they lie?" my father asked.

"That is an excellent question," she said.

"Then when are they coming?" I asked.

"Another two or three days," my father said cheerfully.

I clapped my hands to my head. "Two or three— You can't hide a body in my garden shed for another three days."

"Well, of course not," my mother said. "It's too obvious. That's why we buried it. Susan, *do* use the senses God gave you."

"I wouldn't exactly call it buried," my father muttered.

I stared. "If it's not in the greenhouse, then where—?"

"Better you don't know," my mother said. "Now, don't you have some work to do?"

My jaw clenched. "Yes." I did. I just didn't need my mother reminding me about it.

Because throwing myself in the path of potential killers was a day at the spa compared to a conversation with my parents, I fled. Gathering up Bailey, I loaded him into my Crosstrek.

We returned to Mr. Van Der Woodsen's street, and I parked on the road. I sat there a moment and tried to let go of my frustration.

But beneath that frustration was a thread of pain. My parents and I had never understood each other, and I knew we never would. I'd moved through their world as an irritant, a disappointment. We'd never truly connected.

Not like me and Gran.

I sighed and glanced again at the rooftop of the Tudor mansion.

Turning away, Bailey and I walked up the brick path to the smaller but fashionable cabin-style house across the street. A barn star hung above its porch.

I knocked on the door.

If the neighbor had threatened Mr. Van Der Woodsen, it was time to talk to him or her. True, the neighbor might not be willing to talk, but—

The door opened, and a cheerful round face smiled out at me.

I gaped. I *knew* who lived here. And this was not good. Not good at all.

CHAPTER EIGHT

THE YOUNG WOMAN STOOD in the doorway and tilted her head. "Susan?" Darla Ashfield hastily tied her longish blond hair into a ponytail. "What are you doing here?"

"Darla? You live here?" How did I not know Darla was loaded? And why was someone with a house like this working as the assistant manager at a coffee shop?

And now she was a suspect in my investigation? I *liked* Darla. She was one of those salt-of-the-earth types who keeps the world turning.

Her round face pinked. "I didn't want to tell people, but I won the lottery. Not one of those crazy jackpots, but enough to get this house."

"And you're still working at Ground?" I glanced up at the horseshoe over the door. Between that and the barn star, Darla had gone all out on blinging the front of her house.

"It's because of Ground that my luck turned around. No rhyme intended."

I rubbed my temple. "Really?" What did a coffeeshop have to do with winning the lottery?

"Come on in," Darla said and pulled the door wider. "Bailey too."

Bailey and I eased past a fancy bicycle. My hip bumped the handlebars, and it wobbled. "Sorry," I said, steadying the bike.

We followed her through a hallway lined with Pennsylvania Dutch hex signs. She led us into a living area with a high ceiling crisscrossed by dark-wood beams.

Darla motioned us to a new-looking couch, and I sat, Bailey at my feet. Opposite us, one of those glass, Turkish blue eyes hung on the wall between a row of bookcases. A massive dream catcher dangled in the window.

"The hex signs," I said. "Are you Pennsylvania Dutch?"

"Oh, no. I'm German."

"The Pennsylvania Dutch are..." I shook my head. The Pennsylvania Dutch actually were German, Dutch being a bastardization of *Deutch*. But... *Never mind.*

"What brings you here?" Darla sat in a wide, comfy looking white chair opposite us.

I pulled my planner from my bag and opened it to my investigations page. "I wanted to ask you about the complaint you made about Mr. Van Der Woodsen's garbage cans."

"Why do you ask?"

"My parents are visiting."

"Oh, my."

"So I can't go home."

"That bad?" she asked.

"You have no idea."

"And so... you decided to turn your hand to crime solving?"

I shrugged helplessly.

"Well, okay then." Darla's mouth set. "They left their cans out overnight all the time. A bear got into it three times this year. His butler or whatever always cleaned up the mess. But it's not healthy for the bears to consider humans a food source. If he had to leave the cans out overnight, he should have gotten bear proof cans. But he was too cheap to do even that. I don't know why he didn't just tell that Franklin guy to put them out in the morning. That butler had him wrapped around his little finger."

"He did?"

"It's awful what happened, but... I have to say, I wasn't much surprised when he was killed."

"You weren't? Why?"

She leaned forward and glanced around the room. "Because there's something wrong with Doyle," she whispered.

"Wrong?" I pulled Bailey closer.

"Don't you feel it? All the murders for a town this size? But hardly anyone moves away. There's something... supernatural about this place."

"Supernatural?" I parroted. Doyle had a reputation for UFOs for a reason, but Darla had never expressed an interest in aliens.

She leaned closer. "Have you heard if there's anything... weird about his murder?"

"Well, it was murder, which is horrible and wrong. But I don't think aliens killed him."

Darla reared back in her seat. "Of course not, not aliens. I mean, no offense to your B&B."

"None taken," I murmured, bemused.

She toyed with a horseshoe charm around her neck. "I know the alien stuff has made Doyle a tourist attraction. But after last year's panic, I see UFO tourism can be taken too far."

"True," I said ruefully. We'd been lucky the town hall fire hadn't spread to other buildings on Main Street.

"That's why I took down that squirrel flyer in Ground. The bulletin board is supposed to be for the community, but squirrels were a bridge too far."

I ruminated on that. Darla was obviously superstitious. Dream catchers and hex signs, Turkish eyes and horseshoes—they all pointed to someone obsessed with good luck. But what did she have against what had to be a joke flyer? "Squirrels."

She pressed a finger to her nose.

I mentally shrugged and changed the subject. "I heard Mr. Van Der Woodsen confronted you."

"If by *confronted* you mean *screamed at*, yes. The whole street must have heard him shouting."

"Did he threaten you?"

"I can't remember exactly what he said. All I remember is that butler, standing behind him and smirking. He's such a jerk."

Oh, this was ridiculous. Darla didn't kill anybody. Salt-of-the-earth types don't go around murdering their neighbors. But I couldn't leave a clue unturned.

"Did you see anyone at Mr. Van Der Woodsen's house on Friday?" I asked.

"No, I was working Friday."

"All afternoon?"

"I had a lunch break, but after that, I was at Ground until closing."

I made a note in my planner and relaxed on the couch. *Good.* Darla had an alibi. Not that I'd ever seriously considered her a murder suspect. But at least the sheriff couldn't consider her a suspect either.

Darla promised to let me know if she remembered anything suspicious, and Bailey and I left.

I walked down her driveway and glanced up at the barn star—another good luck symbol. But if memory served, the hex signs and Turkish eyes were about more than good luck. They also were believed to ward off evil forces.

I stopped on the sidewalk. And what was that business about supernatural forces if she hadn't been talking about UFOs? Did she think the town was haunted?

I shook my head. That was just nutty. All those talismans were probably Darla's attempt to win another lottery.

Bailey sniffed her mailbox.

I tugged gently on his leash. "I know new smells are exciting, but this isn't the sort of neighborhood for peeing on mailboxes."

Bailey shot me a sulky look and reluctantly toddled after me toward the Subaru.

"There *are* a lot of murders though," I mused. "It's weird, because Doyle doesn't *feel* like a bad place."

The town was charming with its Gold Rush history, thick forests, and low-key wineries. I'd spent my summers here as a child with Gran, and I'd never felt safer. I still felt safe here.

The back of my neck prickled, and I stopped. Turned.

A trio of clouds shaped like UFOs floated over the mountains behind Darla's house. They were lenticular clouds, and natural phenomena. But suddenly I fancied the clouds were creeping up on me, that if I turned my back...

I shook myself. I'd let Darla's superstitions get to me. There was nothing wrong with Doyle, and I was completely safe. I pulled my keys from my bag and pressed the fob.

My Crosstrek's headlights flashed, and the car beeped. I helped Bailey inside, then rolled down my window and buckled in. I reached for his dog harness.

Bailey whined, and I glanced at the passenger seat. The beagle had somehow managed to wedge his rump between the two seats.

"What on earth were you trying to accomplish?" I bent to dislodge the dog.

Something dark whistled past my ear. I tensed, hunched over Bailey. There was a thud, a cracking noise.

A yellow and black rubber ball ricocheted off something and flew behind me. I yelped and squeezed Bailey more tightly, shielding his head. Another bang. The ball struck my shoulder. I gasped, pain rocketing down my arm.

Cautiously, I raised my head.

The ball, made of hard rubber, lay on the floor in front of the passenger seat. Knowing better than to touch it, I looked around. The street was empty.

A dent the size of my fist had been punched in the strip of metal between the passenger-side windows. My windshield was cracked. My shoulder *really* hurt.

Bailey *awoooed.*

"It's okay," I said shakily and pulled him free. "We're safe."

That ball had dented metal and cracked a window. If it had hit me in the head...

I shuddered, and then hot anger washed over me. Whoever had thrown that ball could have hit Bailey. They could have killed me.

And they might still be nearby.

Hands trembling, I reached for my car keys.

"*This* is what comes from sticking your nose in another murder investigation," a voice graveled at my ear.

CHAPTER NINE

I ROCKETED UPWARD. MY seatbelt cut into my shoulders and jolted me back into my seat.

Mrs. Steinberg leaned on her cane. The old lady blew a stream of raspberry-scented smoke through my open window and studied the cracked windshield.

At least, I *think* she studied it. It was hard to tell behind her Jackie-Kennedy style sunglasses.

She leaned forward on her cane, her long black dress rippling at the motion. "So who's trying to kill you now?"

"Er, I'm guessing you're not?"

"I wouldn't use a ball to kill you," she said. "Inefficient."

That was... What *would* she use?

Mrs. Steinberg blew a smoke ring.

"Did you see who threw it?" I asked.

"Nope. Just the aftermath. Your car was really rocking."

I eyed her. The elderly woman worked in town records. She knew everything about everybody. Mrs. Steinberg could be a source. "What are you doing here?"

"A better question is, what are *you* doing here?"

Okay, she could be a source *if* she wasn't always so darned sphinxlike. "I'm... just... visiting a friend."

"Your parents are back in town."

I started. "How do you know about that?"

"I know lots of things."

"What sort of things, exactly?"

She brandished her e-cigarette. "I know you're in jeopardy again, and not just physically. There's more at stake here than you may know."

I gripped the steering wheel, slippery beneath my palms. "Like what? Do you know anything about the Van Der Woodsen murder?"

"I know you should stay out of it."

"Yes, but what are the odds of that?"

One corner of her wrinkled mouth quirked upward. "This was a crime of greed."

"Was Mr. Van Der Woodsen as rich as people say?"

"Rich in more ways than one. And people can also be greedy in more ways than one. Your parents know about that."

I stiffened. "What about my parents? What did Gran tell you about them?" She and Gran had been close friends. Sadness weighted my chest at the thought of our loss.

"She didn't need to tell me anything. It's obvious they're spies."

My mouth dropped open. "Wait. What?" I shook my head emphatically. "No."

"You're a terrible liar, Susan. Hard to believe they ever thought you might follow in their footsteps."

"I could too be a spy."

She raised a snowy brow.

"Well, I could," I said stubbornly. People told me I couldn't be a detective all the time, and see where *that* got them.

"There's a big difference between detecting and spying."

She leaned closer, smoke pouring from her nostrils like a dragon's. "Don't let them pull you into their world, Susan. You got out once. You may not be so lucky the next time."

A squirrel scampered across the street in front of my car. Bailey lunged, his front paws on the dashboard, and loosed a steady stream of barks.

"Bailey, stop that." I grabbed his collar and tugged him back to the seat. "Mrs. Steinberg—" I turned toward the window.

The old lady had vanished.

I twisted, looking up and down the tree-lined street, but she was nowhere in sight. She used a cane. Where the heck had she gone so fast?

Frustrated, I stepped from the car and peered around some more, but I didn't see her anywhere. *Weird.*

Bailey dropped to the ground beside me and sniffed.

I phoned Sheriff McCourt.

"What?" she asked, her tone bored.

"Someone threw a ball through my car window and nearly killed me."

"Nearly killed you. With a ball."

"It was a very hard ball." I leaned against my car, the Saturday sun warming my shoulders, and adjusted the phone against my ear.

"Someone's playing hardball?" the sheriff asked.

"Funny," I grumbled. "It cracked my windshield." This wasn't the first time someone had broken it. My insurance company was going to raise my rates for sure.

"Where did this happen? What are you up to? Were you investigating? I told you not to investigate."

Uh, oh. This really wasn't the time for the sheriff's little stay-out-of-my-investigation game. But I couldn't lie. There were alibis she'd need to check and evidence. "Outside Darla—"

"Never mind. I don't want to know. Bring me the ball, and I'll see if I can get prints."

"Really?"

"I just said I would, didn't I?"

Bailey whuffed, and I looked down. The beagle dropped the black and yellow ball, covered in dog drool, at my feet.

"Uh, oh," I said.

"Uh, oh? Uh, oh what? What's wrong?"

I covered my eyes with my free hand. "Bailey got to the ball before I could, um, secure it. But obviously there's something going on here in Doyle. Someone just tried to kill me."

"I can't imagine who'd want to kill you," she said dryly. "It's not like you're annoying or anything."

"Well, my parents certainly wouldn't. They didn't attack me with a ball. Van Der Woodsen's killer must have. That means my parents aren't suspects in his murder."

There was a long silence. The sheriff hung up.

I tossed the phone onto the passenger seat and crossed my arms. "I'm right, and she knows it," I told Bailey. "Sure, she has to cross her t's and dot her i's in this investigation. But she doesn't understand the danger that might put her in."

The sheriff needed me.

"I have to help her before she gets into real trouble."

Bailey woofed.

I checked the time I'd called the sheriff and subtracted five minutes. In my planner, I noted my guesstimate of when the ball attack had occurred: one-forty-two.

My phone rang. I checked the number. It was Arsen, and my heart fizzed with happiness. He still had that effect on me.

"Hi, Arsen."

"Hey. I finished up with my client earlier than I expected. Want to meet up?"

"Sure. Where?"

"Ground? We never got our lunch, but I could go for some coffee if you're game."

I glanced at the house with the barn star. "I'll be there in ten minutes."

I loaded Bailey into my Crosstrek and fastened his harness around him. We drove down the hill to Main Street. This being a weekend afternoon, cars lined the old-west street. Tourists thronged Doyle's raised sidewalks.

I found a spot in front of a tasting room covered in ivy, and Bailey and I walked to Ground.

Its sidewalk tables were filled with customers, heads bent over phones and computer tablets.

I walked into the crowded coffeeshop and scanned the oddly silent tables. Or maybe it wasn't so odd that it was quiet—everyone was engrossed in their screens.

Arsen waved to me from a corner. Smiling, I wound through the tables to him.

Marla Merriweather leaned across a table toward her friend, Cindy. "How could I stay friends with someone who thinks squirrels are just squirrels? It's dangerous."

Cindy's long nose twitched. "She could be in denial. Unless...she's one of them."

I banged my hip on a stray chair, and it tumbled sideways to the floor. Bailey yipped.

The two women and pretty much everyone else in the café stared at me. Muttering apologies, I righted the wooden chair and hurried to Arsen's table.

He stood and pulled out a chair for me, then kissed my cheek. "How'd your detecting go?"

I rubbed my aching hip. "You knew I was detecting?"

"I figured. Dixie's manning the reception desk, so you have the afternoon free."

Biting my lip, I sat.

He pushed a cup of iced coffee toward me.

"I would have invited you to come," I said quickly. "But you said you had an appointment."

"I'll forgive you if you tell me what you learned."

I looped Bailey's leash around the back of the chair. The beagle sat on my foot.

"Thanks," I said to Arsen and took a sip of the coffee. *Heaven*. No one made coffee better than Ground. It was like magic.

"My investigation went well," I continued. "It turns out the neighbor who called the authorities on Mr. Van Der Woodsen was Darla."

He glanced at the long, wooden bar. "Our Darla? The assistant manager at Ground?"

"So we can cross one suspect off the list. She obviously didn't kill anyone."

He smiled faintly. "You can't cross off suspects just because you like them."

"Why not? We're seasoned investigators. I have instincts for these things. She's innocent. Besides, she was working all that afternoon. Darla couldn't be the killer."

"That's a better reason."

"But when I was leaving her house, someone threw this at me." I reached into my bag with a napkin and pulled out the ball, set it on the table. "It went through my car's open window hard enough to dent a metal strip in the car and crack the windshield."

Arsen's brow furrowed, but he didn't touch the ball. "That's a jai alai ball. Susan, you could have been killed."

"A what now?"

"Jai alai – it's like high intensity racket ball."

"Well, it's only a ball."

"No, it isn't. When thrown with a cesta, those balls can reach a hundred and eighty miles an hour."

I felt the blood drain from my face. "A hundred and eighty?"

Horrified, I sunk back against the chair. If Bailey hadn't wedged himself between the seats. If I hadn't bent down to pry him free at exactly the right moment... "Oh."

"Keeping the ball in a napkin was a good idea," he said. "I'll take it to the sheriff's department to get it printed."

I winced. I'd used the napkin so I wouldn't have to touch a slimy dog ball. "Don't bother. Bailey used it as a chew toy before I could grab it."

"Bummer. But at least we're honing down on some suspects."

"How?"

"Jai alai's a rich man's sport. We played it at that boarding school."

"Oh," I said, repeating myself. "I suppose you did all sorts of fun things at that school."

The boarding school. It was easy to forget Arsen had money. It had never seemed to matter to him, so it hadn't mattered to me. So why were these reminders bothering me so much?

He shrugged. "Mountain biking, fencing. The place wasn't all bad. But it wasn't Doyle."

"And Malcolm and Maive were both there?" I asked, tentative.

"Both there, and both players." He grinned. "Maive wasn't supposed to play. It's still considered a man's sport. But they couldn't stop her, especially when her old man pitched a fit and threatened to stop donating to the school."

"We need to talk to Malcolm and Maive." I checked my watch. "But not today. I promised Dixie I'd return by three."

"Then we'd better get you back."

I deposited the ball in my purse. We grabbed our coffees, and he followed me in his Jeep to Wits' End. The Victorian was still standing, which was about as much as one could ask for from Dixie.

My cousin, booted feet on the reception desk, glared up at me as we stepped into the foyer. "About time," she said.

"I have five minutes to spare," I said, indignant. "I'm never late. That would knock the entire day off schedule."

Her feet thudded to the faux-Persian carpet. "Whatever. Oh. Some guy called and made a reservation."

"For when?" I asked.

"Tomorrow."

I pulled the reservation book across the desk to me and scanned Sunday. "I don't see any new reservations."

"Was I supposed to write it down?"

I did not roll my eyes, though I really wanted to. "What was the guest's name?"

"Something Slavic-sounding."

I jammed my hands on my hips. How was I supposed to put that in my reservation book? "Did he say when he was arriving?"

"Mm... No."

"How many days is he staying?"

"I didn't ask."

My jaw clenched. She was doing this on purpose. "Dixie—"

My parents strolled down the carpeted stairs.

"There you are." My mother stopped on the bottom step. "We've been looking all over for you."

"I had some errands to run," I said.

"Not you," my mother said. "Arsen."

My insides chilled to absolute zero. "What do you want with Arsen?"

"Anything I can do to help." Arsen rocked on the heels of his hiking boots.

"Thanks," my father said to him. "My back's not what it once was. I was hoping you could help me move something."

Move something? Horror choked my throat. The only heavy object he could possibly need to move—

"I'll help," I said.

"It's okay." Arsen touched my arm. "I'll do it."

"No, really," I said. "They're my parents."

"Give me a break," my mother said. "You obviously have no upper body strength. Whatever happened to that training regime we put you on?"

The training regime they'd put me on had been a hellscape of fitness machines and dumbbells. I'd dumped it as soon as I'd moved out from under their thumbscrews. "I get plenty of exercise gardening."

"Speaking of gardening," my father said, "is there any part of your garden that *isn't* a thin layer of soil over solid rock? How do you grow anything here?"

"No," I said, sweating. Could they be any more obvious? I knew the body had to go somewhere, but not in Gran's garden. "It's all rock."

"What about under that little spirit house?" my mother asked. "The ground looks soft there."

"It isn't," I said sharply.

Dixie squinted at me.

My mother shrugged and pivoted on the step. "So Arsen, a hand?"

"I need Arsen for something else," I said.

Arsen beamed. "Anything you need."

"Great." I'd successfully diverted him from corpse-moving duty.

"So?" Arsen asked. "What do you need?"

My gaze darted around the foyer. There had to be something here that needed fixing, some project I could rope him into. But everything was obviously perfect. Drat my superb organizational skills!

"I think your project can wait," my mother said.

"No," I said, "it can't." My gaze fixed on the stained-glass transom. That worked too. Maybe something outside?

"I can do both," Arsen said. "I'll help your parents move whatever it is, and then I'll help you."

"It can't wait," I blurted, voice rising. "The UFO on the roof is coming loose and it could fall and kill someone and wreck the roof and Wits' End."

The four stared at me.

I shuffled my feet.

Bailey thumped his tail on the carpet.

"Whoa," Arsen said. "That sounds serious. Why didn't you say anything earlier? You're right, I'd better check the roof first. But afterward, I'll be right down to move whatever you need, Mr. and Mrs. Witsend."

My parents stood aside, and he sidled past them, then took the remaining steps two at a time.

"Okay," Dixie said. "That was... weird. I'm going home." She stomped out the front door. It slammed behind her.

I waited for the second porch screen door to bang shut before whirling on my parents. "You can't have Arsen. You can't involve him in your problems."

"Susan—"

"No." I leaned sideways, looking inside the blue breakfast room. It was empty. "I know he's got the muscles," I whispered, "but he's not moving any bodies for you. Arsen has to stay out of this."

My mother shook her head. "Then you shouldn't have sent him up to that UFO."

"Why not?"

"Because that's where we stashed the body."

CHAPTER TEN

I GOGGLED AT MY parents.

I goggled at them some more.

Yes, I had heard my mother right.

No, I was not having a mental break.

"Why would you put a body in my flying saucer?" I asked, my voice level.

My father angled his head. "Well..."

"Never mind." Acid burning my stomach, I raced up the stairs.

How on earth had they made it this far as spies? No wonder they'd once wanted me to join the team. Clearly, they needed someone with strong organizational skills.

Bailey's dog collar jangled behind me. The beagle wheezed. But I couldn't stop for him now.

At the top of the stairs, I pivoted and raced down the narrow strip of hall to the turret room. I jogged through its open door.

Curtains fluttered at a window. Arsen's foot balanced on the sill. The rest of him was outside the octagonal room.

"Arsen, it's okay," I shouted and stuck my head out the window.

He gripped the sloping roof and looked down at me. "The UFO seems to be attached pretty well."

"Oh, great. The guest who complained must have been wrong."

"A guest was complaining about your UFO? What was a guest doing up here?"

"You know... Looking for UFOs." I clenched the sill, realized I was doing it, and jammed my hands in the pockets of my capris. "Why don't you come down?"

"Are you sure it wasn't the smell they were complaining about? I think an animal might have crawled inside your flying saucer and died." He moved his other foot to the low corner where the two slopes of the shingled roof met. "I'll need a toolbox. Can you get yours for me?"

My eyes bulged. "No!"

"Don't tell me you lost it."

"No, I mean, I haven't lost it, but you don't need to do that. Just come down."

"You don't want me to get out whatever's in there?"

My brain churned. "My... insurance company requires me to use a professional um, extermination service for that."

Bailey's collar jingled behind me.

"It would just be easier if I dealt with it," Arsen said. "I'll get some gloves." He swung into the room and landed gracefully on the throw rug.

"Honestly," I said, "I'd rather the exterminator deal with it. They've got the right equipment."

His brow furrowed. Arsen studied me. "You hate dead animals. Why don't you want me to get rid of this one?"

Bailey whined at my feet.

When in doubt, blame mom. "My parents," I said. "They said if I want to run a B&B, I need to be more professional."

"That's not fair. You've got the best UFO B&B in the Sierras."

"But they may have a point in this case. You know. Insurance."

He nodded. "Gotcha. Well, if you'd really prefer an exterminator, I guess I'll go help them." He scooped up the beagle, and I tottered after them as they trooped downstairs.

Arsen scanned the empty foyer. "Where'd they go?"

"Maybe their need wasn't so urgent after all?" I said.

"I'll check the kitchen."

We looked in the kitchen, the yard, and their room, but my parents were in none of those places.

He scratched his head. "You think they ditched us?"

"One can only hope."

"Well, since they don't need me, and we're all alone..." He leered.

"Not on the schedule." I bustled him out the front door.

He stopped on the porch. "You have a schedule for romance?"

"No, that would be weird. But it's still working hours. Lots to do. Gotta do it. Love you. Byeee." I retreated into the B&B and closed the door.

After a moment, I heard the roar of Arsen's Jeep and the crunch of gravel. I sagged against the front desk. Did I want to know where my parents had gone?

No, I did not.

I hurried to the kitchen, grabbed one of Arsen's beers from my fridge and chugged it. I'm not a beer person, or even much of an alcohol person, but the day seemed to call for it.

Bailey eyed me warily from his dog bed, which he'd somehow moved beside the stove.

"Why on earth did my parents decide my UFO made a good hiding place for a body?" I dragged bed and beagle beneath the table and out of the way. "And why hasn't their team removed the cadaver anyway?"

Bailey yawned.

"I mean, I understand budget cuts. My budget is thin. But this is ridiculous. National security's at stake."

The bell on the reception desk pinged.

I started and the bottle slipped from my fingers.

Instead of shattering, it thunked and rolled, dripping beer across the linoleum.

I reached for a dish towel, thought better of it, and hurried into the foyer.

Bailey heaved a sigh and toddled after me.

Maive and Jacob stood in the foyer. Expensive-looking suitcases piled around them on the faded rug.

I slowed. "Hi," I said. "Are you... looking for a room?"

Maive's face reddened. "That bastard threw us out." Her green and brown eyes darkened.

"He didn't throw us out." Her husband stroked his goatee.

She whirled on him, the hem of her violet dress rippling. "He wants us to pay rent!"

"Sorry," I said. "What?"

Bailey's gaze swiveled between us.

Maive gulped. "Franklin. He inherited our condo."

"Why would he—?"

"He inherited everything." Maive vibrated with fury. "This whole time, he's been working on my father, putting a wedge between him and us. And it worked. We're suing."

Franklin Asher had inherited *everything*? That might explain why he'd been lounging around the pool like he'd owned the place. He *did* own the place.

"Of course, we're suing," Jacob said, soothing. "And we'll win, too. A father can't disinherit his children. Not in California." He smiled briefly at me. "But in the meantime, staying at the condo has become rather awkward."

"Infuriating, you mean," Maive said.

"Please tell us you have a room free," he said.

"What about that room in the turret that's on your website?" Maive asked. "That's the biggest one, isn't it?"

The room with the dead body over it? "Yes," I said slowly. "But wouldn't you be happier, er, closer to town?"

"The Doyle Hotel is full up for the week," Jacob said.

Of course it was. It hadn't been likely Wits' End would be Maive and Jacob's first choice.

I scanned the reception book, hoping I'd remembered wrong. But the turret room was the only free room in the B&B until tomorrow. "Have you considered renting a house?" I asked.

"We needed a speedy exit," Jacob said. "Is the turret free?"

"It is," I said, "but—"

"We'll take the turret." Maive climbed the stairs.

"But—"

"She's not used to keys anymore," Jacob said and held out his hand. "We had voice recognition at the condo."

"There are some great luxury rentals—"

"Keep this under your hat," he said, lowering his voice, "but we can't afford one. I'm not sure we could have afforded the Doyle Hotel either. Our finances are a bit of a disaster now that her father's dead."

"Oh."

"But don't worry. We can pay you." He reached into the rear pocket of his designer slacks and pulled out a wallet, laid out a row of hundreds on the desk. "This should cover us for a few nights, right?"

I swallowed. If they were really strapped for a place to stay, I couldn't turn them away. That would be cruel, especially coming on top of the loss of Maive's father.

This would also make interrogating them easier if they were right upstairs. And I couldn't exactly afford to turn away guests. Not if I wanted to get that roof repaired.

Besides, if Arsen hadn't noticed a body in the UFO, Jacob and
Maive wouldn't either. And my parents' clean-up team, whenever
they came, could pretend to be fixing the roof.

"Say, do you have a gym?" he asked. "I like to keep fit." Jacob
flexed his muscles beneath his tweed jacket.

"Sorry. We don't."

His face fell. "That's okay. We can make do for a week. There's
always hiking, right?"

Maive returned to the foyer. "The room is adequate."

I straightened. "How—?" Then I remembered I'd left the door
unlocked when I'd raced out earlier.

"Please have someone bring up our things as soon as possible,"
she said. "I'd like to get settled. This day has been awful."

And at least she'd said *please*. I forced a smile, made new electronic key cards, and handed two to Jacob. "Here you go. I'll take
care of your bags. How long do you plan to stay?"

"Until Friday," he said.

Nearly a week. I checked the reception book. People would be
checking out tomorrow, so there'd be space for our new guest.
This could work.

"Until Friday then," I said. "Enjoy your stay."

"UFO's," Maive muttered, climbing the stairs. "I can't believe you
wanted to stay here."

"It'll be fun," Jacob said cheerfully. "Think of it as an adventure."

I grimaced. Did Maive know they had financial problems? And
how low on funds were they? Jacob had been awfully quick to lay
out those hundreds.

"This isn't over." Maive's faint voice drifted down the stairs.

I counted the money. It would cover their stay, and my muscles
loosened.

Not that I didn't want to help Jacob and Maive, but I'd once gotten stiffed by a, well, a stiff. I'd let him get away with not paying longer than I should have, and then it had been too late. I'd become more militant about on-time payments since.

Bailey whuffed.

"This will work," I whispered to him. "The sheriff can't accuse us of interfering if two suspects willingly came to stay here."

The beagle lifted a gray-flecked brow.

"I know you don't like uniforms, but Sheriff McCourt needs our help."

And she was going to get it whether she liked it or not.

CHAPTER ELEVEN

"WHEN IS YOUR COMPANY getting rid of that body?" I whispered. Hugging an empty orange juice carafe to my chest, I tried to fix my mother with a stern look.

But I just wasn't used to glaring at my parents. They were... my parents. So I found myself slipping again into whiny teenager mode. It was even more annoying in a grown woman than it had been as a teen.

Late morning sunshine streamed through the foyer's stained-glass transom. It cast weird and colorful beams of light across my father's frown.

"There are a lot of moving pieces," he said. "Sometimes we don't see all of them."

"Or something's gone wrong," my mother said to him. "It's those damned bureaucrats. I told you we couldn't trust—"

"Pansy," he said warningly. "There's no need to worry Susan."

I banged the carafe on the reception desk and winced. I hadn't meant to bang things around. "That makes me even more worried. What aren't you telling me?"

"Lots," my mother said. "Are you going to wear that blouse?"

"Yes, and—"

Two pairs of legs appeared descending the stairs. Two suitcases followed, and the rest of Layla and Fred hove into view.

"Checking out?" I asked with forced cheerfulness.

I hurried behind the desk to check their records on the computer.

"Yes," Layla said.

"How was your stay?"

"Amazing." Layla set her suitcase on the rug. "Do you need anything from us, aside from a rave review?"

"No," I said. "You're all taken care of. Is there anything I can help you with before you go? Directions? Maps?"

Her husband grinned. "Nope. We got everything we wanted and more from this vacation. The lights over Wits' End last night made our trip."

My mother's brows pulled downward.

"Lights over Wits' End?" I rubbed the skin below my ear.

Layla nodded excitedly. "We were coming home from dinner last night—"

"They looked like they were right over that flying saucer in the roof," her husband said. "The fake one, I mean."

I flinched. *The one with the body?*

"We were so startled, we forgot to take pictures," Layla said. "But we know what we saw."

"What exactly *did* you see?" My father edged closer and reached behind his back.

"Aliens," the man said. "We could see their silhouettes, moving around your spaceship. It's like the ship was a beacon or something."

"Doyle." I laughed loudly. "You never know what you'll see." I grabbed the suitcase from his hand. "Let me help you to your car." Bustling them out the door, I helped them load their sedan.

The Ford backed from the driveway, and I waved goodbye. My father came to stand beside me on the porch.

"You were the aliens on the roof," I said. "Weren't you?"

"Your mother and I thought we could shift that body on our own, but we didn't have the right tools. Funny how extracting something *from* a fake UFO is harder than putting something *into* a UFO."

"There are guests in the room below that spaceship."

"I am aware. Don't worry, we waited until they'd left for a late dinner. Was that a hardware store I saw on Main Street?"

"Yes, but you could have been seen," I hissed.

"Apparently, we *were* seen. It's a good thing you have gullible clients," he said.

"They're not gullible. They're UFO curious."

"That's not always a positive trait."

"But what are you going to do about..." My gaze flicked upward. "You know."

"That's really none of your business." He walked inside the B&B.

My neck stiffened. They'd hidden a body at Wits' End. It *was* my business. I mean, okay, I might not have a security clearance, but still.

The shadow touched my shoulder blade, and I shuddered, closed my eyes. My heartbeat galloped, out of control. The entire situation was out of control, and oh, God, it was happening again. Not another panic attack. I sucked in healing breaths. *I am calm and serene.*

Oh, who was I kidding? I was not calm. *Breathe, breathe, breathe.*

I pressed my palm to my chest. Arsen had taught me a calming technique. What was it? Oh, right.

"I'm feeling anxious and out of control," I said in a low voice. "Yes." *Accept the feelings. Then locate the feelings.* Or was it locate and then accept? *Whatever.*

"I'm feeling tightness in my—"

A man cleared his throat.

I yelped, jumped, turned, and clunked my head against a hanging fern.

A jowly man in a rumpled suit stood before me. A raised scar traveled from the corner of his eye to his cheek. He looked like a pudgy Bela Lugosi.

I raised my hand to still the swinging fern.

"Hello," he said in a thick Russian accent. "I apologize for startling you." He lifted the fedora from his head, exposing unkempt, graying hair. "May I have room please?"

"Oh. Yes." I rubbed my head. That potted fern had hurt. "I mean, were you the man who called yesterday?"

He nodded. "I made a reservation. A woman took my call. Was she you?"

"No, that was my cousin, Dixie."

He handed me his battered suitcase, and I staggered beneath its weight.

"I'm sorry," I gasped, "but my cousin didn't get your—"

He strode inside, letting the screen door fall back on me.

"—name," I finished. Grimacing, I pushed open the door and staggered into the foyer. I set the suitcase on the rug. My father had vanished.

In his bed beside the desk, Bailey opened one eye and studied the newcomer. He snorted and went back to sleep.

I rounded the desk and studied the reservation book. "May I see some ID, so I can check you in?"

"Of course." He dug into his jacket pocket and pulled out a red passport.

I opened the front page. It was in Cyrillic. "Um, I'm afraid I can't—"

"My name is Sasha Baransky."

His name could have been Boris Yeltsin and I wouldn't have been able to verify it. But I photocopied the front pages and typed his name into the computer.

"How long will you be staying with us?" I asked.

"All week."

I nodded. "And have you got a credit card?"

He handed me one which I also couldn't read. But it worked when I ran it through the machine.

I returned the card to him and bent to the computer, where I got an invoice started.

"You're in room three, upstairs." I handed him a key card. "Breakfast is served from six until ten in the dining room, there." I pointed to the open door.

On my left, the printer whirred.

Mr. Baransky nodded, his jowls quivering. "I was supposed to meet someone at the Doyle Historic Hotel. Maybe you saw him. He is a Russian, like me?"

Russian? My scalp prickled. No. No way. He couldn't be talking about the body in my UFO. "Not... Crimean?"

He chuckled. "You have a good ear. Yes, I was born in Crimea, but as a child I moved to Moscow."

I swallowed. *Act natural.* Baransky might be Crimean, but he didn't say his friend was. "He's at the Historic Doyle Hotel, you said?" I pulled out a map I'd created for just such an occasion (the Visitors Center maps are subpar). "Here you go."

I circled the rival hotel on Main Street and drew a wavering X for Wits' End.

"Thank you," he said.

I turned to the printer. A red light on its side blinked, baleful. "Sorry, I said. "The printer's jammed."

I opened the lid, pulled out the paper tray and squinted inside. The paper was curled like a Christmas ribbon. Carefully, I tugged its edge. The page tore free, leaving a ragged piece behind.

I cleared my throat. "This might take a minute."

"I do not need an invoice." He grabbed his suitcase, and I watched him climb the stairs. His footsteps sounded above me, and a door opened and shut.

I gnawed the inside of my cheek. Russia had a strong UFO mythos. Mr. Baransky wasn't the first from that region to visit Wits' End. He was probably a perfectly innocent Russian. Or Crimean.

I wiggled the torn paper free of the printer's wheels. A torn corner of goldenrod paper emerged with my wrecked invoice. *Strange.* We didn't use colored paper at Wits' End.

Frowning, I flicked it into the waste bin and printed a new invoice.

Should I warn my parents about Mr. Baransky?

But what if he was innocent? He was probably innocent. It was likely a coincidence he was looking for a missing Russian. Or Crimean.

I shifted my weight. If I did tell my parents, what would they do?

It's not as if they ran around killing innocent Russians. But sometimes they could get a little... excessive. I *really* needed to clear up the sheriff's murder mystery before they turned their attention on McCourt.

I noticed the carafe, still on the reception desk, and carried it into the kitchen.

A door banged behind me in the foyer.

I was overthinking this Baransky business. I'd just—

The desk bell dinged. I hurried into the foyer.

Malcolm scowled in front of the reception desk, his green and brown eyes squinting. His wife, Lupita studied the nearby shelf of UFO pamphlets and paraphernalia. Her nose wrinkled.

"Good morning," I said. "What can I do for you?"

"We're looking for my sister," Malcolm said. "She's expecting us. I believe she and Jacob are staying here?"

"I'll just call up and let her know you've arrived." I plucked the old-fashioned phone from its receiver and dialed her room. After a few rings, Maive picked up.

I smiled. "Your brother and Lupita are—"

"Send them up, will you?" Maive hung up.

I swallowed my annoyance. We innkeepers had to make allowances for guests under stress. So she'd been a little short? The customer is always right.

"Go on up," I said to the couple. "Top of the stairs, then make a one hundred and eighty degree turn and walk to the end of the hall to the turret room."

"Thanks," he said.

The two marched up the narrow steps.

I leaned over the desk and watched them disappear. Who would have thought Wits' End would become a nexus for assassins and murder suspects?

I'd be a fool not to take advantage.

The breakfast room lay directly beneath Maive's. Its location made it perfect for snooping, assuming Maive's window upstairs was open.

I hurried into the breakfast room and heaved up the window. Straining my ears, I leaned my head out. All I could hear was the twittering of birds and the whir of a neighbor's lawn mower.

I leaned out farther, craning my neck. Curtains fluttered through an open window above me. Eavesdropping *should* be possible, as long as Maive and her guests didn't speak in low voices.

But darn it, they *were* speaking in low voices. I tapped my foot on the hardwood floor. How annoyingly discreet.

I needed to get closer. Room three shared a wall with the turret suite, but Mr. Baransky was currently *in* room three. He'd hardly let me wander in to press my ear against the wall without wanting to know why.

There was only one alternative. The roof.

Striding from the breakfast room, I jogged up the stairs, and walked down the green-carpeted hall.

My mother stuck her head from the door of room five. "Susan?"

I forced a smile. "Yes?"

"Your father thinks I should tell you..." Her face contorted with distaste. "...that your blouse is... adequate. Even though lilac doesn't suit your complexion. But I do wish you'd put on a dress every now and again."

"Okay. Thanks."

"That wasn't a compliment. You could be lovely, if only you tried harder."

"Thanks," I said again, my voice flattening.

She smiled and shut the door.

I shook off my annoyance and continued to the rear of the B&B. Letting myself onto the wooden landing, I clambered over the railing onto the sloping overhang above the side porch.

I edged across the shingles, my back pressed to the wall. At the first window, I dropped to my knees and crawled, so any guests inside wouldn't see me.

You can't do that *in a dress.* Which my mom, being a spy, should know.

I made it to the corner and the octagonal turret room. Here, the overhang narrowed to three-feet wide. I crouched on one knee beside an open window.

"...need to strategize," Malcolm was saying.

"Shouldn't our lawyer be doing that?" Maive asked.

"She's right," her husband said. "This is a legal battle. Now, I know a lawyer—"

"I have my own lawyer," Malcolm said.

"Are we each going to get our own lawyer?" Maive asked. "That seems a waste."

"It's going to be a waste no matter how you cut it," Jacob said. "Legal fights are never quick, and they're never cheap."

"Are you suggesting we give up?" Malcolm asked.

"No," Jacob said, "I'm suggesting—"

"What are you doing up there?" Dixie hollered.

I flattened against the wall.

Dixie stared up at me from the lawn, her arms akimbo. Bailey whoofed beside her booted feet.

I raised a finger to my lips. A shingle pressed painfully through the fabric of my capris and into my knee.

"What?" my cousin shouted louder. "Should I start cleaning now?"

Frantically, I waved her away.

"Hello?" Malcolm stuck his head out the window, his green-brown eyes burning. "What are you doing here?"

I wobbled. *Dixie.* But this wasn't the time for recriminations. I needed to think fast.

Unfortunately, my thinking was distracted by the smell of Malcolm's delicious cologne.

I scooted away from him, decided that looked guilty, and edged forward. My capris caught on a shingle, and there was a tearing sound. I winced.

"Well?" he demanded.

I bent and tugged the edge of a shingle. "I'm checking the roof. Arsen was up here the other day and said there were some loose shingles."

"They look okay to me," Malcolm said.

I grabbed one and wrenched harder. It didn't budge. "They're tricky to spot. You have to sort of step on them to really know if they're loose." I reached forward with my foot and stamped on a shingle. My foot slipped beneath me.

Malcolm hissed and grasped my arm. "Careful."

"I'll just ask Arsen to mark the ones that need replacing."

"Maybe you should come inside before you fall." He held out his hand.

"Thanks."

His hand closed firmly around mine, and I clambered through the window.

"Good. You're here," his sister said. Maive had changed into a modish A-line skirt and blouse. "There's a strange smell in this room."

Alarmed, I brushed off my capris. "Strange?"

"Kind of like something died," her husband, Jacob, said.

I felt the blood drain from my face and into my sensible sneakers.

"No," Maive said. "Not like that. More like a litter box."

"I don't smell anything," Malcolm said.

"I can't really either," Jacob admitted, scratching his goatee. "But Maive's got a good sense of smell."

"I'll look into it," I said faintly.

"What happened to your slacks?" Maive asked me.

"Susan?" Arsen shouted from outside.

"They're torn," Maive said. "Can't you afford decent pants?"

I stuck my head out the window and waved at Arsen, standing beside Gran's spirit house. "I'll be right..." My insides plunged in horror.

In the side yard, Sasha the Crimean studied a pair of faint parallel tracks on the lawn leading to the gazebo.

"...down," I whispered.

CHAPTER TWELVE

ON THE LAWN BENEATH me, Mr. Baransky rubbed his chin. He nodded once and strode purposefully alongside the tracks toward the gazebo.

My pulse skyrocketed. *Stay calm.* This was okay. The body wasn't in the gazebo. I had nothing to worry about.

Absolutely nothing.

Aside from a snoopy Crimean and possible assassin.

"I'm coming up," Arsen called. He scrambled up the banister. Biceps bulging, Arsen swung himself atop the porch overhang. He strolled to the turret window as easily as if the roof were flat. "Everything okay?"

"No," Maive said from behind me. "There's a weird smell."

"The UFO?" Arsen asked me.

"No," I said. "But I'll call the exterminator today."

"Exterminator?" Maive yelped.

Arsen reached up and grasped the roof's overhang. "I'll do a quick check."

No. "Let's not disturb our guests," I said hurriedly. "I can take care of it later."

"Is that Arsen?" Maive bent and rubbed the small scar on her leg.

I stepped jerkily away from the window. "Yes. Arsen, why don't you come in off the roof?"

"It'll just take me a minute to check the UFO—"

Maive grasped the window frame and leaned out. "It is you. And of course you're on the roof." She laughed musically. "Come inside before you fall off."

"You'd better," her husband said, grinning. "You know how determined Maive can be."

Arsen grimaced and stepped through the window. He looked around the oversized room. "Are all four of you staying here?"

Lupita tossed her long, dark hair. "Here? We're not that desperate." She shot me an embarrassed look. "I just meant it would be awfully crowded. Your B&B is fun."

"No offense taken," I said.

"Asher thinks he owns our condo," Maive explained. "We couldn't stay."

"Did you know someone threw a jai alai ball at Susan yesterday outside your father's house?" Arsen's voice was hard.

"Our father's house?" Malcolm turned to me, his eyes narrowed. "What were you doing there?"

"I was across the street talking to his neighbor, Darla," I said.

Malcolm snorted. "Oh. The lottery winner."

Arsen folded his arms. "Where were you yesterday at one o'clock?"

"Who can remember?" Maive rolled her green-brown eyes.

"We were having lunch," her husband said. "Weren't we?"

"I suppose we were," Maive said. "Why? You don't think one of us of threw a ball at Susan?"

"And you and Lupita?" Arsen asked Malcolm.

"The same." Malcolm's jaw tightened. "And I can't believe you'd think we'd do something like that. Especially when it's obvious who would."

"Who?" I asked.

"Franklin Asher."

"Why is it obvious?" I asked.

Malcolm arched a brow. "He was right there in the house right across the street, wasn't he? None of us were nearby. Honestly, Arsen. You *know* us. We went to school together."

Arsen's tanned skin darkened.

"A jai alai ball could do some serious damage." Lupita studied me. "You were lucky."

"Yes," Arsen said. "She was. I plan to make sure nothing like that happens again."

"But why would someone try to hurt Susan?" Lupita asked. "That is what you're saying, isn't it? That it wasn't an accident?"

No *way*. "It wasn't—" Wait. *Could* it have been an accident?

"I don't see how it could have been," Malcolm said. "But why go after Susan? You're suggesting this is connected to our father. How?"

"A jai alai ball implicates one of us," Maive said. "That's what the connection is. We all played, except Lupita."

"That was years ago," Jacob said.

"Franklin knew we played," Maive said. "There's got to be some old equipment at Dad's house."

The four stared at each other.

I cleared my throat. "Okay. Well. If you need anything, let me know." I hustled Arsen from the room before he could get any more ideas about inspecting the UFO for dead animals.

Arsen trailed me down the stairs. "Why are they staying here?"

"The Historic Doyle Hotel was full." I lowered my voice. "And there seem to be some money problems now that Asher has inherited."

"I don't like this setup. Maive was right. That jai alai ball points straight at one of them."

"I'll be sure to keep the door to my private rooms locked." I nearly always did—a lesson I'd learned the hard way.

Hurrying into the kitchen, I looked out the window above the sink. Mr. Baransky paced inside the gazebo. His head was lowered, as if he were searching for something at his feet.

"Everything okay?" Arsen asked.

"Yes," I said. "Yes. I have a new guest. I was just checking if he was all right."

"Why wouldn't he be?"

"No reason. Lunch?"

We ate lunch in the kitchen with Bailey. Arsen left to ride his new mountain bike. I loaded tableware into the dishwasher and glanced out the window again. Mr. Baransky sat in the gazebo, his back to me.

My parents wandered into the kitchen.

"Any news?" I asked. "About the you-know-what, I mean."

"No," my mother said.

"Well that UFO is metal and it gets hot," I said. "You're going to have to move the body soon. The guests in the room beneath are complaining about a smell."

"I don't know why you put guests in that room," my mother complained. "You knew the body was there."

"We'll move it as soon as we can," my father said. "Was that Arsen we saw leaving?"

"Probably." I closed the dishwasher and glanced out the window. Mr. Baransky was still in the gazebo.

Briefly, I closed my eyes. When I opened them, he hadn't budged. Should I tell my parents about my new guest?

I shook my head. Whatever else they might be, they were professionals. I had to trust they'd do the right thing. "A new guest arrived this morning. A man with a Russian passport."

"The man in the gazebo?" my mother asked.

I nodded. It was easy to forget how good they were at their job. Of course she'd noticed the newcomer.

"And you're worried he might be another assassin?" my father asked. "Don't be. If he was, he wouldn't be carrying a Russian passport."

"Right," I said, relieved. "It's got to be a coincidence."

"Russian passports are no exemption, Hank." My mother drew a butcher knife from its block on the counter. "You remember Tbilisi?"

"Yes," he said, "but—"

She examined the blade. "And Bishkek?"

"It's not so unusual for Wits' End to have guests from Eastern Europe," I said. "They like California and UFOs."

"Don't worry about this new *guest*." My mother slid the knife back into its block on the counter. "We'll take care of everything."

A rush of blood washed into my brain. "Take—take care of it? How?"

She and my father exchanged a nod, their expressions flattening. They moved toward the porch door.

I grasped the back of a chair. "Wait. What if he's a tourist? There could be nothing to take care of. He could be innocent."

"Don't worry," my mother said. "As long as he leaves us alone, we'll leave him alone. What did you say his name was?"

"Sasha Baransky."

"That name... sounds familiar," my father said.

My mother shook her head. "I'm more of a faces person. Let's introduce ourselves." She smiled the sort of smile that could make it snow on Mercury. "It's only polite."

They strode out the porch door. It banged shut behind them, and I started.

Bailey looked up from his dog bed. His brown eyes met my appalled gaze.

I'd just sicced two skilled spies on a perfectly innocent Crimean.

CHAPTER THIRTEEN

My PARENTS WOULDN'T KILL one of my guests. Unless he was an assassin. But if he wasn't...

I had to save Mr. Baransky.

I hurried outside, Bailey at my heels. At the top of the porch steps, the beagle halted and whined. I turned, snatched him up, and set him down again on the lawn.

"You need to get over your stair phobia," I said.

My parents mounted the gazebo steps. Mr. Baransky lounged, unmoving, beneath the climbing roses on a white-painted bench.

I speed walked across the lawn. Collar jingling, Bailey trotted to keep up.

"Mom? Dad?" I shouted.

They turned, twin expressions of annoyance on their faces.

"Wait," I said.

"We are waiting," my mother said. "What do you want?"

I motioned them toward me.

My mother rolled her eyes. They trooped down the gazebo steps and crossed the lawn.

"Wouldn't it be easier if I just gave you a photocopy of his passport?" I whispered. "Then you can send it to your, um, agency, and they can tell you if he's legit."

"You didn't mention having a copy of his passport," my father said.

"I am now. It's in my desk."

"You were always like this." My mother folded her arms across her chest.

"Like what?" I asked.

"Always secretive," she said. "Always withholding."

"What are you talking about?" I said hotly. "All I did was forget—"

"Oh, you *forgot*," my mother said. "Like you forgot all those times when you were young."

"What times?"

"Sneaking out," she said. "Keeping your friends from us."

I laughed weakly. "I had to keep *some* things to myself."

They stared at me, and I felt myself crumpling inward into teenage Susan. The dark shadow slithered closer. "I mean," I said, "wanting independence is part of growing up."

"You were sly," my mother said.

That was rich coming from a pair of spies. "And you were controlling."

Their stares hardened.

Panting, Bailey wheezed to a stop. He leaned against my leg.

I wilted. "You have to admit, you *were* just a teensy bit domineering."

"We were protecting you," my father rapped out.

"And now you're throwing our work in our faces?" my mother said. "You have no idea what sacrifices we made—for you, for our country."

"No," I said quickly. "I do know. I mean, I can guess—"

"Do you know how dangerous our work was back then?" my father asked.

"Of course she doesn't," my mother said. "For Susan, it was always all about her."

"That's not fair," I muttered. And how was *I* suddenly in the wrong?

"Fair's a carnival," my mother said. "Life's not fair."

"So do you want that photocopy?" I asked, desperate to change the subject.

"Yes, *and* we'll talk to this Baransky." My mother turned to the gazebo.

Sasha Baransky was gone.

"Now look what you've done," she said. "This is why we kept you out of our missions."

"That and it would have been too dangerous," my father agreed.

"I'll just get that photocopy," I said.

Fuming, I returned inside. I held the kitchen door for Bailey, and the beagle followed me into the foyer.

"Well, it *wasn't* fair," I told the dog. "Try keeping secrets from *your* spy parents."

I yanked open the desk drawer and thumbed through my files.

Granted, I don't have many of points of comparison when it comes to parenting. But it only makes sense that spy parents are even better than regular parents at finding things out. I'd learned early on not to keep a diary. They'd just read it. And forget email and phone conversations. Hacked and tapped.

"National security my Aunt Fanny," I muttered. "What did a date at the mall have to do with national security?"

"Excuse me?" a man asked.

I started, hunched over the files.

Franklin Asher stood in front of the reception desk, a frown on his handsome face.

I straightened. "What? Nothing."

"You were saying something about national security."

"And... UFOs. The government sort of admitted recently that UFOs are real. Of course, they call them UAPs now. And they won't say UFOs are from outer space. Or even another dimension. It's national security."

He ran a hand over his thick, slicked-back hair. "UAPs?"

"Unidentified aerial phenomenon."

"Right."

He looked around the foyer, and his nose wrinkled. "I'm surprised Maive's here instead of the Doyle Hotel."

I stiffened. The Historic Doyle Hotel wasn't *that* great. "We have excellent breakfasts."

He smiled. "I'm sure that's why they're here. Would you tell her I've arrived for our appointment, please?"

"Sure." I called up to the room, and Jacob answered. "Hi," I said, "this is Susan. Franklin Asher is here to see you."

"Don't let him upstairs," Jacob said. "Bad enough he threw us from our hearth and home. I don't want him tainting our temporary home as well. Have you got a meeting room we can use?"

"There's the breakfast room."

He sighed. "That will do." He hung up.

"Jacob would like you to meet them in the breakfast room," I motioned toward the open door.

Franklin nodded. "Are the others here as well?"

"Malcolm and Lupita?" I asked. "I believe so. At least, they were ten minutes ago."

"No doubt plotting my demise," he muttered.

"Surely not."

"Not literally." He gave a small smile, which quickly faded. "Though one of them did kill the old man. It *had* to have been one of them."

"If you have any definite information, you really should tell the sheriff. Unless you've said something to her already?"

"What good could she do? Cops don't prevent murders. They can only clean up after the fact. So I hope you put all the knives away."

"Of course I—"

Franklin pivoted. Whistling tunelessly, he strode inside the breakfast room.

"Oh," I muttered. "You weren't speaking literally."

Gaze darting to the stairs, I made another copy of Mr. Baransky's passport page and stuck it in my pocket.

The Van Der Woodsens trooped downstairs with their respective spouses. They trailed into the breakfast room. Jacob smiled at me and closed its door.

I drummed my fingers on the desk. So much for listening in.

Bailey's tail thumped the carpet.

Though I *had* opened the breakfast room windows during my first eavesdropping attempt. The odds that Dixie had closed them since were basically nil. Closing windows wasn't in her job description.

I hurried through to the kitchen porch and grabbed a pair of garden shears and a basket. Bailey and I ambled outside to cut roses. And we started beneath the breakfast room window.

Bailey flopped onto the lawn and shut his eyes.

I inhaled, and my muscles unwound. There was something magical about my Gran's roses. I really would have to investigate her special fertilizer. And maybe patent it.

I snipped a fuchsia-colored Charles De Mills rose and dropped it into my basket.

"You can't win," Malcolm growled inside the breakfast room. "You know California courts don't like children being disinherited. And you also know in any court battle, the only real winners will be the lawyers."

"Your father was of sound mind—"

"So you say," Maive said. "We'll say otherwise."

"And how do you know I'm not one of his children?" Franklin asked.

Maive sputtered. "You—"

"Maive," Jacob said warningly.

"It's impossible," Maive said. "He would have told us."

"Would he?" Franklin asked.

"He loved our mother," Maive said in an anguished tone. "It's not possible."

A long silence fell.

"I get what you're saying about lawyers," the butler finally said. "Maybe we can make a deal?"

"What sort of deal?" Jacob asked.

"Half for me. The rest for you."

There were outraged gasps.

"Ah, Susan," a Russian-accented voice bellowed. "I was looking for you." Mr. Baransky toddled across the lawn.

I winced and hurried from the window to meet him beside the spirit house. "Good afternoon, Mr. Baransky. Is your room okay?"

"The room is adequate."

"Only adequate?" I glanced at the breakfast room's window. A blue curtain shifted inside it.

Bailey raised his head and looked at me inquiringly.

"Is good," Mr. Baransky said. "But I wanted to ask you about this place."

"Oh?"

"Many strange things happen here, yes?"

"Strange?" Had he noticed the lights on the roof too?

"People in Doyle acting strangely."

I folded my arms over my chest and nearly impaled myself with the shears. Doyle wasn't much crazier than the rest of the planet. I dropped the shears into the basket. "You mean, last year's UFO panic?"

"That is part of it, yes."

"Panics aren't unique to Doyle," I said. "They're part of the human condition."

"But last year was more crazy than usual, yes?"

"No. I mean, yes, for Doyle the panic was more crazy." I glanced again at the open window. How was I supposed to hear anything from this distance?

"Susan?" my mother shouted.

I flinched. I had to get rid of Baransky. Fast.

"What's wrong?" he asked.

"Nothing. I was just thinking, if you really want to learn about Doyle, you should go to the Visitor Center on Main Street. It's a historic building in and of itself."

"But—"

"Susan?" my mother called. "Where is she?" Her voice lowered, as if she were moving away, and my muscles relaxed.

"You can't miss it," I told Mr. Baransky. "It's a small, round stone building with a thatched roof."

"Will they know about the squirrels?" he asked.

Bailey jolted to his feet and looked around wildly.

"I try not to use that word around Bailey," I said. "He finds it upsetting."

"What word? Squirrels?"

Bailey bayed and bolted for a pine.

"Yes," I said, resigned. "That word."

"Ah. Apologies."

"He hasn't always been this bad."

"So his interest in the squirrels," he said, "of late, it has grown more intense?"

"I suppose... you could say that."

Bailey ran from tree to tree, scanning their branches.

"Interesting." Mr. Baransky rubbed the thick scar on his cheek. "Very interesting. But you must think my own interest strange?"

"In alien sq—?" I glanced at Bailey. *Those stupid flyers.* "No, of course not. We cater to all sorts of interests, including an interest in bushy-tailed alien rodents."

"Alien, er, yes." He stepped away from me, his shaggy eyebrows squishing together. Muttering in Russian, he hurried across the lawn and out the front gate.

"About time." I returned to my post beside the window and snipped a pink blossom.

"...not crazy," Malcolm was saying.

"Grow a spine," Maive said. "The offer's outrageous. You shouldn't have gotten a penny, Franklin."

"I cared more about the old man than you two ever did," he said hotly. "All you ever wanted from him was his money."

"How dare you," Maive said. "So that's your game—undue influence. You played my father just like all those other poor fools with your palm reading."

Bailey sat up and growled, looking past me.

I turned. A squirrel perched on the white picket fence and nibbled thoughtfully on a leaf.

Bailey howled and bolted toward his latest adversary. The squirrel scampered along the fence and raced up a pine. Bracing his forepaws on the tree, the beagle barked hysterically.

It was impossible to hear a thing over his racket. I dropped my rose into the basket and strode after the dog.

"Bailey," I whisper-shouted. "Stop that."

The beagle ignored me. Of course he ignored me. Squirrels were the enemy, and he was the plucky defender of Wits' End.

"I said stop that. Get away from that squirrel." I dragged Bailey onto the lawn and toward the Victorian.

Inside the breakfast room, someone slammed the window shut.

I released the dog's collar. "Thanks a lot."

Maive appeared in the window and studied me through her green/brown eyes. She shook her head and whisked the curtains closed.

Stupid dog.

Stupid squirrel.

CHAPTER FOURTEEN

HEAT SCORCHED MY FACE as I herded Bailey inside the kitchen. Maive must think I'm a stereotypical nosy innkeeper. Tough. Murder is bigger than a little embarrassment. Or in this case, a lot of embarrassment.

The beagle whuffed in annoyance and dropped onto his dog bed.

"Don't you know timing is everything in love and war?" I asked him and opened my planner on the kitchen table. "Yours was rotten."

I reviewed today's page. I'd accomplished everything I'd listed in the *To Do* section. So why did my life feel so out of control?

Maybe I needed to add an evening review to make sure I'd accomplished my goals? Because I *did* enjoy that time in the morning with my planner and a cup of tea. More structure could only help.

Reviewing my suspect grid, I added notes about what I'd overheard at the window. Could Franklin really be Salvatore's son? It would explain the inheritance. But wow. What a bombshell... if it was true.

My gaze slid to the kitchen door. The Van Der Woodsen's muffled voices still emanated from the breakfast room. Maybe I should have stayed at the reception desk?

I moved crabwise into the foyer. The door to the breakfast room was shut. It was also depressingly solid and keyhole free.

I settled myself behind the reception desk and sketched a new design for my daily planner pages. An evening review section would be a tight fit, but I thought it could work.

Footsteps padded softly down the stairs. I glanced up.

My parents marched into the foyer and stopped in front of my desk.

"We wanted to let you know we've taken care of your little UFO problem," my father said.

Thank you. "No more, um, smell?" I asked.

My mother crossed her arms. "No more smell."

"UFO problem?" Mr. Baransky's silhouette loomed behind the closed screen door to the porch. He pushed open the door and peered inside.

How had he gotten back from the Visitors Center so fast? More worryingly, how much had he overheard?

Really, people can be so nosy.

"There was a dead squirrel in the UFO on the roof," my father said smoothly.

I glanced toward the kitchen door. No howls emanated from the kitchen. Bailey seemed not to have heard the S-word.

"Squirrel?" Mr. Baransky opened the screen door and stepped onto the Persian carpet. "I was just talking to Susan about this. There is something interesting about the squirrels here."

My mother's eyes narrowed. "Oh?"

"He means the flyers," I said. "Someone put flyers around town claiming the squirrels were aliens or... something. The sheriff's worried they might cause more disruption, since there've been complaints. Apparently the poster doesn't have permission to post the flyers."

"Yes," Mr. Baransky said. "I'm very interested in flyers. Strange squirrels may be important."

Muffled shouting erupted in the breakfast room. "No," Maive hollered. "No, no, no."

"Because of the UFO connection," I said, edging toward the closed door. "Mr. Baransky's interested in UFOs, like most of my guests."

"No," Mr. Baransky said. "There is no such thing as UFOs. Everyone knows they are a cover for governments doing military tests above their airbases. Do you know who posted these flyers?"

The commotion in the breakfast room stopped. I strained my ears.

"Susan?" my mother asked.

"What?" I blinked. "Oh. The flyers. I haven't actually seen any."

"I have," Dixie said at my elbow, and I started.

Bailey plopped down by my cousin's boots. I'd been so distracted by trying to make Baransky look innocent and listening in on the Van Der Woodsen meeting, I hadn't even noticed her slip inside the foyer.

My cousin reached into the pocket of her Army-green shorts. She pulled out a creased, goldenrod sheet of paper and handed it to me.

I unfolded the flyer and read.

Squirrels Are Out to Get You!

WARNING!

Squirrels are Alien Robots.

Did you know...? Roughly 10-20% of power outages are caused by squirrels? This isn't chance!

Squirrels began appearing in North America in 1639, after a UFO encounter recorded by the governor of the Massachusetts Bay Colony, John Winthrop. It is believed squirrels were created by these alien visitors to spy on the new colony as Europeans expanded into the New World. Small and nimble, these surveillance devices can go everywhere. And because they have cute, fluffy tails and appear harmless, people take no note when they peer in at them through windows, recording everything...

DON'T TRUST THE SQUIRRELS. THEY'RE WATCHING, AND THEY'RE COMING FOR US.

A squirrel in a motorcycle helmet squinted from one corner of the page. A thought bubble floated over its head: *Peace is never an option, Comrades.*

I choked back a laugh. "Well, that's just—"

"Fascinating," Mr. Baransky said.

The din in the breakfast room renewed. Maybe I hadn't blown my chance to listen in after all. Now if Baransky and Dixie and my parents would just *go* and let me do my job. Casually, I took another step toward the door.

My father folded his arms, mimicking my mother. He cocked his head. "It's true that animals have been used for spying in the past."

"Have they?" Mr. Baransky asked. "Bah. It does not matter. I must know who posted these flyers."

My father rubbed his chin. "We could find that out for you."

Mr. Baransky beamed. "That would be very kind. Americans are so helpful." He thrust out his meaty hand. "My name is Sasha. Sasha Baransky."

My father shook it. I hoped he hadn't palmed a micro listening device while he was at it.

"I take it you're a guest here?" my mother asked.

"Yes," Mr. Baransky said. "I'm in room three."

My parents shared a look, and the hair rose on the back of my neck. I knew that look, and I didn't like it.

"And you?" he asked.

"Oh," my mother said, "we're Susan's parents. I'm Pansy."

"And you can call me Hank," my father said. "We thought we'd take a vacation. And since our daughter owns a B&B, why not here?"

"A vacation from what?" Mr. Baransky asked.

"Forensic accounting," my mother said.

"Forensic." Mr. Baransky's brow puckered. "As in... bodies?"

My mother's gaze flickered. "Like digging very deep into a business's accounts searching for signs of wrongdoing."

"Ah." Mr. Baransky pressed a finger to the side of his wide nose. "You look for mafia."

"Something like that," my mother said.

I swallowed. Why did he care what my parents did? It was only making them more suspicious. And why did they care what room he was in? *That* couldn't end well. A bead of sweat trickled down my brow.

"I can tell you about the squirrels," Dixie said.

Bailey leapt to his feet and growled. A ridge of fur rose along his back.

"You can?" Mr. Baransky asked.

"Sure," she said. "I've heard rumors about these alien squirrels before." Dixie took his arm and led him onto the front porch.

Bailey trailed behind, tail low.

"In 1639..." Dixie began.

The screen door banged shut behind them. I stared at it, unsure whether to be worried for Dixie or for Mr. Baransky. If he was an innocent Crimean, Dixie was... Well, odds were she was up to something.

But if he wasn't an innocent Crimean, Dixie might be lecturing a dangerous foreign agent.

"I suddenly find myself strangely interested in the local wildlife," my father said.

"Me too," my mother agreed.

I whipped my head around, studying them. "Why?"

"Because that Crimean was obviously interested in *us*," she said.

My chest constricted. "Was he? I think he was just being polite. You know. Small talk."

"Ha," my mother said.

"But what does that have to do with those silly squirrel flyers?" I asked, bewildered. "There's no way a foreign spy could be interested in anything so inane."

"And yet he asked you and later us about it," my father said. "He is interested. Which means I want to learn more."

"The flyers are a joke," I said, thrusting mine toward my mother. "*The squirrels are watching?*"

"Maybe." My mother plucked it from my hand. "In fact, most likely. But we're here, and he's here, and I can't think of a better use of a Sunday afternoon than tracking down a flyer scofflaw."

My parents had either lost it, or this was all a ruse to divert me. But what could they be diverting me from? They couldn't seriously think there was anything to these flyers.

On the other hand, as long as they were investigating the local—artist? Joker?—they weren't hassling the sheriff or Mr. Baransky. "I... suppose," I said, uncertain.

"Shall we?" she asked merrily and threaded her arm through my father's.

"We shall."

They hadn't told me what they'd done with the body. "Wait—"

The two walked out the door.

I sagged. What exactly had they meant by "taken care" of the problem? Had the cleaners come? Or had they just moved the body to another spot at Wits' End?

And if Sasha Baransky wasn't interested in UFOs, why did he care about alien-robot-squirrels? It didn't add up. At least he couldn't be an assassin. No assassin would be interested in something so dumb.

Could he? Oh God. I might have let Dixie waltz off with an assassin.

I clawed back a hank of my hair, tugging on it. No. No *way*. He was no assassin.

I paced the foyer and gnawed my bottom lip. My planner stared reproachfully at me from the desk. It had gotten me through holiday disasters, UFO panics, and murder. But this... This might be too big even for my planner.

I needed help. I needed Arsen. But if I got Arsen involved... he'd get involved and put himself in danger. No. I couldn't do it.

I should tell the sheriff what was going on. After all, she was most directly at risk. She was the one who'd deal with the fallout of my parents' activities, whatever it might be.

But if I told the sheriff, would I make things more dangerous for her? Why was I willing to risk her rather than Arsen? Shame flooded my chest. I knew the answer to that. I loved Arsen. But I couldn't make decisions like this based on who I loved best. It wasn't right.

I couldn't tell anyone.

This was awful. I was starting to understand better why my parents had been so controlling. Danger and chaos seemed to spiral outward, touching everyone in their orbits.

Okay, one step at a time. Step one: I had to get Dixie away from Mr. Baransky. The man was probably what he claimed—a Crimean with a weird interest in squirrels. But whether he was or wasn't, getting her away from him couldn't be a bad thing.

I started for the front door.

The door to the breakfast room burst open, slamming against the wall.

Franklin stormed into the foyer, his expression thunderous. The butler turned and pointed into the room. "One of you did it. One of you killed him. He knew exactly how you felt about him, and *that's* the real reason he left me the money." He strode from Wits' End.

The double screen doors banged. The Van Der Woodsens and their spouses trailed from the room.

"...stick to the plan," Malcolm was saying. His green-brown eyes narrowed. "If it takes time, it takes time."

What plan? I grabbed my planner off the desk and frantically began transcribing. But they were talking too fast. I really needed to learn shorthand.

His sister whirled on him. "But what if we don't have time?" Maive shook her head. "There are other ways to take care of him." She raced up the stairs.

Take care of him?

"Maive?" Jacob called after her. He turned to his in-laws and lifted his hands in a helpless gesture. "She'll come around. Don't worry." He hurried up the stairs after his wife.

"Come around?" Malcolm's mouth twisted. "That's not the stubborn Maive I know."

Lupita shook her head. "I'm sure whatever her plan is, it's legal. Your sister's not stupid."

Malcolm arched a brow but said nothing as he strode from the B&B. Lupita followed, patting my arm as she passed without glancing my way.

CHAPTER FIFTEEN

JACOB JOGGED UP THE stairs.

I tucked my planner beneath one arm and hurried onto the porch. Lupita and Malcolm backed from the driveway in their impractical gray sportscar.

My front yard was empty. Dixie and Mr. Baransky couldn't have gone far.

I strode around the corner of the house. Roses bobbed, oblivious to any oncoming disaster, in the warm Sierra breeze.

Dixie, where are you? Mouth dry, I paced past Gran's spirit house and toward the gazebo, covered in climbing roses.

Turning the rear corner of the Victorian, I scanned the backyard. There wasn't much of it, only a thin stretch of lawn that vanished into the trees.

Motion beneath the pines caught my eye.

Dixie lounged in a hammock, an open book on her stomach. Bailey lay on the soft earth beneath her swaying figure.

My lips pressed together. I should have guessed. Instead of re-turning to work, my cousin had returned to lounging. Not that I wasn't happy she hadn't been assassinated. But really.

I strode to the hammock.

Dixie squinted up at me. "Hey."

Bailey raised an eyelid, lowered it.

"What are you—? Never mind," I said. "Where's Mr. Baransky?"

"Sasha? He went into town."

Would he run into my parents? I gnawed my bottom lip. It wasn't that big of a town. All the action is on Main Street, which is an easy stroll. My heart plummeted. Of *course* they'd see each other.

I had to face facts. Whatever happened between Mr. Baransky and my parents was out of my hands.

"What did you tell him?" I asked.

She coiled a strip of pink-tipped hair around one finger. "Just the fascinating history of our alien squirrel problem."

Bailey growled.

"Sorry," she said to the dog.

"What alien..." I glanced at Bailey "...s-word problem? I never heard of it before."

"It's on the flyers, so it must be true."

"I know you don't believe that."

"Is it my fault people are gullible?" she asked.

"So what did you tell Mr. Baransky?"

"I just improved on the story in the flyer."

"Improved?"

"I may have embroidered a few details in the long, amazing, and terrible history of Doyle squirrels." She put *history* in air quotes.

Bailey's harrumph turned into a whine.

"Great," I said, sarcastic. "That's just great."

"Why do you care?" she asked. "The whole point of Wits' End is to entertain UFO nuts."

"*You're* a UFO nut."

"No, I'm UFO curious. There's a difference."

My cousin was so UFO curious, she had a battery of radio equipment in her trailer. Not only did she scan the skies for alien activity, she also used the radios to keep tabs on the police airwaves. I was pretty sure the latter was illegal.

"Did he say why he was so interested in the..." I glanced at the dog. "...bushy-tailed rodents?"

"Because they're *alien robot* bushy-tailed rodents. Who wouldn't be interested? You should include the you-know-whats in your UFO lectures. I might be able to find you a flyer for your presentation. But first I promised another one to Sasha."

My fists clenched. I was trying to save my numbskull cousin from a possible assassin. Why did she have to make everything so aggravating? "I don't care about the whatsits. I'm concerned about Mr. Baransky."

"I think he can find his way back to Wits' End. He's a grown adult."

"I'm not worried about his pathfinding skills," I said. "I just think there's something strange about the man. Maybe you should steer clear."

"Strange how? Dangerous?"

"Possibly," I admitted.

"Cool. It's always the innocent-looking ones who turn out to be axe murderers. I'm going to clean his room." She swung one leg out of the hammock.

"No, I'm going to clean his room. You stay away from Baransky."

"You know if you tell me to do something, I'm going to do the opposite."

At least Dixie and I had *that* in common. "So you'll clean his room?" I asked.

"Not if you're going to do it."

"That's so— Fine, I'll do it." I frowned. "What are you reading?" I hadn't ever seen her with a paperback that wasn't the latest alien abduction literature.

She raised the book from her stomach. "What? This?"

Machiavelli's name decorated the cover, and my heart clenched. It was more than a little terrifying Dixie thought she needed lessons from him. "Why are you—? Never mind, I don't want to know." I had enough on my plate without worrying about Dixie's latest scheme.

Turning on my heel, I strode to the Victorian and let myself in through the kitchen door.

We'd already cleaned all the rooms except for Mr. Baransky's and my parents'. The latter had declined room cleanings, which was a break for me. But that's not why they'd declined the service. They didn't like people snooping around their stuff.

I climbed the stairs and collected the bucket of cleaning supplies and the vacuum from the closet. Tilting to one side from the weight of the bucket, I hurried past the hallway's grainy UFO photos.

Baransky had left, but out of habit I knocked on his door. I dug a master key from the rear pocket of my capris and waved it over the lock.

The door sprang open, and I dropped my bucket in surprise.

Mr. Baransky peered out. "Yes?"

"Oh," I stammered. "Hello." I gathered up the spilled bottles and brushes. "Dixie told me you'd gone into town."

"You want to clean my room?"

"I can come back later."

He stepped away, pulling the door wider. "Come in. I have work to do, but you can clean now."

Drat. What good was cleaning his room if I couldn't paw through his suitcase? Well, okay, the room did need tidying up. But this investigation was *not* going according to plan.

I walked inside, dragging the vacuum behind me. The bed was unmade. A window was open, blue curtains fluttering.

He sat at the modest desk and opened his laptop.

I dusted the end tables, the media cabinet, the windowsill. Under his watchful eye, I made the bed, then tackled the bathroom.

Scrubbing harder than necessary, I cleaned the claw-foot tub. I glanced over my shoulder. The faint clack of a computer keyboard drifted from the other room.

I moved his shaving kit to the other side of the sink and took the opportunity to peek inside. A razor. Shaving cream. A toothbrush. Well, what had I expected? A decoder ring?

"My friend, I have not been able to find him."

I jumped, squeaked, and turned.

Mr. Baransky stood in the bathroom doorway.

I sprayed the sink with cleaner. "I'm sorry to hear that. Have you asked at the Historic Doyle Hotel?"

"I called. They tell me he never arrived. It is strange."

"That *is* strange." Unpleasant prickles rolled through my stomach. "Maybe his plans changed?"

"But he did not tell me about change of plans. Strange squirrels. Strange disappearances. There is something going on in Doyle."

"Those old disappearances *were* mysterious," I said, "but most of the people returned."

It was the story that had made Doyle infamous. Over the decades, tourists and locals alike had disappeared into the woods on a regular basis. Everyone assumed they'd gotten lost. People do vanish in the California forests. Because the sign says it's a state or local park, they think they're safe. They don't understand nature wants you dead.

But one memorable night, an entire pub had vanished with the people inside. That had been harder to explain. The sheriff had said there'd been a gas leak, or explosion or something. No one really believed it.

And then months later, the pub-goers reappeared, minus the pub. They'd returned confused, with no memory of what had happened. But there was no way it had been a gas leak.

So, most of the outside world decided it had been a scam to drum up more tourism. But Doyle knew better. It was no scam. What exactly *had* happened was still a matter for debate.

"Tell me more about this Dixie," Mr. Baransky said.

"My cousin?" Why did he want to know about her? She was no spy.

"She told me a very interesting story."

"Oh, you can't take anything she says at face value." I sent a silent apology to my cousin.

"Why not?"

"Because she's... a semi-reformed criminal." This was actually true. Dixie had once stolen a police car. The sheriff still hadn't forgiven her for that youthful indiscretion.

Mr. Baransky's thick brows drew downward. His scar puckered.

"Really," I babbled on, "she's not that smart. I mean, she got caught. You shouldn't pay attention to anything she says."

He grunted and returned to his computer.

Sagging, I wiped my forehead, remembering the rubber gloves I wore too late. Uck. I had bathroom gunk on my face.

Hurriedly, I finished cleaning and fled into the hallway. I returned the vacuum and bucket to their closet.

A door opened at the other end of the hall, and Maive and Jacob emerged.

I stood aside for them to pass. They ignored my welcoming smile.

Maive, teetering on a pair of stratospheric heels, minced down the steps. "I don't see how you can be so calm about it," she said to her husband.

Jacob sighed and followed her. "We can only do what we can do."

"What does that even *mean*?" she asked.

I pushed the bucket beneath a shelf and shut the closet door.

"It means," he said, "there's no use worrying about something that's out of our hands."

Wasn't that the truth? I peeled off my gloves and cocked my head.

"But it's not out of our hands," she said. "We can't just sit back and— oh!" There were two sickening thuds, and my heart stopped.

Neck tight, I ran to the top of the stairs. "Oh, no," I breathed.

Maive lay at the bottom of the steps and rubbed her ankle.

Her husband stood two steps above her, his arms outstretched, as if he'd tried to catch her and failed. Jacob hurried to the bottom, and I raced after him.

"Maive?" he asked. "Are you okay?"

"No, I'm not okay," she snapped.

"What happened?" I gripped the rail. "Can I get you some ice? A doctor?"

Maive's jaw clenched. "What happened was your stairs tried to kill me. My foot caught on something. I told you we should have gone to a more modern hotel," she said to Jacob.

Heavy footsteps sounded on the carpeted stairs, and I looked up.

"Pardon." Mr. Baransky squeezed past me.

He stepped over Maive and ambled out the front door.

"There must be a rental available... something," she gritted out.

Jacob reached down to help her up. "Perhaps if you wore lower heels..." he murmured.

She swatted his hand away. "There's nothing wrong with my heels. It's this B&B. I'll sue."

Sue? I swayed on the stairs. "Maive, I'm so sorry—"

"You will be." She struggled to her feet and lurched out the front door.

Jacob grimaced. "She's upset about her father."

"Of course," I said faintly. Acid burned my stomach. I had insurance, but would it cover everything?

You can't control what other people do. But how I wanted to. "If there's anything I can do—"

"I'll let you know." He strode out the front door. Outside, a car engine roared.

I stared after him for a long moment. A *lawsuit*? I shook my head. I couldn't think about lawsuits now. Who knew how long Mr. Baransky would be gone?

I raced up the stairs and unlocked room three. Heart pounding, I slipped inside and closed the door behind me.

I winced. Had he left a hair on the door to test if it had been opened? I knelt and ran my fingers along the well-vacuumed green carpet. Nothing.

Rising, I went to the computer and opened it, turned it on. It was password protected, so that was no help.

I shut it down and beelined for his battered suitcase. It, too, was locked.

I really needed to get lockpicking lessons from Dixie. If she could hotwire a car, it was a good bet she could pick the lock on an old suitcase.

Defeated, I returned to the hallway and locked the bedroom door. Was the fact that I'd found nothing incriminating in itself incriminating? Or was I overthinking this?

I walked down the stairs. On the third step, I knelt and looked for any rumples in the carpet that might have tripped up Maive. But the green carpet was smooth and flat.

I ran my hands across the bottom two steps and didn't feel anything odd there either. No fishline stretched across the steps. No nails with broken strings had been pounded into the balusters.

She'd probably tripped over her own heels, like Jacob had suggested.

But a chill prickled the back of my neck. I turned, half-expecting to see the shadow. But it was only my own paranoia.

CHAPTER SIXTEEN

A LAWSUIT. A MURDER. An assassin. How could anyone be expected to plan for that? My life had tumbled so far out of control it had shot into another galaxy.

Lunch sitting uneasily in my stomach, I photographed the stairs where Maive had fallen. The photos didn't expose any hidden shadows or rumples in the carpet—nothing that could have caused her fall.

I returned to the kitchen and opened my planner. Noting the time and date of her accident, I thought about calling my insurance company. They'd be open, even if it was a Sunday. But all I had so far was a threat of a lawsuit. I highlighted my notes about Maive's tumble in yellow.

The kitchen's screen door clattered open and shut, and Dixie and Bailey ambled inside.

"It's Sunday," Dixie said. "What do you have to plan?"

Bailey huffed and dropped onto his dog bed.

"Next week," I said. *Whoops.* I really *did* need to plan next week. There were menu items, new guests, shopping... My parents had thrown me off my game.

"Next week will be the same as last week," Dixie said. "People come. People go. You cook breakfast. We clean the rooms." She squinted at me. "Or is this about your parents?"

"No," I said. "Why would planning be about my parents?"

"They're kind of bossy. They ordered me to vacuum the hall earlier this morning."

"And did you?"

"No. I vacuumed it yesterday."

I gave her a skeptical look.

"Okay," she said, "I vacuumed last week. But they're not the boss of me. They're not the boss of you either."

"Of course not." But the carpet outside Mr. Baransky's door had been recently vacuumed. Could he have done it himself? A clean carpet would make it easier to spot any footprints.

"Then why do you jump whenever your parents tell you?" my cousin asked.

Because they might have parked a dead body somewhere on the premises. It's not the sort of thing you can ignore. But I couldn't tell Dixie that.

I shut my planner. "I don't know what you're talking about. And I notice you've been doing a pretty good job of avoiding my mother."

"I've been busy."

I toyed with the planner's elastic band. "Does it bother you?"

"What?"

"My mother and you...the fact she—you don't get along."

"The fact that she thinks I'm a disaster, you mean, just like my mom."

"No," I said, "I didn't mean—"

"Yes, you did. And I don't care. I don't need her approval."

"No, I guess you don't."

She shook her head. "I'm going home." Dixie wandered out.

I stood motionless for a long moment. Shaking my head, I settled down to my planning.

Arsen returned a couple hours later to take me out to dinner. My parents were shut up in their room when we returned to Wits' End.

We didn't disturb them.

I'm not often behind on my shopping and my menu planning. But my go-to recipe when I *am* behind is alien invasion quiche. It's made with whatever random veggies are on hand, sliced into rounds and scattered amidst slices of purple onion. The effect is of a mass of alien ships flying across a yellow sun.

I arranged slices of the two quiches on the side table in the breakfast room. The slices of onion looked like comet tails, and I smiled.

I lit the tea lights beneath the warming trays, filled with country potatoes and bacon. A bowl of cut fruit, a side of bagels and bread for toasting, and an iced bowl with yogurts in it, completed the table.

It wasn't my best effort, but hopefully there'd be something to satisfy everyone.

My mother strode in, lifted the lid on a warming tray, and sniffed. "You know I prefer hash browns."

My hands throttled the neck of the water carafe.

"And your father doesn't eat bacon." She smoothed her olive hiking pants. Today she wore a matching long-sleeved cotton tee. It was almost like she wanted to be camouflaged.

"Did you vacuum the upstairs hallway?" I asked.

"It was obvious Dixie wasn't going to do it."

"But why?"

"Use your head," she said, "and figure it out."

"Were you removing any trace evidence of the man who attacked you?" I couldn't bring myself to say *the man you killed.*

A faint smile played about her lips. "Very good, Susan."

At least that was one mystery solved. I leaned through the open door to scan the foyer. It was empty. "What did you find at the Historic Doyle Hotel?"

"Why would you think I'd go there?" She lifted another lid.

"That's where the assassin was staying, wasn't he?"

"You're two for two. I see you haven't forgotten *everything* we taught you."

"Well?"

"The usual. A garotte. Fake passports. Our employers may find the latter useful in determining who he really was."

"What did you do with the body?" I whispered. "Did the cleaners come?"

"I'd rather not say."

Not say? Why wouldn't she... Oh, no. "Is it still here?" *Tell me it's not still at Wits' End.*

Her head lowered, her eyebrows rising, and she glowered. "Must I repeat myself?"

"But—"

"It's best you stay out of this, Susan."

"But—"

My father, in loose tweeds and a polo shirt, strode into the room and rubbed his hands. "Do I smell bacon?" He raised the lid and inhaled. "Fantastic."

"You don't eat bacon," my mother said sharply. "It's terrible for your gout."

"We're on vacation. A little bacon won't kill me."

"Did the cleaners come?" I asked. "That's all I want to know."

My father shifted his weight. "Er..."

"It's none of Susan's business," my mother said.

"It is too my business," I hissed. "Wits' End is literally my business."

"But our work is not," she said. "You made it very clear when you left home that you weren't interested in that part of our lives."

"And you're diverting me," I said in a low tone. "Have the cleaners come or not? What's going on?"

My father rubbed the back of his neck. "The thing is—"

A middle-aged guest, a pair of binoculars around her neck, toddled into the room. "Good morning," she boomed. "Any sightings last night?"

"Good morning Mrs. Kent," I said. "I didn't hear of any, but be sure to ask Dixie when you see her."

My parents loaded their plates with food.

She chuckled. "That cousin of yours is a fount of information. And she got me a souvenir squirrel flyer."

That was unusually helpful for Dixie. "Did she charge you?" I asked, leery.

"Oh, no."

I relaxed.

Mrs. Kent leaned closer. "But don't worry, I tipped her well. Is that quiche?"

There was nothing wrong with Dixie getting a tip, but suspicion coiled in my gut. "Alien invasion quiche." I motioned toward the folded label card in front of the two pies. "It's vegetarian."

"Ingenious design!" She grabbed a plate off the side table.

My parents sat at the oval-shaped dining table. I noticed my mother had piled plenty of country potatoes on her plate, even if she did prefer hash browns.

"Doesn't like country potatoes, my eye," I muttered and returned to the kitchen. I wiped the counters and slotted plates into the dishwasher, making frequent checks on the dining room to refill the water and juice carafes.

Arsen ambled into the kitchen. "Morning, Sue. What's for breakfast?"

I pointed at quiche number three.

"Awesome. Thanks." Asking me questions about my day, he polished off most of the quiche. Arsen kissed me and rushed off to a client meeting.

I'd just finished cleaning the breakfast room, when Dixie slouched into the B&B's kitchen.

"Good," I said, putting the last quiche dish in the dishwasher. "You're here."

Her green eyes narrowed. "Why?"

"Mrs. Kent said you got her a squirrel flyer."

"So? It's all part of the Wits' End service."

So indeed. "I'm glad to see you're getting into the spirit of things."

"It's just a dumb flyer. I found it on a utility pole."

"Anyway, I need to run into town and get some shopping done. Will you get started on the cleaning?"

She shrugged. "Whatever."

"Thanks."

I collected my purse and planner, patted Bailey goodbye, and drove into Doyle. It being a Monday, the tourist crowd along its old west sidewalks was thin. I waved at the willowy blond bookstore owner, wedging her front door open, and she waved back.

As much as I wanted to stop in Ground for a coffee, my planner said I had to go to the grocery store first. So that's what I did. I paused at the bulletin board outside its glass front door.

A goldenrod flyer with a pop-eyed squirrel was tacked in its center. The squirrel had antennae that had obviously been drawn on with a thick black marker. No one could possibly take these seriously.

I wavered. But the sheriff knew her stuff. If she was worried...

Unpinning the flyer, I made to throw it in a nearby trash bin. I hesitated, then tucked it into my overlarge purse. After all, I was a Doyle UFO specialist. It only made sense I had a copy of the flyers for research purposes.

I strode inside the air-conditioned store and consulted my shopping list, organized by aisle. It was hard to believe I'd let myself get so low on gruyere.

Rounding the end of an aisle, I stepped into the deliciously chilled dairy section.

"Our lives are *literally* in danger." Mrs. Thompson glowered at a store clerk in a red apron. "What do you mean you don't have squirrel repellant? How can you not have squirrel repellant?"

I slithered past the two and took a wedge of cheese from the shelf.

The clerk edged away. "Maybe at the hardware store—"

"They're out," she said. "There's been a run."

"I'm sorry, ma'am. It's just not the sort of thing we stock."

"Well," she said, "you should. How could you not *care* about such a critical issue? This is a horrible, hateful store."

"I didn't know squirrel repellant was even a thing," I said, and the clerk shot me a grateful look.

Mrs. Thompson sucked in her cheeks. "Oh. You! Everyone knows you're just a useful idiot for the man." She stormed off, the wheels on her cart screeching.

Useful idiot? I was no idiot. I'd solved crimes.

"We sell food and kitchen supplies," the clerk said weakly.

"And they're excellent," I said.

And who was *the man*? Sheriff McCourt? I checked out and returned to my Crosstrek. The crack in the window curved like a frowny face. Even my car was disappointed in me.

Sliding into the driver's seat, I consulted my watch and my planner. At least the next step in my investigation was right on schedule. And thankfully, it involved coffee.

I drove past Main Street's false fronts and raised plank sidewalks. A shady parking spot beneath an elm called to me, and I parked beneath it. I crossed to Ground, walked through its red-paned door, and inhaled the rich scent of coffee.

The door closed, jangling the bell above it. A few old timers looked up from their newspapers and coffees. The younger set were engrossed in computers and cell phones.

Ground was quiet. And not to sound clichéd, but it was a little too quiet. Weirdly quiet. No one was talking to anyone.

Looking around, I walked to the long, wooden counter.

Darla smiled from behind the cash register. "Good morning, Susan. How's it going?" Her voice was overloud in the silent coffeeshop, and we both winced.

"Good. I'll have my usual. And..." I looked around. The café wasn't crowded, and I didn't see her boss. "And do you have a minute?"

"Sure." She motioned me toward the pickup table at the end of the counter and busied herself making my drink. When she finished, Darla handed me the paper cup. "What's going on?"

I reached for a cup sleeve on the counter.

"—ALIENS HAVE RETURNED?" a voice blared from an elderly man's computer, and the cardboard sleeve crunched in my hand.

The other patrons swiveled toward him.

Hastily, he pressed a button.

"BUT WHY WOULDN'T THEY? WHY WOULD WE THINK THEY'D EVER LEFT? WHY NOT ALIEN SQUIRRELS?"

Red faced, the man slammed shut his laptop. "Sorry," he said. "It's just Tom's podcast."

The café patrons, muttering, returned to their papers and devices.

I fitted the crumpled sleeve over my cup and turned to Darla. "Last Saturday—"

"That stupid podcast," she whispered. "It's happening again."

"What is?"

She motioned toward the full tables. "It. What if people start disappearing again too?"

"No," I said. "They won't, because the disappearances aren't happening again. It's just a prankster printing flyers."

"But what if it isn't? Things were just getting back to normal. Doyle can't take another panic."

I plowed onward. "Saturday, after I left your house, someone threw a jai alai ball through my car's open window."

"Jai alai? What's that?"

"Some game for rich people, but the ball's really hard. It cracked a window and dented a metal strip in my car."

"That's terrible. I'm sorry that happened in front of my house. If I'd seen anyone, I'd have let you know."

"So you didn't see anyone?" I asked, disappointed.

Darla shook her head. "No." She brightened. "But my security camera might have."

She pulled her phone from her apron pocket and swiped the screen. "Oh. Sorry. Wrong app." She smiled apologetically. "I really should stay off MyNeighbor. The people on it are getting crazy."

I hated that website. People were supposed to share important neighborhood info, but they could get pretty judge-y.

"Okay," she said. "Here's the camera. That was Saturday afternoon...? Oh, there you are, leaving my house."

"Can I see?" I asked eagerly.

She handed me the phone.

A black and white video of me walking away filled the screen. My figure moved off the edge of the shot. I swiped frantically at the screen, trying to get me back.

"It has a limited field of vision though," Darla said.

I blew out my breath. My car wasn't in the video at all. Her camera had missed everything important.

But I enlarged the video. On the screen, the roof of Mr. Van Der Woodsen's mock Tudor house rose behind the iron gate. "Do you mind if I check something else here?"

"Go ahead."

I reviewed the app's library of videos. There were five from Friday. I played the first. A black cat stalked across Darla's lawn. He stopped, one paw raised as if listening, then moved off screen.

I played the second. A Mercedes exited Mr. Van Der Woodsen's driveway at twelve-forty-five. It must have belonged to Mr. Van Der Woodsen—when he was leaving for the spice shop? The Mercedes returned at one-thirty-four.

In the next video, a Tesla with a bike rack drove to his iron gate. The gates swung open, and the Tesla disappeared inside. I checked the time stamp: two-twelve p.m.

The video was black and white, but Maive drove a Tesla. Maive had lied about not seeing her father in ages.

The next video was time stamped fifteen minutes later. The Tesla cruised out of the gate and down the street. The final video showed an ambulance racing through the gate. A sheriff's department SUV followed.

"Has the sheriff seen these?" I asked.

"Yes," she said. "She stopped by my house the day Mr. Van Der Woodsen was killed to ask if I'd seen anything."

My face warmed. Of course Sheriff McCourt had talked to Darla. The sheriff was no dummy.

"Would you mind sending me a copy?" I asked.

"I'll do it now."

I thanked Darla, took my coffee, and wandered up Main Street. Darla's interrogation hadn't taken as long as I'd expected. I wasn't sure what to do with the free time.

Maive emerged from the knitting store a little ways across the street, and I blinked. *Think of the devil, and she appears.* Checking for cars, I jogged across the street.

Maive stood beside her crimson Tesla and scrounged in an oversized bag. A pair of thick bamboo needles speared from the bag's open top.

"Hi, Maive. How are you doing?"

She looked up. Her green and brown eyes narrowed. "I'm not suing, if that's what you're worried about."

"I just wanted to make sure you were okay after your fall."

"I'm fine. Bored, actually." She raised her bag with the needles. "Do you knit?"

"No. My Gran tried to teach me, but I always make mistakes. And UFO tourism keeps me pretty busy."

She laughed. "Those stupid squirrel flyers. They were discussing patterns for squirrel traps in the knitting shop. I suppose you plastered those around town to gin up business?"

"No," I said, offended. I'd never run a scam to make money for my B&B.

"Don't look so shocked. My father taught me there are no rules if you want to win in business."

I wasn't going to speak ill of the dead, but it didn't sound like a very nice philosophy. "That's an interesting point of view for a writer."

She laughed hollowly. "Writing is an art and a business. Something my husband refuses to acknowledge."

"I guess your father would know. He was one of the most suc-cessful writers al—" I'd started to say *alive*, and bit my bottom lip.

Maive scowled. "Not that his success did him any good, thanks to that damned butler."

"Have you heard anything from the sheriff about the investiga-tion?"

"Not a thing." Maive opened the door to her Tesla, parked in a red zone. "It's as if she considers me a suspect. All she has to do is get off her butt and look into Franklin's past. Then his game is obvious."

"His game?"

"It's all there if you know where to look." She slid into her car and drove down Main Street.

I returned to my Crosstrek before my groceries melted in the heat, and I zipped back to Wits' End.

I hurried into the kitchen. The vacuum roared upstairs. I put the groceries away, booted up my computer, and searched the internet for Franklin Asher. And I found... nothing.

He didn't even have a social media account. *Everyone* has a social media account.

Upstairs, the vacuum quieted.

Maive had said it was there if I knew where to look. So I guess I didn't know. I reached for my phone on the kitchen table. Maybe the sheriff had already figured it out.

My hand retreated. But she had been rather shouty the last time we'd spoken. It would serve her right if I solved this mystery myself.

What I needed was to think outside the box, work my other contacts and connections. Who did I know who...?

Ha. I strode into my black and white sitting room and pulled a dog-eared planner off the shelf. There *was* someone I knew who could get the intel I needed. I opened it, found a number, took a deep breath, and called.

"Sterling Investigations," a man said.

Jared Sterling was a private investigator. My parents had hired him to follow me when I'd first moved to Doyle. I'd never have caught him if it hadn't been such a small town. You can only pretend to be a tourist here for so long.

Though in fairness, it had been Dixie who'd brought him to my attention. She'd thought he was one of the men in black, a mysterious group of men connected to UFO mythology.

I hesitated. *Just do it.* "This is Susan Witsend."

"I had every right to follow you," he blurted. "I didn't break any rules, and you have no basis for a lawsuit."

"I don't?" *Lawsuit?* I'd never even considered one. And after Maive had threatened suing, I wouldn't. There was no way I'd inflict that kind of stress on anyone.

He sighed. "What do you want?"

"I need information on a man named Franklin Asher. He's currently employed as a butler or something for Salvatore Van Der Woodsen."

"The dead guy?"

"You heard?" I asked, surprised.

"He's big in the news these days."

"Yes, that Salvatore Van Der Woodsen." I wandered into the kitchen and sat at the round table. "Asher doesn't have much of an online presence. I need a background check, including his parentage."

"My rates aren't cheap."

Darn it. I couldn't exactly afford a splurge.

The PI had been a real jerk when I'd confronted him those years ago about tailing me. Didn't he feel guilty at all? You'd think he could throw me a bone as an apology.

"Are you *sure* you want to charge me your going rate?" I asked.

"I don't work for free."

This was national security! Maybe if I just explained... "The thing is, my parents are here—"

"Your parents?" he yelped. "You three've made up?"

Why did he care if we'd made up? "They're staying with me at Wits' End," I said, confused.

He was quiet a long moment. "All right. I'll check into this guy and forget the bill. But this is the first and last favor you get from me, got it?"

"Got it," I said, pleased. Maybe he *had* grown a conscience since we'd last met. Well, good for him. I'm all about personal growth.

"How do you spell his name?"

I told him, and he hung up. *Ha.* I didn't need the sheriff, because I had my own resources. All it took was a little—

"Why are you blackmailing a private investigator?" Arsen asked from behind me.

CHAPTER SEVENTEEN

"Blackmail, Susan?" Arsen folded his arms across his golf shirt. Frowning, he stood inside the open door to the foyer. "You had your phone volume on high. I could hear everything."

I set the phone on the kitchen table. "That was a PI in San Francisco, Jared Sterling. He's going to do a background check on Franklin Asher, since I haven't been able to find anything on him online. It's a little strange that he's an internet ghost."

"What's strange is overhearing your girlfriend sounding like she's blackmailing a private investigator. What's going on?"

"Blackmail?" I asked, confused. "I wasn't blackmailing him."

"And yet he's going to work for you for free."

"That's not blackmail, that's guilt." Wasn't it? I replayed our conversation in my mind. The detective couldn't have thought...

Oh. Oh, no. My stomach twisted, and I sank back in my chair.

My parents. The detective had gotten a lot more nervous and cooperative when I'd brought them up. But he couldn't know what they did for a living. Could he?

I needed to call the man back and explain. I reached for the phone on the table.

Arsen's face smoothed. "He was the investigator your parents hired to follow you, wasn't he?"

I nodded, my hand retreating.

"He *should* feel guilty," Arsen said hotly. "But you could have asked me for help. I do own a security firm, you know. I've got people on call who do background checks for a living."

"You do?" But one of us would have had to pay those people, and I knew Arsen would try to cover that cost. I wasn't about to let him.

He sat across from me. "So you think there's a real chance the butler did it?"

"I hate to say it, but Franklin makes a good suspect. He found the body. He had means, opportunity, and motive. Plus, it's suspicious for someone his age not to have any social media accounts. And Maive hinted there's something in Franklin's past that needed looking into."

"Hinted? She didn't tell you what it was?"

"No."

"That doesn't seem like Maive." He scratched the back of his head. "She's pretty direct."

"Is she?" I rubbed my forearm. How well *did* Arsen know Maive?

I pulled my phone to me and found the footage Darla had sent. "There's something else. Darla's home security camera caught these the day Mr. Van Der Woodsen was killed."

I handed him the phone.

Frowning, he watched the videos. "The Mercedes belongs to Mr. Van Der Woodsen. It looks like Asher was driving. And that Tesla looks like Maive's car."

"That's what I thought."

"Does the sheriff have these?"

"Darla said she'd already given them to her."

"Are there any others?" he asked.

"No. Just these."

"Maive and Franklin Asher were the only suspects to come through the gate the day Van Der Woodsen was killed."

"But there must be other ways onto the grounds," I said.

"There is. His estate backs onto an open preserve. You can get to it from Dead Horse Road."

"So anyone could have snuck in," I said, glum. At least we were filling in the timeline, but we needed more evidence. We had to break more alibis. "I'm surprised Mr. Van Der Woodsen didn't have a security system."

"None I could see," Arsen said. "And I looked."

Gravel crunched in the driveway.

I walked onto the kitchen porch and into the B&B's side yard. Arsen followed.

Maive's Tesla reversed behind Arsen's Jeep Commander. It swung into the court and zipped away.

"That's odd," I said, staring at the now-empty space. "Maive must have just arrived. I left her in town not thirty minutes ago, and her car was behind yours." Why was she leaving so soon?

"I say odd is worth checking out," Arsen said. "Let's see what she's up to."

We hopped into his massive Jeep, and Arsen backed onto the court. At the end of the road, the Tesla turned a corner.

"Maybe she forgot something at the knitting store?" I said.

"Maive knits?" He pulled from the driveway.

"It's become fashionable again. Gran said it was relaxing."

We trailed Maive out of town and down the winding mountain highway. Tall pines fell away, the landscape opening up to brown grasses and oaks. I suddenly breathed easier, as if a weight of the mountains had lifted from my chest.

We drove through a dry and golden valley into Angels Camp. Its main street was lined with antique stores and frog statues. The frogs were in honor of a Mark Twain story, and added a touch of whimsy to the steep road.

The Tesla turned into the parking lot of a chain hotel. She pulled into a spot and strode through the glass doors into the lobby.

"A hotel," I said uneasily. Tailing a murder suspect was one thing, but this was starting to feel peeping-Tomish.

"Come on." Arsen stepped from the Jeep.

"Wait. We're going in there?"

But he was already striding across the parking lot. I scrambled after him. "Wait."

He paused outside the doors, then walked inside.

"Arsen," I hissed and jogged through the sliding doors.

We walked to the high counter.

Arsen braced his elbow on the gray-streaked marble. He smiled winningly at the desk clerk, in a smart green uniform.

"Hi," Arsen said. "We're meeting a friend of ours, Maive Van Der Woodsen. Could you call up to her room and let her know we're here?"

The clerk consulted his computer. "Sorry, we don't have any Van Der Woodsens registered."

Arsen turned to me. "We are at the right hotel, aren't we?"

"Ah..." He wanted me to improvise? If I was any good at improvisation, I wouldn't need a planner.

Arsen nudged me.

"This is the one she told us to come to," I fumbled. "Unless there are two Jackson Arms in Angels Camp?"

"There's only one," the clerk said.

"Maybe she hasn't arrived yet," I said.

"No Maive Van Der Woodsen has a reservation," he said.

Defeated, we returned to Arsen's car, already baking in the summer sun. Desk clerks were a lot easier to get information out of in the movies.

I climbed inside the Jeep and rolled down the window. "She must be meeting someone here." I'm not totally naïve. I know what goes on in hotels, since I own a B&B. But Maive was married, and this just felt icky.

"Maybe she and Jacob decided to take a break from Wits' End, or maybe something else is going on. But I don't like her lurking around your house, and I want to know who she's meeting."

I was starting to feel like I *didn't* want to know. This was getting really personal. But this was also a murder investigation. Seasoned detectives don't fold at the first sign of something distasteful. "You're right." If Arsen hadn't pushed me, I might not have come here. "You know, we make a good team."

"Between your organizational skills and my high risk tolerance?" He grinned. "Yeah, we are."

My heart warmed. And suddenly, that warmth turned to cold lead. I couldn't lie to him anymore. "There's something I need to tell you about my parents."

"I know their visit's been making you a little tense."

"Only a little?" Either I was getting better at hiding my feelings, or Arsen was slipping.

"What's going on?" he asked.

I hesitated. "Could you believe something completely ridiculous?"

"We live in Doyle. People believe ridiculous things all the time." He sobered. "And last year, we nearly burned the town down because of that. I don't want to go through anything like that again."

I studied his handsome face. His brow was puckered, his gaze distant, as if lost in a bad memory.

"But we got through the panic," I said.

"Did we? We lost most of Town Hall. And I..."

"You what?" I asked quietly.

He stared harder out the window. "I wasn't there when you needed me."

"You were trying to stop the fire at Town Hall from spreading. You saved that clerk's life."

He turned to me, his hazel eyes serious. "And you nearly lost yours," he said.

"Is that why you're helping me investigate? You're afraid I'll get into trouble when you're not around?"

"Partly," he admitted. "But let's face it. Doyle may have amazing outdoor adventure, but it's still a small town. Options are limited. And hunting killers isn't boring."

"No." I smiled. "It's not."

He studied his hands, gripping the steering wheel. "It used to be, when things got rough, I'd tell myself life was a game. That we were all just spirits, come down to Earth for an adventure. Is that crazy?"

At his admission, my heart swelled, overflowed. It wasn't crazy at all. No crazier than running a UFO B&B. "No. Arsen, I love... I love that idea."

"It helped me not take life so seriously when things went wrong. To shake off the bad times and think of the next game play. Maybe I spent too much time not taking things seriously."

"But you're here now," I said. "You have your own security company, a home—"

"Yeah. Now I have things that matter, things to lose. I have you. The stakes are higher. We can lose each other in an instant, and for what? A stupid UFO panic?"

"But it was only a panic."

"People thought aliens had taken over their neighbors and turned them into the enemy. It was a mind virus. The fear and suspicion were contagious."

"I know," I said, the memory twisting my stomach. "It was terrible. I always thought Doyle... It seemed like the bad things that happened only brought the town closer. But it didn't this time."

"What bugs me is more than that," he said. "You asked me if I could believe in something crazy. I'm starting to wonder if that's all I've been doing."

"Arsen, no."

"The military taught me to stay watchful, to look beneath the surface. But I worry I've lost that. Do I really know what's real, or have I somehow deluded myself too?"

"No." Arsen knew what was real and what wasn't, because *he* was real in every way.

I was silent for a long moment. What I was about to tell him would sound like madness. I fiddled with the seatbelt. "But could you believe something real, but improbable?"

"Like UFOs?"

"You think UFOs are real?" Because I was swiftly moving from UFO agnostic to believer. I just wasn't quite ready to admit it.

"They could be," he said. "It makes sense that we're not alone in this big universe. Why couldn't there be races out there with more advanced technology than we have?"

We'd had variations on this conversation before, and I shook my head. We were getting off track. "I guess I'm talking about something as improbable as UFOs, but definitely true."

"Then, if I were being honest, I'd need to see evidence."

Evidence. I sank in my seat.

My parents didn't carry around cards identifying themselves as spies. I couldn't even point to the assassin's body as evidence, because I didn't know where it was. But it was a good bet it was still at Wits' End.

"What does any of this have to do with your parents?" he asked.

"What? Oh. Nothing." I smiled brightly. "Just... stupid childhood drama."

"That's not stupid."

The breeze shifted. The scent of tomatoes and melted cheese wafted through the car window.

"I'm starving." I pointed at the brick pizza parlor across the street. "Why don't we move our stakeout?"

"No argument from me."

We migrated to the pizza parlor and watched Maive's Tesla from a wide, front window.

I checked my planner and winced. I'd blocked this time for doing online research into the suspects, not chasing Maive.

"What's wrong?" Arsen asked.

"I was wondering—how do you win?"

"What?"

"The game," I said. "The game we came to play."

"Feel grateful for every minute, and be the best human being you can."

I don't know if I'd spent a lot of time being my best, but Arsen had. My heart filled with warmth. I was grateful for *him*. My eyes burned, and I looked away.

"I never said winning was easy," he said.

"No, but it's worth a try." I swallowed. "Would you mind if I ruined this metaphysical mood to do a little internet sleuthing?"

He grinned. "Go ahead. I'll keep watch on Maive's car."

I typed Salvatore Van Der Woodsen's name into my phone. The screen filled with articles. Notice of his death topped the list.

Salvatore Van Der Woodsen, Legendary Novelist, Dies.

Salvatore Van Der Woodsen, self-taught novelist of bestselling spy novels, died Friday under suspicious circumstances in Doyle, California, police say.

The Doyle Sheriff's Department said that deputies responded to Van Der Woodsen's home at 3:30 p.m. Friday. First responders found the author non-responsive and were unable to revive him.

The department has not said what caused Van Der Woodsen's death. Fans have taken to social media to express their grief and speculate about the content of his upcoming book.

Roughly, I shoved my crumb-strewn plate aside.

Arsen looked away from the window. "No luck?"

"It's frustrating." I skimmed more articles. None had any real intel.

I clicked on Van Der Woodsen's website. The last blog post was dated the day before his death. According to it, Salvatore had been putting the final touches on his new book.

"What does Jacob write?" I asked Arsen.

"Something post-modernist."

"What's that?"

"No idea."

Fortunately, Jacob had a website. Unfortunately, after reading it, I still had no idea what genre he wrote in. Not that it mattered much.

"A small press published a four-hundred-page essay by Jacob," I said. "It says the essay's a meditation on swimming pools and manicured lawns."

Arsen yawned. "Unless the pools and lawns blow up, I'm not interested."

I clicked on Jacob's bio.

Jacob Parker *is a multidisciplinary writer and artist. His works seek to redefine literature, and provide an important contribution to the ongoing postmodern conversation about social responsibilities and emotional consequences. He holds an MFA from the Iowa Writers' Workshop and lives in Doyle, California.*

I splayed my hands on the wooden table. Jacob's bio didn't help either.

Arsen nudged my foot with his boot. "There she is."

I looked out the window.

Maive emerged from the hotel, stepped into her Tesla, and drove off.

I checked my watch and noted the time in my planner. We'd been here nearly two hours.

"Now," I said. "Who was she meeting?"

After twenty minutes, Franklin Asher strode from the hotel. His lips puckered in a whistle. Franklin stepped into a Mercedes, and the butler peeled from the driveway.

"Huh," Arsen said.

"No," I said. "I hadn't been expecting that either."

CHAPTER EIGHTEEN

HAD MAIVE'S ARGUMENT WITH Franklin been a ruse? We followed Franklin Asher up the highway into Doyle. The butler's Mercedes peeled off Main Street towards the Van Der Woodsen House.

Arsen glided into an empty spot in front of the old-west building that was Antoine's Bar. Its batwing doors swayed gently, slowing.

"Franklin and Maive," I said again, because I still couldn't believe it. Could they have colluded in her father's murder?

But when it came to detecting, organization came first, speculation second. I checked my watch. It was five-ten, and I made a note of it in my planner.

"There aren't a whole lot of good reasons for those two to meet in a hotel," Arsen said, grim. "But I thought she was better than that."

My chest squeezed. "Were you two very good friends?"

"I thought we'd been, once." He shook his head and made a U-turn. "She's a helluva performer."

Maive wasn't the only bad actress in Arsen's life. "What's next?" I asked brightly.

"We know where Franklin's going. But I'm curious about where Maive went. Have you got time?"

"The beauty of owning a B&B is, things are only busy around breakfast." Also, I was lying to him about my parents, so he could pretty much ask anything of me and I'd say *yes*.

"Great." He smiled the sort of smile that usually made me warm and gushy inside. Now, all I felt was guilt. "Thanks," he said.

We took a private road that led up a steep hill lined with pines, and I realized we were headed to Maive's condo.

I shot Arsen a glance but didn't say anything. We pulled into the driveway, and I scanned the parking lot, packed with luxury cars.

"I don't see her Tesla," I said.

He parked beneath a redwood tree. "She's got a valet and a private parking garage," he said. "You wouldn't."

A red Tesla zipped into the lot. Maive parked in the carport, and a uniformed valet hurried out. She strode past him without a word.

The door to the foyer opened, and Jacob walked out, stopped short. He smiled and opened his arms, and the couple hugged.

Maive stepped back, both hands on his chest. Her head lowered.

Jacob's face contorted with shock. He shook his head once, as if to knock an unpleasant idea free, and said something.

Maive shook her head.

He held her briefly. Then, one arm over her shoulders, he led Maive inside.

"What was that about?" Arsen asked.

"No idea." I squinted at the closing glass door. "And I thought they'd been kicked out of their condo. What are they doing here now?"

"Maybe picking up more of their stuff?"

I shrugged. "It's possible."

"I'm starting to feel creepy about this," Arsen said.

"You're *just* starting?" I propped my elbow on the open window. "I've been feeling creepy about this all afternoon."

"Not about the hotel business. About what a good actress Maive is."

"We don't *know* she's having an affair with Franklin," I said.

He raised an eyebrow.

"Okay," I said, "I don't know why else they'd meet in a hotel either. Or how we beat her here."

"She must have stopped at a gas station or something, and we drove past without noticing."

"That was a long stop for gas," I said. "Over thirty minutes."

A pinecone the size of my thumb pinged off the Jeep's hood.

"You're right. But if we'd stayed on her, we wouldn't have known about Franklin." Arsen's hands squeezed the wheel then slid to his muscular thighs.

"Do you want to stay here a while?" I rolled down the window.

"If they are picking up more of their things," he said. "They won't be here long. Let's wait and see if we're right."

I nodded.

We sat quietly for forty minutes, my discomfort growing. I needed to tell Arsen what was going on with my parents, evidence or no. *Tell him.* I opened my mouth and shut it in confusion.

I fiddled with my window control. *Just say it.* I drew a long breath.

"Something's off," Arsen said.

Huzzah for timely interruptions. "It does seem weird that they're still here," I babbled.

My phone rang, and I checked the number. "It's that PI." I answered. "Hello?"

"I'm texting you what I found, and then we're done." He hung up.

My phone pinged.

I opened the files and enlarged the top on my small screen. "It's a rap sheet."

"For Franklin?"

"Yes." I swiped up and read on. "Franklin was arrested for some sort of palm-reading scam."

I

I moved on to the next file, a brief newspaper clipping about a scheme involving curse removal. And then another, briefer article, about how Franklin had gotten off. "He wasn't convicted."

"I'm surprised that detail escaped Salvatore's notice. You'd think he'd run background checks on his employees."

"Maive accused Franklin of using undue influence to inherit the estate. If he was a professional conman..."

"We need to talk to Franklin."

"Now?"

"We aren't getting anywhere here." He started the Jeep. "Let's shake him up, ask him what he was doing in Angels Camp, let him know we know."

I loved Arsen's direct approach. "There's another file." I opened it. "It's a birth certificate."

"What did you want that for?"

"Franklin suggested he might be Salvatore's son." And I really hoped that wasn't true considering what we'd just seen.

"He told you that? When?"

"I might have overheard it," I admitted, and Arsen laughed.

I opened the copy of the birth certificate the PI had sent.

"Well?" Arsen asked.

"Franklin was born in North Dakota to Wallace and Geraldine Asher." It didn't mean he *wasn't* Salvatore's son—those new DNA tests were revealing all sorts of family secrets. But it made it less likely.

"So he's a liar." Arsen's mouth compressed. "No surprise there, but it's something else we can call him on."

We returned to Main Street. Arsen took a right, and we drove slowly up the hill to the Van Der Woodsen's neighborhood.

A mountain twilight had fallen. Shadows thickened and blended together on the twisting, treelined street. The mansion's iron gates hung open.

Arsen cruised to a halt on the street. We walked down the curving driveway to the faux-Tudor house.

I pulled my purse closer against my body. How was I supposed to tell Arsen about my parents? I couldn't *start* with the dead body. That made my parents sound awful, and they'd only been acting in self-defense. The man had been an assassin.

We stepped onto the brick stoop.

Or maybe I *should* start with the body. Yes, rip the bandage off. "Arsen—"

He rang the bell, and it gonged loudly.

I waited for the tone to fade, then realized this was a terrible time to tell Arsen. We were about to interrogate a suspect. I couldn't blurt out *my parents are spies*. It would put Arsen off his game.

No, that was an excuse. *Just say it.* "Arsen—"

"Susan?" a feminine voice hallooed behind us.

We turned.

Darla waved and trotted through the gates.

"What's she doing here?" Arsen muttered.

"No idea, but she lives across the street."

Panting, Darla slowed at the bottom of the brick step. "I thought I recognized your car," she said. "What are you two doing here?"

"We came to talk to Franklin," I said, "but no one seems to be answering."

"It's a big house," Arsen said. "It might take him a few minutes to make his way to the front door."

Darla nodded, her loose blond hair swinging. "He's home. I saw him drive in about an hour ago." Her voice dropped. "Did you learn anything more about the squirrels?"

"Squirrels?" Arsen asked.

"The gag squirrel flyers someone's been posting around town," I explained. I looked to Darla. "Has something else happened?"

"No. Well. Yeah," she said. "Mr. Parnassus saw a squirrel outside Ground yesterday and threw his coffee at it."

I pressed my hands to my chest. "That poor squirrel!"

"The squirrel was fine," Darla said. "But he accidentally hit Mrs. Brandenburg. Then Mr. Brandenburg upended his table and went after Parnassus."

"Whoa," Arsen said.

"I know," Darla said. "It was lucky the sheriff was nearby. She calmed everyone down."

"That's... not good." Arsen rubbed his eyebrow, his forehead wrinkling.

"I know," Darla said. "I didn't think it would be possible to have two UFO panics in one town. Everyone was so embarrassed the first time, but..."

"I'm sorry," I said. "I still don't know who's posting those squirrel flyers." I hadn't even put it in my planner. But honestly, between the murder and my parents, something had been bound to slip.

Darla rubbed her bottom lip. "I know it seems a small thing after what happened to Mr. Van Der Woodsen—"

"No," I said. I was the UFO expert. I was duty bound to investigate. "I'll figure this out."

She motioned toward the wide front door and sighed. "I didn't like Mr. Van Der Woodsen much, but murder's still a terrible thing to happen. I can't believe it happened right across the street, and I didn't see— Oh well, I'll leave you two to it. Have a good night."

We murmured goodbyes and watched her walk back to the high gates. Darla vanished behind the hedges.

"I wonder why she really stopped by," Arsen said.

"You don't believe she's worried about a squirrel panic?"

He shook his head. "Now *I'm* worried about a squirrel panic. But why'd she come to us?"

"I am sort of an authority on all things alien and UFO related," I said modestly.

He grinned. "How could I forget?" Arsen rang the doorbell again.

The gong echoed. Franklin didn't answer.

"Maybe he's at the pool," I said.

Arsen nodded and strode away. I hurried to keep up. We rounded the corner of the brick house, our shoes whispering on the lawn.

"I wish Wits' End had a swimming pool," I said. The day's heat had only just begun to fade as the blue of the sky deepened.

"There's always the lake. Let's go to Lake Alpine tomorrow."

"Are you kidding? With my parents here?"

"We could take them with us."

"Taking them to the lake is hardly going to be relaxing. I'm not sure they even can relax. And I can't leave them alone."

"Why not? They can take care of themselves."

We turned the other corner. The lawn expanded before us, the swimming pool turning inky as the light faded. Franklin was nowhere in sight.

"We may as well take advantage of the lack of security," Arsen said. "I'm going to check the rear windows." He walked to a set of French doors and peered inside.

Feeling more and more like a peeper, I ambled toward the pool. I had to tell Arsen the truth, but how?

Lights flashed on in the box hedges. I halted, my breath catching in my chest. The metal pineapples around the pool lit, shining long, crisscrossed shadows on the cement. I relaxed. It was only the timed garden lights, uplighting trees and elegant shrubbery.

The pool lights switched on next. An odd shadow drifted along the water's surface.

Frowning, I walked toward the pool.

Sinister spirals darkened the water around the shadow like spilled ink. But the color...

I stopped, swaying.

A man floated face down in the pool, his blood tinting the water crimson.

CHAPTER NINETEEN

ARSEN MOVED IN A blur, rushing past me. I sheared away and nearly stumbled on the thick lawn.

He dove into the pool. Flipping Franklin onto his back, Arsen tugged him to the pool's edge.

I raced to help. But it was mostly Arsen who pulled the butler onto the cement. He began CPR, and I called 9-1-1, a dull feeling settling into my chest. We both knew it was too late.

The sky above the mountains darkened to cobalt. Sirens wailed. The sheriff and paramedics arrived.

Arsen moved away for the paramedics to work. He ran his hand across the top of his head, flinging droplets to the cement.

The sheriff adjusted her hat and scowled. "Why. Why? Why come here? No, don't tell me. I already know."

I glanced at Arsen, speaking with a paramedic. "But—"

She held up her hand. "No. When did you find him?"

"Just before we called 9-1-1." I checked my phone. "At six-twenty-seven."

"And before that?" she asked. "What were you doing?"

I pulled my planner from my over-sized bag and flipped through its pages. "We were, um, outside Maive and Jacob's condo."

"You needed your planner to tell you where you were today?"

I hadn't *needed* it, but I'd felt better squeezing its leather cover between my hands.

Her lips whitened. "For how long have you been stalking two of my murder suspects?"

I glanced toward the pool. The paramedics stood around Franklin Montrose's motionless body. Arsen shook his head.

"From about five-thirty to ten after six," I whispered. He really was gone.

"Were Maive and Jacob home?"

"We saw them outside their condo and then go in. We didn't see them leave."

"And before that?" she asked in a strangled voice.

"Susan!" My parents hurried across the sloping lawn.

My parents? Could this night get any worse?

"And before that?" the sheriff repeated.

"Arsen and I were in Angels Camp. Maive met Franklin there in a hotel."

"You saw Franklin Asher?" she asked sharply.

I flipped to the page in my planner. "He left the hotel around ten to five."

"Which hotel?"

"The Jackson Arms, right off the highway."

My father clapped a hand on my shoulder. "What are you doing here, Susan?"

"What are *you* doing here?" the sheriff asked him.

"We were driving past and saw the police lights," my mother said. "Since Susan wasn't home, I got irrationally worried she might be involved." She smiled thinly. "You know how mothers can be."

My jaw slackened. They were just driving past? Did they think the sheriff was stupid? OMG, had they been *following* me?

"You *happened* to be driving by?" The sheriff raised a blond brow.

"And Pansy, your intuition wasn't so irrational, as it turned out," my father said. "What's happened?"

"This is a funny neighborhood to go for a drive in," the sheriff said.

"Not really," my father said. "Pansy likes looking at big houses."

"And dreaming about the not-so-simple life," she said. "Though our home in San Francisco is lovely. I really shouldn't complain. But it's the city, with big city problems."

"Looks like little Doyle has some big city problems of its own, eh Sheriff?" My father guffawed.

Inwardly, I groaned. Were they *trying* to make her mad?

The sheriff's face tightened. "And what were you doing before you arrived here?" she asked them.

"Relaxing at our daughter's B&B," my mother said.

"Can anyone confirm that?" the sheriff asked.

My mother tapped her chin. "I don't *think* we ran into any of the other guests."

"Don't go anywhere." The sheriff strode to the men clustering around the body.

My mother's eyes narrowed. "I don't think I like that sheriff."

"She is disturbingly suspicious," my father agreed.

"Why wouldn't she be with *just driving by* as an excuse?" I hissed and glanced again at the pool. The sheriff paced around its kidney-shaped edge and shone her flashlight at the cement. "What are you two really doing here?"

"We were listening to your cousin's police scanner. Imagine our shock when we heard your name over the airwaves," my father said.

"Dixie let you in her trailer?" I asked, alarmed. Dixie was the ultimate conspiracy theorist. If she got even a hint that my parents weren't what they said they were, she wouldn't let it go.

"Your father is something of an expert on radio equipment," my mother said. "They got to talking, and Dixie offered to show hers off."

"Wait. No one's at the B&B?" I frowned. I *did* leave the guests to their own devices on occasion. That was one of the beauties of a B&B. And no one was checking in this afternoon. But I'd expected Dixie to be there.

"You're missing the bigger picture," my mother chided. "That sheriff is looking more and more like trouble. We're only minor players in your murder drama, and she's all over us."

"No," I said quickly. "She's not. It's our thing. I uncover a vital clue in an investigation, and the sheriff snaps and snarls. But we're really good friends. She trusts me."

The sheriff strode toward us.

"Hush," my mother murmured. "Here she comes."

Sheriff McCourt stopped in front of us. "Did you see anyone else around when you arrived here?" she asked me.

"No," I said. "Do you think someone pushed him in?"

"Since Arsen will tell you anyway, there's no use me trying to keep it secret. Something struck the back of his head. It's likely he was unconscious when he went in."

"You don't think our daughter was responsible?" my mother asked huffily.

"Oh!" I snapped my fingers. "Darla came over. She saw us walking down the driveway and came to chat. She can confirm when we arrived."

"Darla Ashfield?" the sheriff asked.

Oh. I'd forgotten Darla was a suspect. I squeezed my lips together, and my gaze flicked heavenward. A bat pinwheeled above us in the darkening sky.

"Who is this Darla person?" my mother asked.

"No one," I said. "Just a neighbor."

"So she had opportunity to commit the crime," my mother said, "assuming there was a crime. This poor man's death could have been an accident. Susan, I think you should come home now."

"I have more questions," the sheriff said.

"I don't see why you need to talk to my daughter now," she insisted. "She's obviously distraught."

"She doesn't look particularly distraught to me," the sheriff said.

"You can see she's on the verge of one of her anxiety attacks."

My face heated. Why did my mother have to bring *those* up?

The sheriff frowned at me. "Anxiety attacks?"

"Really," I said. "They're no big deal. I haven't had one in ages."

"You had one the day we arrived," my mother said. "She has them at least once a week."

"Not anymore," I said, my voice rising. "Sheriff, if you have more questions—"

"They're nothing to be ashamed of," my father said. "It's a chemical imbalance."

"Susan, a word." The sheriff tilted her head toward a pine tree.

"She's not having any words without a lawyer," my father said mildly.

My insides froze. I knew that mild voice. It usually came right before the hammer dropped.

The sheriff's face reddened. "Or we can go to the station."

"Hey, Sheriff." Arsen strode up to us. "I notice one of the pineapple lights is gone."

"Where?" she barked.

He pointed, and the sheriff and Arsen walked to the border where lawn met concrete.

"Something must be done about that sheriff," my mother said.

"No," I said. "Something doesn't have to be done. Nothing's to be done. Don't do anything."

Arsen pointed at the cement, and the sheriff squatted, examining the spot.

"That's your anxiety talking, dear," my mother said.

"It isn't." My fists clenched. "I'm not anxious."

"Obviously, you are. Look at her, Hank."

"You look anxious," he said.

"I'm only anxious you're going to do something awful to the sheriff," I said.

My mother rolled her eyes. "As you well know, since she's a US citizen, we wouldn't hurt her. There are strict rules about that sort of thing."

My shoulders relaxed. I'd thought so. "Good."

"We'd just put in a call or two—"

"You can't," I said loudly. A call? That might wreck the sheriff's career. Doyle needed Sheriff McCourt. Arsen and I couldn't do *all* the crime solving in this town.

"There." My mother flapped her hand in my direction. "See? Anxiety."

"I like the sheriff," I said. "She's good for Doyle—"

"She can't be that good," my father said. "Do you know what the murder rate is in this little town?"

The sheriff and Arsen returned.

"You can go," the sheriff said. "But I may have more questions for you two later."

"Thanks, Sheriff." Arsen nodded.

We hurried across the lawn and around the side of the house to the gravel driveway.

"What was that about missing pineapples?" my father asked.

"The pineapple lanterns around the pool," Arsen said. "One of them was missing. I picked one up. It was pretty heavy."

"The murder weapon," I breathed.

"Maybe," Arsen said.

"You shouldn't jump to conclusions," my father said.

My mother laughed, her expression shadowed. "That's Susan all over though, isn't it? Seeing murder and conspiracies wherever she turns."

My neck stiffened. "Are you returning to Wits' End?" I asked them.

My father checked his watch. "I don't think so. We haven't had dinner yet. Can you recommend a place?"

"Alchemy," Arsen said promptly. "It's on Main Street, and you shouldn't need a reservation on a Monday."

"I'm not quite hungry enough," my mother said. "Perhaps a walk before dinner? We have that lovely trail map to explore."

"Excellent idea," my father said.

We watched them get into their car and drive off, then we walked to Arsen's Jeep Commander.

"What were your parents doing here?" Arsen asked.

"They were listening to Dixie's police radio and heard my name mentioned," I said. "But don't tell the sheriff. They said they were just driving around and saw the lights."

He opened the passenger door and helped me climb inside. "Huh."

"Dixie could get in trouble. I don't think she's supposed to have that radio."

Arsen made another noncommittal sound.

"What?" I asked.

"Nothing. I was just thinking about Maive and Jacob."

A vast improvement over thinking of my parents, and one to be encouraged. "They do seem to have the strongest reason to want Franklin Asher dead. Aside from Malcolm and Lupita."

He shut my door and walked around to the driver's side.

"They could possibly have slipped past us to come up here," I said when he got inside. "Maybe their condos have another exit." I unlocked my phone and looked at a map of the place. "Though I don't see any driveways on this map."

"Then we'll have to go old school and check it out ourselves." Arsen started the Jeep. We drove to the condos, their high walls inset with river stones.

Instead of parking in the front lot, however, Arsen cruised around the building to the rear. There, a covered garage sat hidden beside a stand of pines.

"Valet only?" I asked. "Or do you think residents can use it?"

"Let's ask."

We drove to the front of the building. Arsen let the Jeep drift to a halt beneath the covered driveway.

A valet hurried to his door, and Arsen stepped out.

"Hi," Arsen said. "I'm not parking. I'm thinking of moving in here. Is there a garage for tenants, one with self parking?"

"Oh, sure," the valet said. "It's around back."

"I heard the Parkers might be moving out," Arsen said.

"Yeah, I heard that too." He shrugged. "Who knows?"

I leaned across the seat. "How many spaces per unit?"

The valet shook his head. "Two. People in these condos usually have more than one car."

"Thanks." Arsen slipped him a bill, and he got into the Jeep, shut the door.

"So they *could* have left without us knowing," I said. "Assuming they took Jacob's car."

"When are they planning on checking out of Wits' End?"

"They've booked through the end of the week."

"That's not soon enough. Maybe you should stay at my place."

Horrified, I studied his profile. What was he thinking? "With my parents at Wits' End?" I couldn't leave them alone. What if another assassin turned up? They were running out of places to hide bodies.

Arsen shifted uncomfortably. "They must know we're, er, serious."

Heat raced up my cheeks. That hadn't been what I was worrying about. "They're old fashioned," I lied.

"A little embarrassment isn't worth risking your life over."

"Oh, yes it is," I said fervently.

We drove through downtown and turned off Main Street to my neighborhood. On Grizzly Court, Arsen slowed. The lights from Wits' End glowed beneath the first stars dotting the sky. Moonlight shimmered on the curve of the roof's flying saucer.

He pulled into the driveway behind a blue Jaguar with a bike rack on the back.

"That's Jacob Parker's car," Arsen said. Parked in front of it was Maive's red Tesla.

"They are staying here," I said, uneasy. "They have parking rights." But why did it feel like they were lying in wait?

CHAPTER TWENTY

I REVIEWED MY PLANNER and nodded, satisfied by the morning's progress. Sunlight gleamed off my newly cleaned counter, and the scent of pine and summer mingled with baked berries and bacon. I couldn't take credit for the glorious weather. But I could for my Strawberries are from Venus French Toast.

Breakfast had been served. We had no new check-ins or outs today. Dixie was upstairs vacuuming. And last night's evening planner review had been a success. I'd accomplished quite a bit yesterday.

Now all I needed to do was solve two murders and get my parents out of Wits' End. But they couldn't leave until *their* little body problem was cleaned up.

I added *get alibis for yesterday's murder* to my list.

The kitchen door swung open, and Bailey lifted his head from his dog bed.

Maive strode inside. She jammed her hands in the pockets of her brown skirt. With her green blouse, she looked a bit like a tree. "There's no more orange juice."

I forced a smile. Guests aren't really supposed to come inside the kitchen, but it isn't like I had an "off limits" sign on the door.

"Breakfast ended at ten," I said, "so I cleared the room."

"But I want orange juice."

My smile grew tighter, and I reminded myself the customer is always right. "There's some in the fridge."

I pointed with my pencil, because I'd learned putting a plan in ink was a fools game. Except for highlighter pens. They didn't count.

She stalked to the refrigerator and pulled out a carton of OJ.

I rose and got her a glass from the cupboard. "How are you doing?" I asked. "The last week..." I motioned vaguely with the glass.

"How am I doing with a murdered father? And now his servant's dead, and it doesn't sound like it was suicide?" She laughed, the sound hard-edged and bitter. "You must have heard the sheriff when she was here last night, getting our alibis. How do you *think* I'm handling it?"

I passed her the glass. *And what was your alibi?*

Our fingertips touched. The glass slipped in her hand. Maive caught it before it hit the linoleum floor.

"Whoops," I said. "Good catch. But you must be dealing with a million details. What can I do to help?"

"Nothing." She poured the juice and stared into its orangey depths. "My father was a great writer, you know, even if he did write spy novels." Her mouth twisted. "The literary establishment hated him because he was successful. They sniped and sneered, and he despised them right back."

"I heard the critics could be vicious."

"Vicious? They delighted in making him miserable. It was a game to them. The internet's only made it worse. The uglier the reviews, the more clicks they got. Though bad reviews didn't hurt my father. His fans knew what they liked."

"I'm still not sure if the internet is a blessing or curse."

"A curse, definitely. People get so nasty online. They forget there are other human beings on the receiving end of their bile." She sipped the juice. "I was a literature major, you know. My father hoped I'd follow in his footsteps. But of course I didn't."

"Why not?"

Her green and brown eyes flickered. "I didn't have the knack or want to put in the time. Not like Jacob." She shuddered. "You should see what he goes through. He's a literary writer, real literature. He doesn't need to hide his prose in genre fiction. He's beyond writing boring narrative arcs that start at the beginning and go through to the end. Jacob's the real deal."

If stories didn't start at the beginning and go to the end, where *did* they go? "I like genre fiction," I said mildly.

"You and most every other American." Maive swigged the rest of the juice and set the glass on the butcher block counter.

"You said the sheriff talked to you?" I said.

"And it was utterly disheartening because it was so predictable. *Where were we between five and seven? Who might have wanted Franklin Asher dead?* As if we knew."

"What did you tell her?"

"I told her Franklin was a conman, and all sorts of people probably wanted him dead."

I fiddled with my pencil, rolling it between my fingers. "At least the sheriff couldn't blame you. You had an alibi," I hazarded.

"Yes, fortunately, because the sheriff isn't the sort to look beyond the obvious suspects. But Jacob and I were together all last night."

"Oh? I didn't hear you come in."

"You wouldn't have. We'd gone for a walk in the woods. Jacob says it clears his head."

"My favorite is Fairy Creek trail," I said. "Which one did you take?"

She made a face. "That one's so creepy. We took Bear Head trail."

Which would be fairly deserted on a Monday at that time of day. The hike wasn't much of an alibi, and I gnawed the inside of my lip. "Did the sheriff ask if anyone saw you?"

Maive rolled her eyes. "Of course she did, and we *did* see people, but I couldn't tell you who they were. Does she expect me to know the names and numbers of every hiker in Doyle?"

She strode from the kitchen, and the door swung shut behind her.

"So she's got no alibi except for Jacob," I said to Bailey. "And they're married. Who can trust that?"

I pulled my laptop toward me and typed in Salvatore's name.

There were several new articles in literary journals about the writer's death. I sensed something contemptuous in their tone. But maybe Maive had colored my impressions.

The journalists couldn't argue with Salvatore's success though. His books were still selling like hotcakes. He dominated the top ten on Amazon.

I opened another article.

Salvatore Van Der Woodsen's Book Sales Get Healthier

As the thriller world mourns Salvatore Van Der Woodsen's death, his book sales are skyrocketing. His next manuscript is expected to generate extreme interest at auction, and his extensive backlist is benefiting.

"His death has definitely changed the picture," his agent, Waldorf Manners said. "But he was a good friend, and a great writer, and I'd rather focus on his life and work rather than his untimely death."

Manners confirmed Van Der Woodsen had completed a manu-script before he was brutally murdered at his home in Doyle, CA, but said that he had not reviewed it.

Huh. His children would now get the proceeds from that once the book was published. Though if Franklin Asher had any family, maybe his heirs would instead?

I grabbed my phone and pulled up the files the PI had sent. According to his background search, Franklin had no siblings or children. The inheritances would likely revert to Salvatore's kids.

And Maive had a weak alibi.

I returned to the online bookstore and searched for Jacob Parker's books.

He had three for sale, and none had reviews. Even I knew that wasn't a good sign. But I downloaded one to my e-reader anyway.

"Are you a fan?" Jacob asked from behind me, his voice hard. "Or just snooping?"

CHAPTER TWENTY-ONE

I STARTED. IT WAS a little embarrassing that people kept sneaking up on me. My parents are spies, after all. *Something* should have rubbed off.

At least I'd closed the window with the article about his father-in-law. I pressed a hand to my thudding heart. "I didn't hear you come in."

Jacob stared, unblinking. "Must be my catlike reflexes. And my book?"

"I don't think I've had a famous writer as a guest before," I gushed. "I wanted to read it."

His shoulders relaxed inside his rumpled, tweed jacket. "Sorry I startled you," he said stiffly. "And for biting your head off. I guess I'm more defensive than usual these days."

In the dog bed, Bailey yawned.

"Who wouldn't feel defensive with the sheriff poking around?" I said.

"You heard about that?"

"Well..."

He sighed. "It wouldn't be hard to deduce I'm a suspect. It's just... I know I'm innocent. I know my wife would never do anything like this. But how can I prove it? How does one prove innocence?"

"I think," I said quietly, "the only thing to do is find the killer."

He hung his head. "Maybe we should hire a PI. The quicker this is put to bed, the better for everyone. You have no idea how it's tearing us all apart."

"I'm sorry."

Jacob shook himself. "No, I'm sorry. And I'll stop whining now. I was looking for my wife." He scratched his goatee and glanced around the kitchen. "But it appears she's not here."

"No," I said. "You just missed her."

"So. You appreciate literary collage?"

"Excuse me?"

"My book." He nodded toward my e-reader on the table, his book cover prominent on the screen.

"Oh. Literary collage? I don't think I've heard of that before. It sounds innovative," I said, wincing on the inside. Was my faux-fan-girling obvious?

He smiled. "It's taking pieces of existing fiction and collaging them into a unique work."

And that wasn't plagiarism? "They, er, let you do that?"

"Oh, yes. It's creating something new from something old."

"I suppose there really is nothing new under the sun."

"That's right." His cocoa-colored eyes lit with enthusiasm. "It's impossible to be original. So you may as well embrace that fact. Not that the average reader will." He motioned to his publisher's webpage on my open laptop.

"I'll be sure to leave a review."

His jaw set. "I *have* reviews. Important reviews from important critics and literary journals." He smiled. "But every review helps. Thanks."

"What's it like living in a literary family?" I asked brightly.

"There was nothing literary about Salvatore," Jacob said ruefully. "He wrote genre fiction. But that's what sells. Maybe I should try it. Maybe I should stop trying to create art and just write about sex and spies."

"Spying's not as sexy as you think," I muttered.

"What?"

"Nothing," I said. "I'm sure you could write whatever you want."

"Of course he could." Maive strode into the kitchen, and I bit back a frown. What was this? Invade Susan's Kitchen day?

"Jacob's a literary genius." She placed a hand on his arm. "My father understood that."

Her husband's face spasmed.

"Are you ready to go?" she asked him.

"Go where?" I asked.

"That's not really any of your business, Susan, is it?" she asked.

"Maive..." Jacob muttered.

"I just thought... Sorry," I said. "I'm so used to giving directions to tourists, the question is automatic. But of course, you're not tourists. You live here."

"And we're moving back into our home today," she said, "now that it's ours again."

"So soon?" Jacob asked. "Are you sure? We still don't have the legal details."

She lifted her chin. "Franklin's dead. Who's going to fight us for my father's estate now? There's no reason why we shouldn't go home."

"But—"

She turned on her stiletto heels and strode from the kitchen. The door swung in her wake. At least her ankle seemed okay.

"It looks like we'll be checking out sooner than expected," Jacob said cheerfully. "I hope that's not a problem."

I smothered a sigh of disappointment. "Nope. No problem at all." But their departure would make sleuthing more challenging.

I hadn't even had a chance to ransack their room. No wonder the sheriff had been giving me the stink eye. I was falling down on the job. "I'll bring the invoice upstairs."

"Thanks." He hurried after his wife.

In the foyer, I tallied their bill and pressed print. The printer ground alarmingly, wheezed like an aged turtle, and spat out the invoice.

I walked upstairs and knocked. Soft voices came from inside Maive and Jacob's room. I bent my head, but couldn't make anything out. Thwarted by the solid Victorian architecture, I slipped the invoice under the door.

The couple checked out an hour later. Maive walked straight to her Tesla, and Jacob and I finalized the bill.

I helped Jacob lug suitcases to his Jaguar, Dixie having conveniently vanished. Bailey watched us load the car from the top porch step.

The two cars backed down the gravel drive and zipped away.

I blew out my breath. *Rats.* I'd let two prime suspects slip through my fingers.

Dixie came onto the porch to stand beside Bailey. "Do you need help carrying their luggage?"

I glared up from the base of the steps. "Really? Now?"

She shrugged her bare shoulders. "What?"

"I've got to go shopping," I said. "Can you manage here? No one else should be checking in or out today."

"Don't I always manage?"

Mr. Baransky shuffled past her and down the porch steps. He touched his head and chuckled. "Good morning. Did Bailey encounter any strange squirrel activity?"

Bailey howled, bouncing on his forelegs.

I winced. "No."

"Lots," Dixie said.

"We must talk more later." He bustled past us.

"Did you ever find your friend?" I called after him hopefully.

Mr. Baransky stopped and turned, his thick scar creasing. "No. It is like he disappeared into the earth." He snapped his fingers. "Like that."

"Maybe the squirrels took him," Dixie said.

Bailey growled, scanning the pines.

"It would explain why so many people go missing in the woods," she finished. "That's where the you-know-what's are."

Mr. Baransky looked at her askance. "Yes. Well. I am going now. Good day." He strode down the drive, footsteps crunching, and turned onto the court.

"Do you need to encourage the S-word stories?" I asked.

"Yes," she said. "Yes, I do."

"But what if this business sets off another panic like last year? They're *still* rebuilding town hall."

She folded her arms. "I can't help it if people are delusional. I mean, it's obvious the flyers are a gag. Besides, a little mockery is just what this town needs. If we hadn't taken things so seriously last year, we wouldn't have had a panic."

"But people might—"

Dixie pivoted and strode inside. The screen doors clattered shut behind her.

I stood on the gravel and my vision clouded. The flyers seemed like a joke to me too. So why were some people taking them seriously? Was I the delusional one?

Bailey sneezed and shook his head, his collar jingling.

"At least I'm not delusional about my parents or these murders," I said. "What's happening now is real." But unease quivered through my bones.

I shook myself. Enough self-analysis. Maive and Jacob may have evaded my clutches, but there were still Malcolm and his wife Lupita.

Taking out my phone, I checked Lupita's social media feeds. According to one of her accounts, she was currently at a tasting room on Main Street. The timing was perfect. Modern life made detecting so much easier.

Though it did seem a little early for wine tasting. It wasn't even noon. Not that I was judging—I was worried. Lupita's father-in-law had been killed, and that was enough to throw anyone for a loop.

I nodded crisply, collected my purse and drove into Doyle.

The wine tasting room was set back from the road in a tiny green Craftsman-style home. I crossed its concrete patio. Oversized planters overflowing with colorful impatiens. I opened the door and stepped into a distressed wood tasting room.

A vertical succulent garden climbed one wall. Behind the long, metal bar, a chalkboard promoted the day's tasting. The air conditioner hummed.

Lupita sat at the counter, a wine glass before her.

I smoothed my blouse and approached the bar.

Francine, one of the workers, smiled at me from behind the bar. "Hi, Susan. Have you got another event coming up?"

Since that made a good excuse to be here, I nodded. "I need some good summer wines."

"We have some terrific Prosecco and a great dry White Zin. Would you like to try them?"

"Absolutely."

Lupita shook her head. "Why do they call it white when it's rosé? Blech. Pink wine should be illegal."

"I don't know," I said, sliding onto a high seat. "Pink champagne is fun."

"Oh, don't mind me, Susan," Lupita said. "I'm in a mood. Though FYI, I think white wine should be banned as well."

Francine uncorked a bottle with a pop. "But a lot of older people prefer it. It's easier on the stomach."

Lupita snorted and turned to eye me. She grimaced. "I heard you found Franklin's body."

I shifted and glanced at Francine, but her back was turned. "Arsen and I did."

"I also heard Arsen tried to save him. It was good of you to try." She sipped her wine, a deep, bloody red.

"You liked him?"

"No. But he didn't deserve to die."

"How well did you know him?"

"Not at all, it seems. He hid behind a mask, like everyone else."

"What do you mean?"

Lupita's shoulders caved inward. "You and Arsen say what you think. You have no idea what it's like, living in all this fakery."

I swiveled my chair to face her. "Fakery?"

"This family," she said, morose. "When you're rich, no one tells you what they really think. You can't trust anyone. So you put on armor—either because you want to feed the image, or because you can't stand the thought of all the phonies and toadies getting to the real you."

How much wine had she had? "That does sound... rough." I looked down at the polished bar. "I hadn't thought of the downside of wealth." I had, however, thought of how nice it would be not to have to worry about the new roof I'd soon need.

"Here. Watch." She turned, raised her phone and her glass, and smiled brilliantly, snapping a picture. "See what an amazing life I have and how much fun I'm having? And it's all garbage."

"It can't be *all* garbage. I mean, what happened to your father-in-law was terrible. But there is a light at the end of the tunnel. There are still good things in your life."

"Tell that to—" She clamped her lips together. "I know. I know. But when you're in the middle of it, when something like this happens, it's hard to remember that."

And somehow, I got the feeling she wasn't talking about herself. "Lupita—"

"Here you go," Francine said to me. She set down a glass with a touch of pink liquid. "It's perfect for picnics, goes well with fish, and is light and crisp."

"Thanks," I said.

Francine moved off down the bar.

Unsure how to pick up the conversational thread, I said, "Jacob and Maive are moving back into their condo."

"Jacob." She shook her head. "All he wanted was approval from the great man, Salvatore Van Der Woodsen. But Salvatore wouldn't give him the time of day. Would it have killed him to give Jacob a little help? But no, Salvatore hated the establishment too much, and saw Jacob as a part of that. I'm afraid Jacob was the real reason Malcolm and Maive were cut out of the will, not Franklin. I almost wish Franklin *had* gotten the money. Maybe then..." She fell silent.

I braced my elbow on the bar. "What do you—?"

"What do you think?" Francine bustled along the bar, a wine bottle in her hand.

"It's great," I said. "I'll take a case."

"You haven't even tried the Prosecco yet." The bartender poured a helping into a tall glass and drifted away.

"Sorry," I said to Lupita. "You were saying?"

"Too much."

Augh! "Jacob mentioned he might try his hand at genre writing," I said.

"Too late for that. If he'd done it sooner, Salvatore might have liked him better. Salvatore despised postmodernism."

"And he really disinherited his kids over... a literary dispute?"

She sighed. "It's not that simple. Nothing is. For instance, how did you happen to stumble over Franklin's body?"

"What does that have to do with anything?"

"Is it a simple story?"

"No," I admitted.

"And?"

I couldn't tell her about following him from a rendezvous with her sister-in-law. "We just found him," I said lamely.

She sipped her wine. I tried the prosecco. She put her glass on the bar and said nothing.

Fine. Sometimes you have to give something to get something. "You wanted to know how we found Franklin. We saw him in Angels Camp earlier that day. Franklin was, er, acting strangely, and with all that's going on, we went to the house to ask him why."

She raised a brow. "Strangely?"

"I suppose the sheriff's talked to you about all of this already?" I hedged.

"Not a thing. All she did was ask questions."

"Such as?"

"She wanted to know where I was between five and six-thirty."

I turned the champagne flute on the bar. "Did she like your answer?"

"That I was returning from a paddle board yoga class up at Lake Alpine?" She shrugged. "Who knows?"

"And Malcolm?"

She shrugged. "This has been more difficult for Malcolm than he lets on."

That wasn't very helpful. "I've been thinking about that jai alai ball—"

"I would be too if someone had thrown it at me. That... wasn't very nice."

"No," I said.

"If you want to know about the game, ask Maive. It's how she met her husband." Lupita stood, grabbed her purse off the bar, and strode from the tasting room.

Francine hefted a box onto the counter. "How was the Prosecco?"

"I think I'll stick with the White Zin," I said hastily. I couldn't afford another case of anything.

"Sure thing." Francine rung me up.

A woman shrieked. I started, knocking over my glass. The remains of my Prosecco spilled across the bar. Other wine tasters stared, eyes wide.

"There! There!" Another worker at the tasting room, Jean Shelton, clambered onto the bar. She pointed with a trembling hand at a shelf lined with upscale crackers. "It's inside!"

"What is?" Francine's brow creased with annoyance.

Something rustled on the shelf. A box of crackers slipped to the floor. Jean screamed, a high-pitched sound that drilled into my eardrums.

A squirrel peeked around a mustard jar and twitched his whiskers.

Shouts and squeals reverberated through the tasting room. Customers stampeded toward the door, knocking over displays of t-shirts and wine paraphernalia.

I squeezed closer to the bar. A man knocked a barstool sideways, and it toppled, banging into my thigh. A table full of wine glasses crashed to the wooden floor.

The tasting room emptied except for a shaking Jean, Francine, and me.

"Where is it?" Jean crouched on the bar, her head lashing back and forth. "Where'd it go?"

A bushy tail scampered through the slowly closing screen door.

"It's gone," I said. "It ran out with everyone else."

"Are you sure?" Jean asked.

"She's sure." Francine groaned, poured herself a measure of Zinfandel, and swigged it down. "Look at this mess."

The floor was littered with souvenirs and high-end foodstuffs. It looked like an earthquake had hit, but the destruction was down to one, solitary squirrel. Speechless, I handed Francine my credit card.

"At least *your* wine survived." She motioned toward a broken glass on the floor. "Jean, sweep that up before someone steps in it."

"But what if there's another squirrel?" Jean asked, plaintive.

"Then it doesn't want glass in its paws either," Francine said.

Jean clambered off the bar.

Francine rang me up and shoved the box of wine across the bar to me. "Do you need help getting this to your car?" she asked.

Jean nudged some t-shirts away from the broom with her foot.

I hefted the box. "I can manage."

On the patio, I wove around the planters, the box of wine weighting my arms. I staggered onto the sidewalk.

There was a whirring sound. I flinched backward.

A blur of blue and red and yellow jolted my arm and crashed into the box, sending it and me smashing to the concrete walk.

CHAPTER TWENTY-TWO

I ROLLED ONTO MY side, cool pavement pressing into my skin, and watched the bicyclist's swiftly departing backside. A man shouted. Wine soaked through the cardboard box, my spending money trickling down the sidewalk.

"Seriously?" Wasn't the universe going to cut me a *single* break?

A coil of raspberry-scented smoke wreathed my head.

"You shouldn't lie in the sidewalk," Mrs. Steinberg said.

I started and glanced behind me.

"Someone may step on you," she continued. The old lady stared after the bicyclist. He whipped around a corner and vanished.

"Very funny." I sat up and rubbed my arm. "Did you see what happened? He could have really hurt me."

"Or she." The old lady leaned, one-handed, on her cane.

I clambered to my feet and brushed tiny bits of stone and dirt from my palms. "Was it a woman?"

Mrs. Steinberg shrugged. "Impossible to tell in all that gear. But either that bicyclist was blind as a bat or aiming for you."

"Aiming…" My breath quickened. Had the hit-and-run been intentional? It made sense. I *was* an experienced investigator, with an inside track on the murders.

I was a threat.

"Maybe he thought you were a squirrel." She barked a laugh.

"A squir—? That isn't funny either. What do you know about the squirrels? The squirrel flyers, I mean."

"I know lots of things," she said darkly.

I stood and brushed off my capris. "Do you know who posted those flyers?"

"No," she admitted. "Most people aren't taking them seriously. But a dangerous few are."

A tremor shivered up my spine. "Dangerous?"

She gazed at the sky. Not a single cloud floated past. "I used to work in town hall, you know. Now half of its gone, burnt to a crisp, and I work in a trailer. It's undignified."

"Yes, but—"

"Panic is part of human nature, but it's a destructive force, and it only takes one spark."

"And you think these flyers may be the spark?"

"I hope not. I'm old, Susan. I don't want to go through another riot."

I shivered. The sheriff. Arsen. Mrs. Steinberg. They all thought these flyers were more dangerous than they seemed. And after the scene in the tasting room, I couldn't say they were wrong.

I gathered up the soaking box and checked to see if any bottles had survived. Two had. I set them aside and dumped the sodden box in a nearby trash bin.

"Do you think someone's intentionally trying to cause another panic?" I turned toward her.

The sidewalk was empty. My hands dropped to my sides. The old woman had pulled her disappearing act again. If I didn't know better, I'd think she was a witch.

Clutching a damp bottle in each hand, I trudged to my car and returned to Wits' End.

The noon sun reflected off the rooftop UFO as I stepped from the Crosstrek.

Laughter sounded from the side yard. Cautiously, I walked around the corner of the Victorian.

My parents and Mr. Baransky lounged in the gazebo, and I stumbled. Nothing good could come from the three of them lounging around like they were innocent. Because my parents most definitely were not.

I hurried toward the gazebo. "Hi, everyone!"

Their laughter stopped as if a switch had been thrown. Was I that big of a killjoy? At the bottom of the white-painted steps, Bailey raised his head.

"Is that wine?" my mother asked. "Isn't it a little early in the day?"

"It's for an event," I said, pulling the bottles to my chest.

"It mustn't be a very big event if you only have two bottles," my father said.

"I had more, but a bicyclist nearly ran me down, and I dropped the box."

"That was careless of you," my mother said.

"A bicyclist?" Mr. Baransky's wide brow furrowed, and the scar on his cheek wrinkled, darkening. "Some of these bicyclists drive too fast. Were you hurt?"

"No," I said. "Just some scuffs. How has your stay been so far?"

He frowned. "My friend still has not responded to my calls. I am starting to worry."

"The reception in these mountains can be dicey," my father said. "What did your friend look like?"

"Very tall, very big. He looks like an angry bear. But he is a very kind man. Kind angry bear."

My parents exchanged a significant look, and cold sweat broke out on my brow. The assassin had looked big—or at least the leg I'd seen had. The rest of him had been out the window.

I needed to get Baransky out of here and away from my parents. "I've been thinking about your sq—your question about the flyers," I said. "Have you spoken to Mrs. Steinberg?"

"Mrs. Steinberg? Is she a squirrel researcher?"

Bailey started to his paws and looked wildly around the yard.

I bent to stroke the beagle's fur. "No, she works in the records department at town hall. Well, it's a trailer now, but she hears everything that's happening in Doyle."

"Mrs. Steinberg?" my mother asked. "Wasn't she your grandmother's friend?"

"Yes, she's—"

"Absolutely nuts." My father circled one finger around his ear. "She was crazy as a bedbug when I knew her. She's still employed?"

"What were you doing spending time with a lunatic?" my mother asked.

"I—She's not a lunatic," I said, my voice rising. "She's... eccentric."

"There's a thin line between insanity and eccentricity," my father said. "Mrs. Steinberg crossed that years ago."

I shook my head. *Never mind.* "Anyway, you might want to ask her about the flyers. The trailer's in the parking lot behind town hall." Mrs. Steinberg had admitted she didn't know anything, but it didn't matter. He'd never find her. Mrs. Steinberg was like a ghost.

Mr. Baransky's eyes lit. "Old crazy lady in records. Thank you. I will go find her now." He shook hands with my parents and trotted down the gazebo steps. The Crimean hurried away, across the lawn.

My mother's eyes narrowed. "I don't recall saying Mrs. Steinberg was old."

"You implied it when you said she was Gran's friend," I said, grasping the wooden railing. "And please tell me you didn't kill Mr. Baransky's colleague."

My father rubbed his chin. "Unclear. The man who attacked us *was* large. I thought I was going to throw my back out dragging him all over your B&B. Have you got any heating pads?"

"Yes, but... How can you still not *know*? You've obviously been interrogating Mr. Baransky. And what about all those fake passports you found?" I was starting to worry for our national security. How long did it take to identify and remove a body?

"They haven't actually gotten back—" my father began.

"If Baransky's a foreign spy, he's good. We searched his room—" My mother rose from the bench, and a rose blossom fluttered to the wooden floor.

I stared, aghast. "You what?" That was so unfair. I had the key. I should have searched his room.

"—and we couldn't find anything," she finished. "That could mean he is what he says or he's very good at his *real* job."

"You can't just invade my guests' rooms," I said.

"We have to know what we're dealing with," my father said. "We need to know if he's another assassin or an innocent Russian."

My mother scowled. "There are no innocent Russians."

"I thought he was Crimean," I said.

"Now, now," my father said to her. "You know that isn't true. What about Slava?"

For some reason, my mother pinked. "Baransky is no Slava."

"We don't know that," my father said.

"But he hasn't tried to kill you," I said. "That's got to be a good sign."

My mother shot me an annoyed look. "He may not know what his targets look like. That other fellow surveilled us for days before he made a move."

My nostrils flared. "Surveilled—" I struggled to rein in my temper. "You knew someone was watching you, and you came here anyway?" They could have put the whole B&B in danger.

"Well what good would staying away have done?" my mother asked.

I gave a slight shake of my head. This conversation was futile. "And the body?" I asked.

My parents glanced away. A warm breeze kicked up and soughed in the pine branches.

"Oh, for Pete's sake," I said. "I know this is the government we're talking about. But this is glacial levels of slowness. DMV levels of slowness. Why haven't they removed it yet?"

My father rubbed the back of his neck. "The thing is, we're sort of—"

"Frank," my mother said sharply.

"I don't see what the harm is in telling her," he said.

"Susan's made it clear she doesn't want to be involved in that part of our lives."

"Which is over," my father said.

My mother's mouth flattened.

"Wait," I said. "Over? What do you mean?"

"We've... retired," he said.

I stilled. My parents, retired? I couldn't imagine it. I set the bottles on the steps. "If you've retired, then why did that man attack you?"

"It's not as if a memo goes out to all the other agencies," my father said.

"But..." I sputtered. "If you're retired—"

"Don't worry," my father said. "Our agency will take care of this. It's just taking a little longer to get things moving, since we're not on the inside anymore."

"But—"

"So you see," my mother said, "there's no reason for you to hide out in these mountains anymore. I've called a local realtor, and she's very interested in selling this property."

"Hiding out?" This was my B&B, my livelihood, my life. "I'm not hiding out."

And spying had been their life, their passion. They *loved* spying. Suddenly, my heart warmed with realization. To give that up— "Did you retire because of... me?"

"Don't be ridiculous," my mother snapped.

"It would be more accurate to say we *were* retired," my father said. "There's a strict age limit on what we do."

"Oh." I toed my tennis shoe into the lawn. "Okay, but I'm not selling Wits' End. I'm happy here."

"You can go back to your accounting job." My father removed his glasses and polished them with the hem of his knit vest. "And we'll be near each other again."

A cold shadow touched my shoulder. My mouth went dry, my heart galloping. I forced myself not to look behind me, because I'd never catch it. No matter where I turned, the shadow would always be behind me.

Don't think that way. I was in control. I was an adult, and they couldn't control me anymore. "I don't like accounting," I said. "I've never liked accounting. I mean, it's useful, but—"

"Think of all the great restaurants in San Francisco we can go to," she said. "And the culture, the shows, the museums. Now that we've retired, we'll have time to enjoy all the things we want to."

I was sinking, drowning. The shadow's chill spread across my upper back. "There are good restaurants here."

My mother's gaze flicked to the gazebo's octagonal ceiling. "Oh, please. In this village? That restaurant you sent us to last night was very sub par."

"Well, okay, it is small, and we may not have the variety of San Francisco, but..." Why was I talking about restaurants? Who cared about restaurants? None of this was the point.

"You can thank us later." My mother strode off.

"She really does have your best interests at heart," my father said and followed her.

"But—"

Bailey looked up at me, his brown eyes somber.

"But why don't they *listen?*" I asked him.

The beagle sneezed and looked longingly toward the kitchen.

I jammed my fists on my hips. "You can't possibly be hungry." But I grabbed the bottles in one hand and walked with him into the kitchen.

Bailey trotted to his dog bowl.

Thinking hard, I refilled his water. My parents couldn't make me sell, so what had they been up to? It must have been another attempt to divert me. But divert me from what?

There was a lot I didn't know about my parents' work. But killing a foreign agent, even in self-defense, was no small affair. Contra all the spy movies I've seen, there's a ton of paperwork and panels involved. If my parents were no longer real spies, they could be in serious trouble.

I fixed a grilled cheese sandwich with tomatoes and set it on a plate. The scent of melting cheese lifted my spirits, and I carefully folded a napkin beside my meal.

Opening the refrigerator, I leaned in, looking for any leftover pasta salad. I'd figure this out and put the shadow in its place. I'd solved crimes before. I'd been under pressure before. I'd get through this disaster.

The foyer door banged open, and Dixie strolled into the kitchen. "I finished cleaning the rooms." She grabbed my sandwich and took a bite. "This is good," she mumbled. "What kind of cheese did you use?"

I frowned. "Cheddar and Gouda. And that was mine." I spotted the tub of pasta salad and extracted it from the fridge.

She held out the sandwich to me. "Want it back?"

I surveyed the bite mark. "No. Thanks." I set the tub on the counter.

"Anyway." She swallowed. "I cleaned all the rooms. Did you know your parents are armed?"

I went cold. "What?"

"How'd they get a concealed carry license in California? I hear that's near impossible."

"I don't know," I said faintly.

She shrugged. "I'll ask them when I see them."

"No, don't."

"Why not? And why do you look like you're in labor?"

I realized I was puffing quick gasps, and I inhaled slowly through my nose. "Because then they'll know you've been snooping in their room."

"Cleaning."

"Snooping. They specifically said they didn't want anyone cleaning. But I'll cover for you, and I'll ask them about the license. You stay out of it."

Her green eyes narrowed. "You seem awfully jumpy."

"Someone nearly ran me over with a bike today. And that was my sandwich."

"At least it wasn't a minivan." She ambled outside with my lunch.

Bailey followed, no doubt hoping for scraps.

I fried another sandwich and set the plate on the kitchen table with the leftover pasta salad.

The kitchen door banged open behind me.

"This sandwich is mine, dammit." I pulled the plate closer and twisted in my chair.

Maive glowered from the kitchen door.

"Oh, hi," I said, my ears turning hot. "Did you forget something?"

She folded her arms. "A bird defecated on my husband's Jaguar in your driveway."

"You can borrow the hose, if you want," I said, half rising. "I can show you where—"

Her nostrils flared. "Do you have any idea how expensive that paint job was?"

"No," I said slowly, straightening. "But if you wash it now—"

"The damage was incurred on your property."

"I can't control the birds," I said slowly. I didn't have superpowers. And bird control would be a pretty dumb superpower even if I did.

Maive's face reddened. "It happened in your driveway."

She was out of her mind. What did I have to do with birds? Next thing, she'd be blaming me for the alien squirrels. But she was a customer, if an ex-customer. And the customer was... usually right.

"I don't know what you want me to do about this," I said.

"I nearly killed myself on your stairs." Her tone deepened. "My husband's car was extensively damaged on your property—"

"Extensively?"

"Jacob is seriously considering a lawsuit."

The hair rose on the back of my neck. "Another lawsuit?" I repeated stupidly. I'd just escaped the first one.

"If you know what's good for you, you'll stay away from the both of us." She stormed out the door into the foyer.

Hands shaking, I set my plate on the small table. It was okay. I had insurance. And right now they were only *threatening* to sue. Or was Maive the one doing the threatening? I had a hard time imagining Jacob going after me for something so trivial.

They couldn't really sue me over a bird, could they? Birds were everywhere, like squirrels. And why were small animals suddenly turning into such pests?

I sat and took a bite of the sandwich but couldn't taste it. I knew it was hot, because I'd just cooked it. But I couldn't sense the heat either.

The shadow edged closer. *Stop panicking. Think.*

I gulped a hard lump of bread and cheese. Maive had implied if I stayed away from them, they might not sue. And that was... suspicious, wasn't it? If she wanted to sue me, she'd sue me.

Was she really upset about a bird? Or was she worried I might figure something out about her father's death?

Ha. Maybe I *was* on the right track.

Unfortunately, I didn't know where that track was going. I raked a hand through my hair.

Could Maive possibly know that we'd seen her meet Franklin in Angels Camp? I hadn't said anything to her, and I was pretty sure Arsen hadn't either.

But I had told Lupita we'd seen Franklin there. If she'd told her sister-in-law, Maive might have put two and two together.

I shoved aside the grilled cheese, pulled my laptop toward me, and booted it up.

I scanned Maive's social media accounts. She hadn't posted anything for the last two days. If there were clues as to what she'd been up to recently, they weren't online.

I typed her name into the search engine. A new article about her father popped up.

Anticipation Builds Over Van Der Woodsen's Final Novel

Buzz in the publishing industry is building over Salvatore Van Der Woodsen's last novel. Van Der Woodsen was an American novelist whose books regularly landed on the bestseller charts. Fifteen of his stories, to date, have been translated into films. His final manuscript is said to portray the complex relationships between rival spies.

"I haven't read the manuscript," his agent, Waldorf Manners said. "However, I don't need to. Salvatore was at the top of his game when he was killed. His books rarely needed much editing. I fully expect the manuscript to fetch at least seven figures at auction."

Salvatore was murdered by person or persons unknown in his Doyle mansion. He is survived by his twin son and daughter, Malcolm and Maive Van Der Woodsen.

I whistled. A seven-figure deal? I printed the article in the foyer, clipped it to fit, and pasted it into my planner.

Seven figures...

If that wasn't a motive for murder, I wasn't a plucky amateur detective.

CHAPTER TWENTY-THREE

CLEANING UP AFTER SOMEONE else's breakfast is weirdly satisfying when no one's died. I'd gotten through another night without my parents causing more trouble. Dare I hope it was the beginning of a trend?

Mr. Baransky stretched and pushed the blue-cushioned chair away from the breakfast table. His jacket sleeve caught in the tablecloth, tugging it toward him. The vase of roses on the table wobbled.

He disentangled himself. "Thank you for sending me to Mrs. Steinberg," he said. "She knows a lot about Doyle."

I blinked, surprised, and picked up an empty carafe. "You found—? Oh, good." I guess it was harder for Mrs. Steinberg to stay elusive in a twenty-foot trailer. "Did you sleep well?"

"Yes, in spite of the strange dream. There is something about the air in the mountains."

"Strange dream?"

He chuckled. "A mad dream. I dreamed your parents were in my bedroom, searching my suitcase. What would Jung say about that, eh?"

My hopes of normalcy crashed to the wood floor. If I knew my parents, that had been no dream. "I have no idea," I croaked.

He stood. "I am off to find a strange squirrel."

"Okay then." Rubbing my forehead, I watched him leave, then hurried into the kitchen. Arsen strolled in through the porch door.

"Morning, Susan. Happy birthday eve." He pulled me into his arms and kissed me, and my heart turned over.

I rested my head against his chest, and a warm glow washed through my body. So my parents had returned to ransack Mr. Baransky's room? They'd gotten away with it, and all was well. "Thanks for remembering."

"Of course I remembered. Rough morning?"

"My parents—" I snapped shut my mouth. "Never mind."

"You've been a real champion with them."

"They want me to sell Wits' End."

He chuckled. "That's not going to happen."

"No. It isn't." Because at least I was in control of that.

He stepped away from me. "I wanted to hold this for your birthday, but I don't want to wait any longer. How would you like to go to Iceland?"

"Iceland?" Briefly, I fantasized about Arsen, half-naked in a hot spring.

"A ten-day vacation for the B&B owner. I've already talked it over with Dixie, and she can run the place while you're gone."

I wasn't so sure about that. Lately, my cousin had been more cavalier about the B&B than usual. My Arsen fantasy evaporated.

"All you have to do is name the date," he said. "As long as it's in September, because that's one of the best times to see the Northern Lights."

The Northern Lights. I sighed. I'd always wanted to see them. Why not go? I deserved a vacation.

My gaze fell upon my planner, open on the kitchen table. The sight of its clean lines snapped me back to reality. What was I thinking? My parents were killer spies. My life was a disaster.

How was I supposed to go anywhere with Arsen with that kind of baggage?

He grinned and took my planner off the table. "Consult the oracle." He handed it to me. "And let me know."

He grabbed a leftover waffle and ambled out the door.

Iceland. Arsen. My eyelids heated. I remembered our earlier hug, and how it had felt like home. It was a poor sort of home though, because I was lying to the best man in the world. Had he sensed it? Was that why he'd gone on about seeing what he wanted to see?

Miserable, I opened my planner. But instead of looking at September, I flipped to the orange tab with my murder files. I couldn't think of Iceland or Arsen. All this stress was just distracting me from crime solving. And I needed to help the sheriff solve these murders.

My parents had thrown me off my game. All I needed was to push my organizational skills a bit farther, and I'd figure this out like I had the others.

Maybe I should use some of that Japanese Washi tape for the page edges in my planner? A different tape design for each suspect? That *would* be a tighter system.

I opened my kitchen drawer and pulled out six rolls of tape. Now, which pattern to pick for which suspect? I nodded. Since Franklin was dead, he should get the black tape with stars.

I placed tape around my transcript of my conversation with him. It would have been better if I'd recorded it on my phone for accuracy, but that might have been off-putting.

I carefully snipped the end of the tape.

Now for Maive... I turned the page to my notes on Maive. She'd get pink and orange tape. She and Franklin seemed like an odd couple, but I couldn't deny they'd been in that hotel together.

But what if they *hadn't* been fooling around in that hotel room? It wasn't likely, but a seasoned investigator never assumes. They could have met for a reason other than hanky panky...

To discuss the new manuscript? If Franklin was the heir, he wouldn't have wanted to give that up. Maive and Malcolm must have been gnashing their teeth over all that cash.

And where *was* the manuscript? Why hadn't Salvatore's agent seen it yet? If he didn't have the manuscript, who did?

Franklin had lived in the mansion with Salvatore. The butler would have had the best chance of finding and selling the manuscript. But he hadn't sold it yet, or it would have gone to the agent, wouldn't it?

Or had Salvatore's killer taken it?

I needed to ask the sheriff who had that manuscript. My face tightened. She'd no doubt shout at me for interfering in an investigation. But that was life. Sheriff McCourt would tell me in the end. She always did. It was the way we worked.

The kitchen door banged open, and Dixie clomped in with a pair of garden shears. "What are you doing?"

"Organizing."

"Again?"

"Organization is an ongoing process," I said loftily.

"Yeah," she said. "And it's a great way to put off actually *doing* anything real."

I stared at the pastel tape sticking to my finger. Dixie... might have had a point. But she knew better than to interfere with my process.

"Speaking of doing things," I said, annoyed, "you know where the vacuum is."

She sniffed and dropped the shears onto the kitchen table with a clatter. Dixie stomped from the kitchen.

I peeled off the tape. Now that I'd started, my planner would just look weird if I stopped.

I selected purple tape for Lupita and stuck it to the edge of her transcripts. Lupita had said she was at a paddleboard yoga class when Franklin was killed. That alibi should be easy enough to check.

I found the paddleboard yoga class online and called the number. It went to voice mail. I squinted at the web page. The next class was scheduled for one o'clock. If I left now, I could catch the instructor before class started at the lake.

I rechecked the computer in the foyer. As I'd thought no one was checking out. So I grabbed my purse and planner and drove up the mountain toward Lake Alpine. The road snaked and narrowed. The mountains rose higher, their weight pressing upon me, squeezing, crushing.

I loosened my grip on the wheel. The mountains had never made me feel this way before. I'd also never spent much time here with my parents. But of course the problem wasn't the mountains. It was the situation—the body at Wits' End, the sheriff's lack of faith, my lies to Arsen, the murders. The car chilled, the shadow creeping closer.

Don't think about what might happen. Don't think about the shadow. Move forward and figure this out.

I found a parking spot beside the bike trail that bordered the lake and walked through the pines to the shore.

Lake Alpine is packed on summer weekends, but this was Wednesday, and its blue surface was serene. Granite islands dotted the shimmering water. Pines sprouted from islands of smooth, pale stone.

A woman in violet yoga pants and a matching tank arranged paddleboards along the shore. She turned and adjusted her baseball hat. Her black ponytail looped through the hole at its back. "Hi! Are you Janice?"

"No, I'm Susan Witsend."

She picked a clipboard off the pine needle-strewn ground and studied it. "I don't see your name on the list."

"I'm not a student. I wanted to ask you about Lupita Van Der Woodsen."

"Lupita?" The instructor squinted at me. "Why?"

"Was she in class with you Monday afternoon?"

"That's confidential."

My mouth slackened. "A paddleboard yoga class is confidential?"

"It is if you're not in the class," she said.

Of course, I *could* suggest the Sheriff check into the class. But she'd probably done it already, and I wanted to know if Lupita had an alibi or not.

"And if I was in the class?" I asked. "Would you tell me then?"

She shrugged. "I guess. You got thirty bucks?"

This was blackmail. I dug into my purse and handed her the cash. "There. I'm in the class. Now about Lupita—"

"Hey!" Three women made their way down the bank. "Is this the yoga class?"

"It sure is," the instructor said. "You must be Fran, Maria, and Nicki. I'm Deepa, and this is Susan. She's joining us today."

"I am?" I looked down at my clothing—stretchy khaki capris and an olive-green tank. "No. I didn't bring my—"

"You'll be fine," Deepa said and handed me a life vest.

I didn't have yoga gear or even a swimsuit. "But—"

"Now," Deepa said, ignoring me, "we're going to be wearing the life vests to paddle out to our yoga spot. You can take them off once you get there, or you can leave them on for the class. It's up to you."

She instructed us on the finer points of paddleboarding, then pulled the boards out to where the water was knee deep. The other women clambered onto them. Deepa attached a paddle strap to their ankles.

The instructor smiled. "Your turn, Susan."

"I just want to know if Lupita was in class Monday afternoon," I said, plaintive.

She smiled. "It's yoga or no info."

Uh, oh. She must be one of those crazed, yoga fanatics Mrs. Steinberg had once warned me about. I edged backward.

"So what'll it be?" she asked.

My jaw tightened. I was a hardened investigator, and sometimes, one had to make sacrifices. This was murder.

Besides, how difficult could paddleboard yoga be? I'd done yoga. I'd even paddleboarded, thanks to Arsen.

I toed off my tennis shoes, rolled up my hems, and splashed through the chill water. Though the lake was shallow, the water was the cold of snowmelt. If the rocks hadn't been so slippery, I would have bolted for shore.

Deepa got me onto the board and attached the strap to my ankle. "I'll see you at the meeting point." She shoved my board forward.

It wobbled beneath me, and I gritted my teeth. *I've got this.*

Soon I was gliding across the small lake toward a granite island. I back paddled to a halt twenty feet from its tallest pine.

"Knock the weights at the end of your boards into the lake and anchor," the yoga instructor called.

I stretched my foot back and nudged the pink weight off the board. The board wobbled, and I stilled, heart thumping.

"All right, everybody," Deepa said. "We'll start on our hands and knees for cat/cow."

I gripped the edges of the board, arched my back, and didn't fall in. I began to relax. This really wasn't hard at all.

"And now straighten your legs to downward dog," the instructor said.

I straightened and looked between my knees. Sky and lake switched positions, two fishermen along the shore hanging upside down. For a moment, I felt like I'd stepped into an upside-down world.

Then we pushed down into a plank, and the spell broke. I wobbled a bit when we moved into a lunge, but I breathed through it and steadied.

"Now," Deepa said, "pivot so you face the long edge of your board."

Paddleboard yoga was easy. *And* it was a good core workout, because you had to pay attention to balance more than you would on solid ground. Why hadn't I tried this class earlier?

I should be doing paddleboard yoga once a week. Or at least once a month. The lake, the sun, the gentle lap of water were like meditation on steroids.

"Slowly bend forward and grab the edge of your board," Deepa called.

I bent. The paddleboard tilted. I gasped, heart seizing.

The surface of the lake rushed toward me, and I plunged head-first into the water. I came up gasping.

The fishermen on the shore guffawed.

In spite of the icy water, my face felt impossibly hot. Shivering, I clambered onto my board and stuck with a dripping corpse pose for the rest of the class.

When the torture finally ended, I waited on the shore for the other women to leave. My clothes stuck uncomfortably to my body.

"I'll email you links to the photos of today's class," Deepa said to me.

"Links? There's photographic evidence of the class? Online?"

"I post the pictures I take on social media so people can share. Don't worry. Students fall in all the time. There's nothing to be embarrassed about."

My neck stiffened. Forget embarrassment. I hadn't had to take this class at all to learn if Lupita had been here. "Was Lupita here Monday or not?"

"Yeah, she was. She's an amazing yogini."

"Whatever." I stuffed my damp feet into my tennis shoes and trudged, fuming, to the Crosstrek.

In my car, I checked the social media site on my phone. There Lupita was, smiling in tree pose in the Monday class. How the heck had she managed tree pose on a paddleboard? It's a one-legged pose. That just wasn't fair.

At least I had hard evidence she couldn't have killed Franklin. Now I had to cross Malcolm, Maive, and Jacob off the list.

Briefly, I considered Darla. I didn't peg her as a killer, even if she lived across the street from the victim and had had an altercation with him. Her motive didn't seem strong enough, and she was Darla. But it would be unprofessional not to confirm her alibi for Salvatore's death. After all, she didn't have an alibi for Franklin's.

I called Darla's boss at the coffeeshop.

"Ground, how can I help you?"

"Hi, Jayce. I have a weird question."

"Cool. I love weird."

"Was Darla working at Ground all Friday afternoon?"

"Um, yeah," she said. "Why?"

"And did she leave at any time to take a long break?"

"Darla?" Jayce laughed, her voice rich and warm as hot cocoa. "Darla doesn't take breaks. She's the most dedicated assistant manager anyone could hope for. What's going on?"

"Nothing. Thanks." Hurriedly, I hung up.

I made notations of what I'd learned in my planner and drove to Wits' End.

I turned in to my gravel drive, and my foot hit the brake too hard. The wheels skidded on stones.

I lurched forward, dismayed. The sheriff's SUV was parked in front of my B&B.

CHAPTER TWENTY-FOUR

I HURRIED INSIDE. IN the foyer, Sheriff McCourt's furious gaze stopped me cold. "Hello, Sheriff. Is everything—?"

"What the hell is going on?" she asked.

"I fell into Lake Alpine," I stammered. It was my house, and that should have given me some advantage. But who's at their personal best with cold, sodden clothing stuck to their body?

"I don't mean your wet clothes," she snapped. "Jai alai balls? Interrogating murder suspects? How many times do I have to tell you not to interfere in official investigations?"

"I told you about the attack with the ball."

"And you never brought it to me."

"Oh." Guiltily, I hunched my shoulders. I *had* dropped the ball—no pun intended. "I thought you didn't want it since Bailey got to it first?"

"Get. Me. The ball."

I squished into the kitchen, and Sheriff McCourt followed. Meekly, I collected the ball, in a plastic bag, and handed it to her.

Beneath the table, Bailey whined, watching a potential toy slip away.

She studied my evidence through the clear plastic and shook her head. "I thought you were over these delusions about being a crack investigator."

"I'm not." Heat rose in my cheeks. "I mean, this isn't what you think."

"That you're once again playing girl detective?" She dropped her broad-brimmed hat on the kitchen table.

"Sheriff—"

"I told myself it wasn't happening again," she said. "I didn't want to see the truth."

I tried again. "It's not that I *want* to solve two murders—"

"This is my fault. I never should have let you help during last year's panic. It only fed your delusions. Are your parents here?"

"You don't want to talk to my parents."

"Oh, don't I?"

Briefly, I closed my eyes. They could wreck the sheriff's career.

Whoa. But they were retired. Telling the sheriff about them wouldn't be a breach of national security anymore. At least, I didn't think it would be. "My parents aren't what you think."

Her lip curled. "Are they aliens?"

"Of course not." I took a deep breath. "They work for a government agency—"

"Not the men in black thing again."

I scuffed one foot against the other. My feet were starting to itch in their wet tennis shoes.

"No," I said. "They're real agents. Not men in black. I mean, men in black may be real too. But my parents have nothing to do with UFOs, or trying to stop people from talking about UFOs, like the men in black. Who may or may not be real."

She raised a brow. "So they're not accountants?"

"They're actually really good accountants. They know how to follow the money, and that's part of what they do, but the other part..." *Just tell her.* "They're spies."

Bailey thumped his tail on the linoleum floor.

The sheriff stared, impassive. "Spies."

"Spies. Here's the thing. A Russian assassin followed them to Doyle for some reason—"

"Russian assass—? You mean Baransky?"

"No. Well, I don't know. He could be an assassin too. We're not sure."

The sheriff smiled and took my arm. She pulled out a kitchen chair and gently forced me into it. "It's going to be all right."

"I hope so. It would help if you had evidence Mr. Baransky is who he says he is. Because then my parents could stop worrying about him and focus on... other things."

"I'll look into this Baransky for you."

"You will?" I *knew* we were still on the same team. "Thanks."

She patted my damp shoulder. "No problem."

The door from the foyer swung open, and my parents strolled into the kitchen.

My mouth went dry. It was one thing to tell the sheriff they were retired spies, another to tell my parents what I'd told the sheriff. This was not going to go well.

"Sheriff?" my father paused beside the knife block on the counter. "Has something happened?"

"Everything's fine," she said. "Susan's just a little stressed out."

My father's hand slid across the butcherblock, toward the knives. The blue curtain fluttered behind him over the sink.

"Not really," I said. "Everything's fine. This is pretty normal stress for me."

"Mr. and Mrs. Witsend, a quick word, if you don't mind?" The sheriff walked onto the kitchen porch and held the screen door for my parents.

I shook my head frantically. The sheriff didn't know what she was doing.

"Susan," she said, "wait here."

My parents exchanged baffled looks and followed her outside.

I hurried to the sink, and the open window. My scruples about eavesdropping had dropped to a dangerous low. But I'd worry about morality later.

"...I like Susan," the sheriff was saying.

I smiled. I'd always known she'd liked me, even if she could be a bit gruff.

"But I'm worried about her fantasies of being an amateur detective," she continued.

Fantasies? I gripped the counter's edge.

"Amateur detective?" my father asked.

"She's inserted herself into several investigations," the sheriff said. "In the past, I thought she was simply an eccentric, and that her delusions could be managed—"

"Delusions?" my mother asked sharply.

My knees buckled. I gripped the counter for balance.

"But now I'm not so sure," the sheriff continued. "She's involved herself in the Van Der Woodsen investigation. I expected that. But she seems to think..." The sheriff laughed shortly. "She told me the two of you were spies."

I clapped my hands over my mouth and stifled a moan.

"Spies?" my father asked. "We're accountants. Well, we *were* accountants. We've recently retired."

"I'm assuming your international work was what led Susan to this spy fantasy," the sheriff said.

"How did you know we worked internationally?" my mother asked.

"You just told me," Sheriff McCourt said. "But Susan mentioned you traveled."

My mother laughed. "I suppose she would. And I'm glad Susan has such a good friend watching out for her. But you don't have to worry. She's selling Wits' End and returning to San Francisco with us."

No!

"That's great news," the sheriff said. "I only want to make sure she gets the help she needs."

"Oh, she will," my father said. "Don't worry about that. Susan's our only child. We'll do anything to protect her."

The sheriff said something in a voice too low for me to hear. Footsteps clomped down the wooden steps.

The kitchen door opened, and I leapt away from the sink. This was it, the confrontation I'd been dreading. And now that it had come, it was *way* worse than I'd imagined.

My parents walked inside.

My mother crossed her arms over her loose blouse. "You told that woman we were spies?"

"Retired spies," I squeaked.

"Do you have any idea how many national security laws you've breached?" she asked. "And who cleaned our room yesterday?"

"I did," I said. "It had to be cleaned."

"Never mind that," my father said.

"Oh," my mother said, "I do mind. And I mind her blowing our cover."

"The sheriff doesn't believe her anyway," my father said.

And that was the worst part of it. My neck corded. I'd thought the sheriff and I were friends.

"We'll have to report this," she said.

Bailey came to lean against my leg. His warm, gentle pressure did nothing to slow the blood pulsing in my temples.

"Why?" my father asked sharply. "Do you think HQ will be any more responsive to that call than to our others?"

"I was trying to explain to Sheriff McCourt why I had to help solve this case too," I said.

"Too?" my mother asked.

"I've solved several murders here in Doyle," I explained.

My father smiled. "That's my girl. You remember your observation training." He turned to my mother. "I told you detecting was easier than it looked."

"It really is." I nodded.

"That isn't the point," my mother said. "Susan's done something reckless and stupid. We can't put this off any longer." She grasped my shoulder. "You're coming back with us to San Francisco. Tonight."

I jerked away. "What? No. I'm not leaving Wits' End. This is my home and my job."

"And the sheriff thinks you're insane," my mother said. "Do you think she'll leave a mad innkeeper alone?"

"She's right, Susan," my father said. "The situation has changed."

"But I'm *not* delusional."

My father shook his head. "It doesn't matter. Appearances must be maintained."

"It's home with us," my mother said, "or to an institution."

I swayed on my feet, feeling the blood drain from my skull. "An institution?"

My mother's expression turned steely. "A mental institution."

CHAPTER TWENTY-FIVE

SHAKEN, I STUMBLED FROM the kitchen and down the porch steps.

Bailey wriggled after me through the dog door. The beagle clambered down the stairs and onto the thick lawn. It was the first time in a long time he hadn't demanded I carry him. Even he must have known the situation was dire.

Could they institutionalize me? The idea seemed like something out of a gothic novel. But from an outsider's perspective, I guess some of my behavior could look a little... odd.

I walked, dazed, past the gazebo. I'd no objective in mind except to get away. We followed a partially hidden deer trail that climbed the hill behind Wits' End. Bailey's collar jingled behind me.

If the sheriff really thought I was mentally ill... I swallowed. That hurt most of all, because I *had* helped the sheriff on occasion. How could she think I was crazy? She *knew* me.

Reaching a break in the pines, I sat on a fallen log.

Bailey, panting loudly, dropped to the earth by my feet.

I looked out over the Doyle rooftops, peeking through the trees. The houses—symbols of home and hearth and everything that mattered—blurred, and I blinked rapidly.

I wouldn't leave Doyle willingly. But would I leave my town *unwillingly*? I gripped my knees hard.

Mrs. Steinberg sat beside me. The hem of her black dress whispered across the dead pine needles scattered on the ground.

I turned my head. "Where did you come from?" I asked, not much interested in the answer.

"I like to walk." She propped her cane between her knees and sank her chin on its handle. "Bad news?"

My shoulders slumped. "The sheriff thinks I'm delusional." I hunched, bracing my forearms on my thighs.

"Welcome to the asylum." The old lady blew out a stream of smoke. "She's convinced I went around the bend decades ago."

"But she didn't tell *your* parents to get you professional help."

"And I suppose they threatened to do it?"

I nodded, and she chuckled.

"Good luck with that in California," she said. "It's near impossible to commit someone even when they really do need the help."

I shook my head. But would it be impossible for a sheriff and two ex-special agents?

"Besides," she continued, "delusional? That's the pot calling the kettle black."

"My parents and the sheriff are under no illusions. Trust me."

She snorted. "Don't they? Everyone's deludes themselves to some degree or another. Most of what we tell ourselves about the world, and even about ourselves, is sheer fantasy. We create a story populated by villains and allies, and we're the hero."

"I guess," I said, morose.

"The Hindus call it *Maya*. I call it human nature. Normally it only hurts us. But it takes a darker turn in crowds." She shuddered.

"You mean the UFO panic."

Mrs. Steinberg didn't respond.

"You're probably right," I continued. "We're all a little nuts. But the thought of the people I care about putting me away is still..." Something blocked my throat, stopping me from speaking.

The old lady dug in her black handbag. "Then think about something else."

I studied Wits' End's gabled rooftop. Suddenly, the loss of my grandmother pierced my heart again, as fresh as if she'd just left us.

My throat squeezed. "I miss her." And I knew I didn't need to say whom I meant.

"As do I."

"She was..."

"One of those people who seems to have a light inside them," Mrs. Steinberg said softly. "She attracted good people to her like moths to a flame."

"Did she... what did she tell you about my parents?"

"She told me enough." She puffed her e-cig.

"I'm so... grateful for the time I had with her. But I miss her so much. I wish... I wish, growing up, I'd appreciated those summers more, known what I had. I mean, I loved my summers here. They were light years better than what I had in San Francisco. But it was all her, you know?" I said inarticulately.

"She would have been proud of you."

I laughed, hollow. "Wits' End is barely making a profit. I need to replace the roof—"

"I'm not talking about Wits' End." She faced the horizon. "You've come a long way, Susan. And you've battled and beaten many demons."

We sat in silence for a time, because once again, I couldn't speak. I was too busy blinking back tears.

"Speaking of which," she said, "how's your murder investigation going?"

I wiped my eyes.

She puffed her e-cig. "Don't think I don't know what you're up to."

I reached for my planner and realized I'd left it in the kitchen.

"Well?" she asked.

I hung my head. I'd forgotten to ask the sheriff about Van Der Woodsen's final manuscript. "I don't suppose you know anything about Salvatore Van Der Woodsen's latest manuscript?"

Her snowy brows drew together. "That is an interesting question."

"It is?"

"Why do you think it matters?" she asked.

"Well, it sounds like it's worth a lot of money."

"His entire estate is worth over a hundred million."

"Dollars?" I squeaked. I couldn't imagine that much money.

"Dollars," she confirmed. "One manuscript, more or less, shouldn't make much of a difference."

She was right. If he'd been killed by an heir, the manuscript would simply be icing on the cake. I'd been on the wrong track.

Mrs. Steinberg blew a vanilla-scented smoke ring. "But money isn't the only reason people kill. There's prestige too, and desire."

Desire? I straightened on the log. "You seem to know a lot about Salvatore's estate."

Bailey woofed an agreement.

"I told you, Susan, I know a lot of things. For example, Salvatore never let anyone read his manuscripts before they went to his agent. But he didn't lock them up either. Anyone with access to his computer would have been able to read them. Salvatore didn't have a password. He thought they were annoying."

"Wait," I said. "Computer? His manuscript is electronic?"

"You weren't expecting a bundle of typewritten pages, were you? This is the twenty-first century."

Would the sheriff have gone through Salvatore's computer files? She must have. Unless someone else had gotten to them first. But again, did one manuscript matter in the big picture of his entire estate?

There's prestige too, and desire... I leapt to my feet. "I need to talk to someone."

"By all means. I'll just sit here for a while longer and enjoy the view."

I walked into the manzanita and hesitated on the narrow trail. She was an elderly woman, and the hillside was uneven. "Why don't we go together?" I turned.

Mrs. Steinberg had vanished.

By now, her sudden disappearances seemed almost anticlimactic. But the hillside was steep, and she was a little tottery. I hoped she was okay. "Mrs. Steinberg?" I called, scanning the manzanita.

No one answered, and I bit my bottom lip. I would have seen if she'd fallen. Ergo, she must have left on her own. But I was damned if I could see how she'd done it without me noticing.

I shivered and walked down the hill, Bailey at my side. Mrs. Steinberg never dropped hints that didn't lead somewhere interesting. And this was a trail I thought I could follow.

We emerged from behind the gazebo to find Mr. Baransky pacing in my backyard.

"Good morning," I said.

He raised a plump finger. "Do you smell that?"

I sniffed and smelled Sierra air and rose blossoms. "Smell what?"

"That rotting smell. I think a deer must have died somewhere in those trees." He motioned toward the hillside. "Did you see anything?"

"Um, no." I rubbed my arms. He couldn't possibly be smelling... a body, could he? "And I don't smell anything rotting."

"I have a very sensitive nose." He tapped it. "It helps with my work."

"I wouldn't worry about it," I said rapidly. "I'm sure nature will, er, take care of whatever's there."

"No, no. This is of great interest to me. I've called my friend, and he will help me find it. Don't worry, he'll get rid of whatever has died."

"Your friend?" I squeaked.

"From the forestry service. He is a ranger." He smiled, his scar crinkling, and looked past me. "And there he is now. Right on time."

A ranger in a green uniform strode across the lawn and raised his hand in greeting. "Sasha! What have you got for me?"

"A dead animal," he said. "A big one, I think."

"I don't smell anything," I said.

"Sasha's got a nose for these things." The ranger stuck out his hand. "I'm Wolf Gray."

He had a firm, competent handshake, and my insides plummeted. I had to derail these two. "Hi," I said. "Susan Witsend. But honestly, Mr. Baransky's probably smelling last week's deer."

Wolf quirked an eyebrow. "Last week's?"

"There was a dead deer just off the trail up there," I lied and pointed toward the hillside. "The coyotes got it. There may be some, um, remains left that Mr. Baransky's smelling. So how about those squirrels?"

Bailey howled and charged into the pines.

"Should you get him?" The ranger's eyebrows drew downward.

"He won't go far," I said.

Wolf grinned. "Has Sasha told you his crazy theory?"

"It is not crazy." The Russian drew himself up. "It is very well reasoned. Those flyers—"

"Are a hoax by some prankster," Wolf said.

"Who would play a prank like that in a town that just had a UFO panic?" Mr. Baransky asked.

"Would you two like to come inside for coffee?" I asked. *And get away from whatever Mr. Baransky is smelling?*

Bailey trotted to the gazebo, a sullen expression on his doggy face.

"Sure," the ranger said.

"But the deer," Mr. Baransky objected.

Bailey huffed.

Wolf knelt and rubbed the beagle's head. "Are you sure it was a coyote kill?" he asked me.

"I heard them howling," I said.

"And it's a week old?" The ranger wrinkled his nose.

"You Americans are so soft." Mr. Baransky snorted, and for a moment he sounded like my mother.

"I could go for some coffee," Wolf said.

"Bah." Mr. Baransky said. "So could I."

Relieved, I herded Bailey and the men into the kitchen. I settled them around the table with mugs of coffee. "Stay as long as you want, and feel free to help yourself to more coffee."

I grabbed my purse and hurried into the foyer.

My father walked down the steps from the rooms. "Susan. Your mother didn't mean it about the institution. She was only worried about you."

"Then she can stop worrying."

"But you have to admit, you have been behaving erratically. Leaving a good job in the Bay Area—"

I lowered my voice. "And by the way, a local ranger is here to look for a deer corpse on the hillside."

My father's eyes widened. "What?"

"So the clock's ticking on that body," I whispered angrily. *Behaving erratically?* That was rich coming from a couple of spies. "You need to get it away from Doyle once and for all."

"But—"

"He's in the kitchen with Mr. Baransky. Good luck. I have to go." I hurried out the door. I was done with letting my parents derail my plans.

CHAPTER TWENTY-SIX

WHAT'S THE GOOD BEING sane if everyone else thinks your nuts? My knuckles whitened on the wheel of my Crosstrek. My parents might not be serious about putting me away, but if the sheriff really questioned my sanity—

The shadow's chill brushed my shoulder. "Go away!" I slammed my hand on the steering wheel. But the shadow didn't retreat. It would always be there, waiting for a weak moment to pounce. And it had been having a field day since my parents had arrived.

And this time... I wasn't sure I could beat it back. It hadn't felt this close in a long time.

I released a slow breath and tried to remember my new coping technique. *I am peace and serenity. Peace and serenity.*

Mrs. Steinberg hadn't been wrong about the power of thinking about something else. Changing the channel in my mind to a new internal conversation didn't always shake my worry. But my muscles relaxed slightly.

I am peace and serenity.

Slowly, I drove down the residential street. And I *wasn't* crazy. I knew what was real and what wasn't. I'd helped solved crimes in the past. I'd helped calm the UFO panic.

But.

Anxiety was based on blowing up things in the mind that *might* happen, things that weren't yet real. And that was kind of irrational.

This self-analysis wasn't making me feel better.

Peace and serenity. My hands twisted on the wheel. "I am peace and serenity."

I reached for my planner on the seat beside me and touched only faux-leather. My chest tightened. The planner was at Wits' End.

I took yogic breaths. *Never mind the planner.* It was a crutch. I didn't need it. I'd just take notes on my phone and transcribe them later.

Now, what was the plan?

I couldn't bother Maive and Jacob again. They'd made it clear they were done talking. And though I had liability insurance, I didn't want to encourage their threatened lawsuit. Lawsuits?

But Malcolm hadn't threatened me with anything lately.

I turned onto Main Street. Its old-west false fronts glided past. Tourists browsed t-shirt shops. A trio of raucous teens emerged from the ice cream parlor.

"Squirrel!" The boy leapt onto a wooden bench and pointed toward a towering pine. His female companions laughed.

An elderly woman shot them an annoyed look and gave them wide berth.

I didn't need social media to guess where Malcolm would be. One of the good/bad things about small towns is you notice people's habits. I'd noticed Malcolm spent his Thursday mornings reading the paper at Alchemy. If I was lucky, he'd be there now.

And he was.

Malcolm hunched at the bar in a high, metal chair. A newspaper and near-empty coffee mug sat before him on the gold-veined, marble counter.

I slid onto an empty seat beside him. He glanced my way, his green and brown eyes dull.

"Oh, hi, Malcolm. Is this seat taken?"

He looked over the row of empty chairs. His gaze returned to rest on me, and I noticed his eyes looked a little pink today as well.

"No." He swallowed the last of his coffee. "And I'm getting the feeling you didn't choose this seat by accident."

"I *was* hoping to talk to you," I admitted.

He sighed. A whiff of alcohol crested on his breath. Had that coffee been spiked?

"So talk." Malcolm pushed aside the newspaper. "Did my sister stiff you on the bill? Because I'm not responsible for her debts."

"Stiff me? No. I thought—"

"That she had money? No. Maive always liked the good life. Her spending drove our father crazy. Did she threaten to sue you?"

Stomach butterflying, I shifted on the high chair. The only reason he'd jump to that... "Sue me? Does she do that a lot?"

He nodded. "I can't help you with that either. When Maive makes a decision, she won't let go, no matter the cost."

Damn. Would she have a case? Of course she would. This was California. If you hadn't been sued at least once, you weren't living.

"Don't look so worried," he said. "You have insurance, don't you?"

"Yes, but I still don't want to be sued."

Forget the lawsuit. Cowgirl up and detect. "I have a favor to ask." I fiddled with a red paper napkin on the counter. "It's about your father's last manuscript. My cousin Dixie is a huge fan, and I promised if I saw you again I'd ask if you could tell me anything about the plot."

"She's out of luck." His shoulders hunched. "I haven't seen it."

As usual, it looked like Mrs. Steinberg had been right. But Malcolm was still a suspect until I could prove otherwise. "This is a little awkward. But I thought I saw you Monday afternoon between five o'clock and six thirty," I lied.

"You were at the police station too? That *is* awkward."

"Police station?" I said, surprised. That...was a pretty good alibi.

"Ah." He shot me a fleeting smile. "You thought I killed Franklin."

"Sorry. I didn't mean—"

"I didn't. And I don't like it that someone killed him." Malcolm's brow furrowed. "I never liked the man, but I admired him."

"I heard he was something of a con artist."

His full lips crooked. "Maybe. He had my father's number, all right."

"What do you mean?"

"My father went through a new assistant or butler or whatever every few months. But Franklin stayed. He didn't put up with my dad's crap, and Dad thought he was funny. Franklin did good by my father, and for that, I'm grateful."

"Even if it meant disinheriting you?" That was hard to swallow.

"You mean that bit about him being a long-lost half-brother?" He shook his head. "Franklin was just yanking Maive's chain."

"I meant your father leaving him the estate in his will."

"But we're not disinherited anymore."

No, now that Franklin was dead, Malcolm and Maive were sitting pretty.

We sat in companionable silence. I'd never realized how restful interrogating possible murderers could be. Soothing, even. Maybe it's because I knew what I was doing. Maybe it was because I was away from my parents. But for a moment, I'd found that still center of the spinning wheel.

"At least Franklin *did* things," he burst out. "Not like me."

Automatically, I began to deny it. "You—"

"What? I do things too? But I don't," he said bitterly. "And my father knew it. The last thing he said to me was I was a failure. I can't stand it, but I don't know what—."

Lupita slammed her purse on the bar beside him, and we both jerked on our seats in surprise.

Her brown eyes flashed. "You don't like being a failure? Then stop acting like one."

He reared back, his eyes widening. "Lupita—"

"Don't you Lupita me." She rounded on me. "Do you know he has three half-finished screenplays sitting in his desk drawer? Three."

I shrank in my chair and willed myself invisible. But of course, that never works.

Malcolm half shrugged. "No one wants to read my—"

"How do you know no one wants? Have you sent any to an agent, or whatever one does with screenplays? No, because you haven't finished a single one. Not one!"

"You don't understand," he said. "It's not easy—"

"I understand perfectly. I have been too understanding of your artist's temperament and your fine feelings. Finish one of those damn manuscripts and send it off, or I'm done."

He straightened in his chair. "Is that an ultimatum?"

"Call it what you will. Decide what's more important to you—feeling sorry for yourself or being with me. Choose." She smiled at me. "Goodbye, Susan. Have a good day." With a toss of her long, dark hair, she stormed from the restaurant.

"Well," Malcolm said weakly, staring after her.

I slid from the chair. "I'll just... go."

Embarrassed by the scene, I hurried onto the sidewalk. I knew what it looked like when someone had been pushed too far. If I was any judge of human nature, Lupita had meant every word of her tirade.

"Susan," Arsen shouted.

He jogged across the street, a wrapped paper package beneath one arm, and pulled me into a bone melting kiss. Releasing me, Arsen handed me the package. "Happy birthday, Susan."

I blinked. I'd forgotten my own birthday. "Thanks." And I hadn't thought about Iceland either. Arsen would want an answer soon.

My chest tightened, my mother's words echoing in my mind. *You've been behaving erratically.* I swallowed. What if I *was* crazy? What would I be doing to Arsen? "But I thought Iceland was my birthday gift."

"We can't go to Iceland today, so you may as well open it."

I slipped my finger beneath the tape and pulled the paper free, revealing a leather-bound planner. "Arsen—"

"Open it," he urged. "I had it made special."

I unhooked the latch and opened the planner.

My breath caught. The pages had all the details I want-ed—monthly, weekly, and daily calendars. At the bottom of each day's page he'd added check boxes for FUN THINGS TO DO TODAY and TOMORROW'S BREAKFAST.

He'd upgraded my planner.

"Check the yellow tab," he said.

I opened to a tab marked CRIME. Instead of my ad-libbed notes pages. He'd upgraded these too. He'd included labeled columns organized by color for means, motive, and opportunity. And there were timelines and color-coded areas for clues and transcripts of conversations.

My heart caught. It was perfect.

"Do you like it?" he asked.

"I love it," I choked out.

"What's wrong?"

"The sheriff thinks I'm delusional," I blurted, "and my parents are killer spies."

"She thinks your parents are spies?"

"No, my parents *are* spies. That's why she thinks I'm crazy. She thinks it's all a fantasy, but I had to tell her the truth."

"Why?"

A Prius honked, drawing my gaze. The car edged around a trio of men in the street. They craned their necks and pointed at the pine outside the ice cream parlor.

I shook my head. "A Russian assassin attacked my parents last Friday. They killed him in self-defense. His body caused that smell in the roof UFO. They've been moving it around Wits' End all week."

"You'd think their organization would have some sort of cleaning crew to take care of that."

"I know, but they've recently retired and..." I stared.

His forehead was furrowed with concern, his hazel eyes serious. He should have been laughing or arguing with me. Anything but this calm acceptance.

"And what?" he asked.

"You... you believe me?"

"Yeah, sure."

"Are you crazy? It's a totally unbelievable story."

More people gathered around the tree, beside the ice cream parlor.

"I know what your parents do. Did," he corrected. "Well, I suspected."

My skin heated. I'd been shielding him for nothing? "How did you know?" I demanded.

He shrugged. "I asked around before I went to visit them last year. After hearing about their international work and what they'd put you through, I was suspicious. I admit, I didn't expect to learn what I did."

I collapsed against a Honda, and its alarm blared. I jerked away. "You... Who told you?" He would need serious government connections to get that kind of intel.

In front of the ice cream parlor, a man shouted and gripped the pine, shaking its slim trunk. Needles and pinecones plummeted to the pavement. A squirrel leapt from the tree and onto a wooden balcony. It scampered to the next building.

Arsen steered me away from the Honda. "No one told me anything. It's what they *didn't* tell me that put me onto it. Besides, your parents have all the classic tells. They seem completely average, boring even. But when I went to San Francisco to tell them about us, there wasn't a single souvenir from all their travels. Their home looked staged, fresh out of a department store. Most people who work overseas return loaded with carpets and kimonos. And it explains why they kept such close tabs on you. They wanted to protect you, and keep you from blowing their covers."

"That's... Well, that's just. *Right.* But Arsen, how can you...? They killed a man," I said quietly.

He took my hands. "Susan. What do you think I was doing in the Seals?"

I stared at him. *Arsen.* Happy, devil-may-care Arsen.

I'd never thought too much about what he'd done overseas. For most of the time I'd known him, I'd thought he'd been bouncing from one resort to another, romancing bored, better-looking women than me. But when I'd learned the truth, my image of him had in many ways stayed the same.

I covered my mouth with my hand, sickened. I'd seen what I'd wanted to see, and that had made me blind.

"Sue?"

But whatever had happened, whatever he'd done, he was a good man. He wasn't just a rock for me, he'd helped others too. I'd seen his kindness. If he'd killed, he wasn't a killer.

"I'm... I didn't think. Arsen, I'm so sorry. I'm such an idiot." *Idiot. Awful person. Self-centered.* "I don't know how you could stand me."

"Stand you? You're the only thing that keeps me sane. When you look at me—" He swallowed, looked away, coughed.

"What?" I asked.

"I'm a little worried about this body. Something's not right. Even if you're parents are retired, their agency should be taking care of this."

When I look at him, what? But he'd changed the subject for a reason, and I'd respect that. My heart swelled, my throat thickening. "I know," I said. "They're concerned about it too."

"And it's not a good sign that someone tracked them here," he said. "It sounds like their cover's been blown." He shook his head. "I'm sticking to you like glue until this is resolved, one way or another."

"You have no idea what this means to me." Not that he was protecting me, though that was lovely. But the way he'd taken my revelation in stride. The way that *he* looked at me—the way he always did. "Thank you."

"You're my girl," he said simply.

We stood there, gazing into each other's eyes, uncaring of the shouts echoing down the street. He loved me. He loved me in spite of my blinders and blunders. And I would do whatever it took to make him happy.

He sighed, breaking the spell. "Something else. I have a hard time believing the sheriff thinks you're crazy."

"She does. I overheard her talking to my parents. Well, I was eavesdropping. She suggested they get me professional help."

"What?" His brows slashed downward. "That's bull. We helped her solve all those murders."

"I know."

"And you helped her calm the UFO panic last year."

"I *know*."

"You're not crazy, Susan. If that's what the sheriff really thinks, she's the one with problems." He rubbed his chin. "Are you sure you didn't mishear?"

"I didn't catch the entire conversation," I admitted. "But I don't see how I could have misinterpreted what she said."

He shook his head. "Either the sheriff has lost it, or something else is going on. We're going to figure this out." He grasped my hand, and my heart thumped harder.

"We have to do it soon," I said. "If the sheriff finds out about the other body, I'm not sure what will happen."

Twin lines appeared between his eyebrows. "Then let's talk to your parents."

CHAPTER TWENTY-SEVEN

"My parents?" I stepped backward and stumbled over the uneven sidewalk. "Haven't you been listening? They can't know you know."

There was a shout down the street, and a beefy man pointed toward us. The squirrel raced along the wire fence bordering the dirt walk. It scampered up the side of an old barn.

"But I do know," Arsen said. "There's no sense pretending." He stroked my cheek. "You're not afraid I'll believe the sheriff's right?"

"No." I squeezed his hand. Arsen was my North Star. He was the one person I'd always been able to count on.

"Because you and I and the sheriff have been through too much together to think that," he said.

"I know. And yes I'll go to Iceland with you." Anything to get away from my parents. "Er, do we need to worry about that squirrel?" I pointed at the small crowd charging down Main Street.

The squirrel whistled, and with a flick of its bushy tail, scrambled onto the barn's rooftop.

"He can take care of himself," Arsen said. "It's that crowd I'm more worried about. We should tell the sheriff about this too—after we find out what McCourt's up to."

He walked around my Crosstrek and opened the driver's door for me.

"Wait. Sheriff? What?"

"Because we all know you're as sane as anyone in Doyle."

"In Doyle" was a big qualifier. The town *had* nearly burnt itself down once over an imaginary alien invasion.

But Arsen was right. The sheriff and I had worked together. She knew me. For her to say that to my parents was strange.

"All right," I said. "Let's talk to the sheriff."

A blur of brown leapt from the barn roof. With a whisk of his tail, the squirrel vanished safely into the pines.

The Doyle sheriff's station was a modern, three-story building of aqua-tinted glass. We walked through its high atrium dotted with Ficus trees and to a reception desk.

Behind it, a grizzled deputy gazed at us impassively. "Can I help you?" the beefy man asked, his tone disinterested.

"We're here to see Sheriff McCourt," Arsen said. "Arsen Holiday and Susan Witsend."

"Have you got an appointment?"

"Yes," Arsen lied.

The deputy picked up a phone receiver. Turning slightly away from us, he muttered into it.

I shot a look at Arsen, and he shrugged.

The deputy hung up and turned to the window. "I'll take you back."

We followed the man through a maze of air-conditioned hallways.

"That was easy," I muttered. And that worried me. I pursed my lips.

The deputy knocked on a frosted glass door. Plain black lettering read: SHERIFF MCCOURT.

"Come in," the sheriff called.

He opened the door and motioned us inside, closing the door behind us.

"Have you solved the murders yet?" Sheriff McCourt asked, her tone caustic.

She sat behind a battered metal desk in one of those luxury executive chairs. Her broad-brimmed hat hung on the coat rack between her desk and a wide window overlooking a stand of pines.

"No," I said. "Though as I'm sure you know, Lupita and Malcolm both have alibis for Franklin Asher's murder. Maive and Jacob alibi each other, though I'm not sure—"

"You didn't come here to review the suspects," she said.

"Did you find a new manuscript by Salvatore on his computer?" I asked.

"Susan," Arsen said warningly. I knew I was supposed to be clearing up this whole insanity business. But it was easier to stick to murder.

"No," she said. "Though it wasn't top of our list. Salvatore's fortune is extremely large. One more manuscript won't make much of a difference."

"But maybe there's more to it," I said, disappointed. I'd really thought the manuscript might be connected to these murders.

"Like what?" the sheriff asked.

"I... don't know," I admitted. "But that's only because we haven't seen the manuscript."

The sheriff shrugged. "Like I said, it shouldn't change the shape of Salvatore's estate much, especially when it's split between Malcolm and Maive."

Arsen whistled. "That's some estate."

"Then his children *are* the heirs now that Franklin is dead?" I asked, once again putting off the inevitable.

She nodded. "Is that all?"

"We saw some people chasing a squirrel down Main Street," I said.

"Great." She propped her head in her hand. "Just great. Knowing this town's luck, they'll all get rabies. I'll send some deputies. Anything else?"

I drew a deep breath. I couldn't put it off any longer. "Why did you tell my parents I was insane?"

She leaned back in her chair. It didn't squeak, didn't creak, didn't do any of the things the chairs at Wits' End did. "I'm sorry you overheard that."

"Then you did say it." Arsen's voice turned hard.

"I couldn't very well let your parents think I believed you," she said. "They were listening outside the door the entire time."

I blinked. "You... what?" The sheriff had been protecting me? My heart lifted. I'd been a fool to doubt.

"A friend of mine once stepped into a federal investigation," she said. "It had international ramifications, and he was warned off. But he didn't like how things were being shuffled under the rug, so he did his job." One corner of her mouth tilted upward. "That was the sort of guy he was." Her lips flattened. "He was out of that department so fast it would make your head spin."

"He was fired?" I breathed.

"Transferred," she said. "To Death Valley."

"Yikes," Arsen said. "I mean, the singing sands are awesome, but the temperatures..."

"I'd prefer to continue as sheriff of Doyle, where I might be able to make a difference. Now, what's going on that I need to know about?"

Doubt once again quivered inside me. Did the sheriff really need to know about the assassin buried somewhere at Wits' End? I glanced at Arsen.

He gave a small shake of his head.

I swallowed. "I'm not sure. My parents seem to have gotten themselves into something... international. But their agency hasn't given them the expected support."

"Because they've retired?"

"I don't know. It doesn't make sense. Retired or not—" How much could I risk saying?

"What sort of *something international*?" she asked.

I hesitated.

"If it affects Doyle," she said, "I need to know."

"It doesn't," I said.

She looked to Arsen for confirmation.

"If it did," he said, "we'd tell you."

Her nostrils flared. She nodded. "Fine."

I relaxed back in my chair. She wasn't going to make me tell. "Were you able to find anything on Baransky?"

The sheriff shook her head. "As far as I can tell, he's a wildlife biologist visiting from the Ukraine. Crimea, actually, though the territory's disputed between..." She shook her head. "Anyway, since he hit Doyle, Baransky's been spending most of his time with the forest rangers. So if he *is* a spy..." Her brow wrinkled.

"What?" I asked. "What are you thinking?"

Sheriff McCourt shook her head. "There's nothing that could interest a spy in our forest," she said firmly. "Anything else?"

"No," I said. "Thanks for your time."

We rose and made for the door.

"And good job on the pineapple lantern," she said, stopping us. "We found it on the trailhead behind the Van Der Woodsen property. There was blood on it, but no prints, unfortunately."

Arsen nodded.

"And Susan?" the sheriff asked.

I turned in the open doorway. Arsen paused in the hall.

"Happy birthday," she said. "Consider the fact I'm not arresting you for interfering in an investigation—again—your gift."

"Thanks." It was a backhanded congratulations, but warmth fizzed through my veins. The sheriff and I were a team again.

I drove Arsen to his Jeep, parked on Main Street. He left me with promises to return tonight for a birthday dinner, and I continued home.

An early arriving guest, a UFO enthusiast from Wyoming, pulled into the drive behind my Crosstrek, and I checked him in.

Pensive, I walked inside the B&B's kitchen. Bailey's dog bed was empty. The beagle was probably sunning himself in the garden.

What next? If Sherriff McCourt and I were a team again, I needed to pull my weight.

Stumped, I consulted my planner. It provided no helpful ideas to pursue. So I went online and ran another search for Salvatore's name in the news section. An article dated this morning popped up.

LOST MANUSCRIPT NEVER EXISTED?

Did bestselling thriller writer, Salvatore Van Der Woodsen, destroy his final manuscript? Or did it never exist? The author's much anticipated final work is now officially missing.

"I received a call from his daughter," his agent, Waldorf Manners, said. "She told me that in his final days, Salvatore was distraught and dissatisfied with his work. He felt that he'd grown too old to produce quality literature, and he destroyed the entire manuscript. Salvatore had spoken to me about difficulties with the new manuscript, but I had no idea he'd go so far."

When asked if the estate would try to recover the file from the author's computer, the agent said he'd strongly suggested the heirs do so. But his daughter said she would honor her father's wishes and let the manuscript "stay gone."

Calls to Ms. Van Der Woodsen were not returned.

Salvatore Van Der Woodsen was murdered by person or persons unknown. The police investigation is ongoing.

Missing? Deleted? Gone forever? It was worth millions. How did something that valuable disappear, and no one seemed to care? Salvatore's estate might be enormous, but still.

Baffled, I wandered into the side yard and inhaled the scent of Gran's roses. I bent to study President Lincoln. The bush had recovered remarkably well for having had a body dropped on it.

Bailey yipped from the gazebo. I glanced the beagle's way and sucked in a breath.

Mr. Baransky sat slumped, motionless, on the bench beside him.

CHAPTER TWENTY-EIGHT

MY HEART LEAPT INTO my throat. Oh my God. My parents had finally done it. They'd killed a guest.

I raced to the gazebo. "Mr. Baransky!"

The man straightened on the bench and turned toward me.

Stumbling over a tuft of grass, I slowed and pressed a hand to my racing heart.

He wasn't dead. Of course he wasn't dead. What had I been thinking? My parents wouldn't have left a dead body lying around. They may be retired, but they were still professionals.

He waved. "Hello, Miss Susan. I understand birthday felicitations are in order?"

"Thank you." I climbed the gazebo step. Behind me, the beagle shook his collar. "How's your day going?"

He frowned. "Have you ever had a theory, but the facts refuse to cooperate with it?"

"Frequently." And that was usually when you were supposed to get a new theory or search for more facts. The missing manuscript had been such a good explanation for Salvatore's death. "It's frustrating," I said. "You know the puzzle fits together, but the pieces don't add up."

"Exactly. I know there is something wrong in Doyle. The evidence of *what* is wrong is clear. No offense. Your town is charming, but that riot last year, and all the murders..." He shook his head.

Scalp prickling, I sat on the bench opposite him. What did a wildlife biologist know about murder?

Bailey rose and lumbered to me. The beagle dropped down and laid his head on my foot.

"But what does that have to do with...?" I started. "I mean, I thought you were a wildlife biologist?"

"Yes, of course. You cannot believe I blame UFOs for Doyle's high murder rate because I stay in a UFO hotel."

"B&B," I corrected absently, considering. But no. No one could think little gray men had killed Salvatore and Franklin. "It's obvious people were responsible for the riots and for the murders. Not the wildlife."

"Yes. This. And people are difficult. We still do not understand the human mind. Oh, we scientists poke and prod, and neuroscientists analyze, and quantum physicists predict. But science does not understand the *why* at the heart of things. Why do large objects bend spacetime? Why do people have subjective experiences? Why, why, why?"

That was precisely my problem. Why had Salvatore been killed? His money was the obvious explanation. "And the simplest explanation is usually the correct one," I muttered.

"Why?" he asked. "Why does the simplest explanation have to be right? Why can't the answer be complicated? People are sometimes simple, yes. But sometimes, we are not. Sometimes we do things because our feelings were hurt as a child, and it colors how we interact with the world. But as scientists, we don't see that why. We only see the reaction, and then we wonder."

"That's..." *Interesting.* An idea blossomed in my mind.

"You think it is crazy?"

"No, I think it's useful." I sprang to my feet. "Thank you."

I hurried into the Victorian and held the screen door open for Bailey. He huffed up the porch steps and into the kitchen.

Dixie stormed through the swinging door, a broom in her hand. "You're selling Wits' End?"

"No."

"Your parents told me you were selling. You can't sell."

"I'm not selling."

"Wits' End is your home," she said hotly. "It's your life. It's *my* life. You have no right to sell."

I jammed my fists on my hips. "I'm not selling Wits' End."

She drew breath to shout some more, then huffed it out. "Then why did your parents tell me you were selling?"

"Because they don't listen." A defect that seemed inherited, if my cousin was anything to go by.

"Oh. Well. Good." She turned and strode into the foyer.

Bailey looked up, his graying eyebrows twitching.

"So much drama." I opened my laptop on the kitchen table and looked up the number for Salvatore's agent. And then I called him.

"Manners, Manners and Manners," a woman answered.

"Hi, this is Susan... Sanders with the Doyle Times." I didn't think I'd get in too much trouble for impersonating a reporter. But it was better to play it safe and use a fake last name.

"Doyle?" she asked sharply.

"Yes." I leaned forward on the wooden chair. "We're doing a retrospective on Salvatore Van Der Woodsen's life and work. I'd hoped to get some quotes from Mr. Manners."

"Hold please."

Bland music played over the phone. Since the agent got a cut of Salvatore's earnings, any publicity was a potential paycheck. I hoped that meant he'd talk to me.

"This is Waldorf Manners," a man cut in.

"Hi, this is Susan Sanders from the Doyle Times." Whoops. I'd inadvertently created a name that rhymed with Waldorf's. "We're doing a—"

"Retrospective," he slurred.

I frowned. Had he been drinking?

"My assistant explained," he continued. "How can I help?"

"What can you tell me about his final manuscript?"

He hiccupped. "It was a new character, the first in a new series. He'd spent so much time with his hero, Jack Slone, it was blor—boring. Boring. So he created a new hero, a woman. So that would make her a heroine. I made a joke that he might get some blowback for that."

"For what?"

"For him being a man, writing a female heroine."

"What's wrong with that?"

He laughed caustically. "Readers—no scratch that, reviewers can be more sensitive these days. If you're not offended, you're not *living*. It was just a little joke on my part. He was Salvatore Van Der Woodsen. He could publish whatever he wanted and it would sell, and I told him so. We knew the critics would come down on him regard...regardless—they always did. He wasn't *literary*. But the readers loved him, and I knew the readers would buy. Hell, some controversy might even have squir—spurred book sales."

"Waldorf?" a woman's voice cut in. "Are you talking to a reporter?"

"No," he shouted.

"Your assistant told me you were talking to a reporter."

"Yes," he said, his voice muffled. "And I don't care. I'm tired of playing games. The literary world be damned. I'd set the whole thing on fire if—"

"Give me that phone," the woman snapped. "You're drunk."

"No." He belched. "It's mine. My phone. My opinions. I can say what I want. It's still a free country—leggo."

"Hello?" I asked. "Waldorf?"

"They'll come for you next," he bellowed. "They'll come for us all. Put that down. No, don't! Put it—"

A dial tone rang in my ear.

Okay... So Waldorf might be a *little* upset over the loss of his client and the manuscript. But he hadn't sounded irrational.

Much.

Could I trust what he'd told me?

I drummed my fingers on the table. How had a simple interrogation gotten so complicated?

Realization lightened my chest. "Why *can't* the answer be complicated?" I asked Bailey.

Because there was only one person who could steal that manuscript and get away with it.

Best. Birthday. Ever.

CHAPTER TWENTY-NINE

GRABBING MY OLD PLANNER, I strode into the foyer, Bailey at my heels.

Dixie stood at the printer. It whirred behind the reception desk.

"Printing an invoice?" I asked.

My cousin whipped around. "Um, yeah." She edged sideways, blocking my view of the printer.

"For whom?" No one else was checking out today. I opened my planner and scanned its pages to confirm there were no check-outs. In my frenzy of crime solving, I might have let a few things slide at the B&B.

Dixie shifted her weight. "Ah..."

Bailey's gaze ping-ponged between the two of us.

"Dixie, if you want to print something, I don't care."

"Okay. Thanks." A goldenrod sheet slipped off the printer tray to the rug.

My eyes narrowed. "What's that?"

"It's private."

I hurried around the scarred desk and snatched the flyer off the rug. A squirrel with two alien antennae goggled from the page.

"You're the one posting those alien..." I glanced at Bailey. "...S-word flyers."

She folded her arms. "So what if I am?"

"The sheriff's really worried about these." I shook the flyer at her.

Dixie snatched it from my hand. "The sheriff's paranoid."

"Para... After everything that's happened, of course she's paranoid. People are getting into fights over these things."

Dixie's brow crinkled. "That's not what they're supposed to do."

"What *are* they supposed to do?" I asked, exasperated.

"Show just how ridiculous these alien conspiracies are."

"Huh?" Dixie *loved* alien conspiracies.

I sat against the wooden desk. "The panic last year," I said hollowly. "The riot. You were trying to stop another riot, not spark a panic."

"Well, we can't keep tearing each other apart." She wrenched the paperback she'd been reading from the back pocket of her cargo shorts. "I thought this guy was supposed to know his stuff." Dixie brandished the book.

"You can't trick people into acting rational."

"Then what's the use?" Dixie dropped the slim book on the desk. "Everyone's dividing into camps. And everyone thinks the other camp isn't just wrong, they're infected by an evil alien virus. What'll be left? People are making themselves crazy. And stupid Tom Tarrant with his stupid podcast is making it worse."

I nodded. Dixie really hated that podcast. "They were listening to that podcast in Ground the other day."

"Tom's stupid podcast is the only thing benefiting from this craziness." She threw up her hands.

"You're probably right," I said. "But I don't think the answer to people being manipulated is to do a better job of manipulating them."

"Why not?"

"Because..." An appeal to morality wouldn't have much sway with my cousin. "Because it isn't working."

"Then what are we supposed to do?" she asked, voice tight.

I sighed and glanced at Bailey. "The alien you-know-what conspiracy was a noble and... unique effort. But it's gone wrong. It's
time to abort."

Dixie's head lowered. "There've been fights? Really?"

"Darla saw one herself." I told her about Mr. Parnassus and the
flying coffee cup. "The sheriff had to break it up. And I've seen
things too. People are getting tense. Arsen and I watched a gang
chase a squirrel down Main Street earlier today."

"And you didn't help the squirrel?"

"He escaped over a roof. He didn't need my help."

"Oh, forget it." She sagged and tugged on her pink-tipped hair.
"I can't believe Machiavelli was wrong."

"Not even Machiavelli could have predicted Doyle."

Her chin lifted. "Unless..."

"Unless what?" I asked, alarmed.

"Never mind. I have an idea. Thanks, Sue." She grabbed the book
and hurried outside. The twin screen doors banged in her wake.

I swayed, tasting bile. *Idea?* When Dixie got ideas, all sorts of
disastrous things happened, alien squirrels being a case in point. I
am peace. I am serenity. And I couldn't control Dixie—only myself.

I dug my phone from my pocket and called Sheriff McCourt. At
least I could put the sheriff at ease on one score.

"What?" she answered.

"The squirrel flyers aren't going to be a problem anymore."

Bailey bolted to his feet and howled.

I clapped a hand over the receiver. "Oh, come *on*," I whispered
to Bailey. "You've got to get over this."

There was a long silence on the sheriff's end of the call.

"Good," she finally said. "Thanks."

"And I have a theory about the murders."

"Of course you do."

A beam of reddish sunlight gleamed in the stained-glass transom above the door and struck me dead in the eyes. I winced and turned away.

"It has to do with that manuscript," I said.

She sighed. "Why wouldn't it? Okay. Tell me your theory."

I did, and there was an even longer silence.

"The timing might fit," she finally said. "But we're going to have to break that alibi."

I bounced on my toes. She'd said *we*. It felt good to be back on Team Sheriff.

"And by we," she continued, "I mean my department. It's a solid theory, and I'll take it from here."

"Right." *Sure.* The sheriff always told me to drop the case, and she never meant it. "Wait," I said. "Do you mean it?"

"Of course I mean it. Why wouldn't I mean it?"

Did she mean *that*? People really were complicated. "Okay. Got it."

"Do you get it? Because—"

"Gotta go, bye!" I hung up. Because in the end, it didn't matter what the sheriff meant or didn't mean. I knew how to crack this case, and it was my birthday. I couldn't think of a better day to stop a killer.

Also, it's usually considered good form to stop them as soon as possible, so they don't kill again.

I made another call.

"Hello?" Maive asked cautiously.

"Maive, it's Susan Witsend."

"I thought I told you—"

"I know what you told me, and I'm sure my insurance company will be devastated to hear about your lawsuit." I sat against the desk. "That's not why I'm calling."

"Why *are* you calling?"

"It's about your father's missing manuscript." I flattened a lump in the faux-Persian rug. "I read in the paper he deleted the file?"

"Yes."

"And you don't plan on trying to undelete it."

"If he didn't want that book to see the light of day," she said, "the least I could do is honor his wishes."

"But it's worth a lot of money."

"I already have plenty of money."

Now that Franklin was dead. "And Malcolm feels the same way?"

"Leave my brother out of this." She hung up.

I smiled.

Bailey looked up at me with a concerned expression in his brown eyes.

"It doesn't matter if she won't talk to me," I told the beagle.

I'd already gotten what I wanted.

CHAPTER THIRTY

NOW ALL I HAD to do was call the sheriff back and tell her about my strategy. I wasn't about to taunt a killer without backup from law enforcement.

I reached for the phone. Outside the B&B, a truck beeped, reversing. What was a truck doing outside Wits' End at this hour?

I hurried outside and around the corner of the Victorian. An exterminator truck sat parked in my driveway. A man carrying a spray cannister squirted the latticework beneath the front porch.

"Hello?" I asked. "What are you doing?"

"Exterminator," he said briefly.

I bristled. "You're not my exterminator."

"Subcontractor," he said.

"But my next appointment isn't for another two months," I said.

"It's a new treatment. Don't worry, you won't be charged. It's all part of your regular service."

I shook my head and returned to the kitchen.

Bailey was gone. The door to the foyer swung gently.

I opened my planner and found the number for the exterminator company. The exterminator may have been right about not being charged. But I couldn't risk being double-billed.

The porch door opened, and my mother strode inside. "Don't make that call."

"Why not?" And how did *she* know what call I was making?

"Put down the phone."

"I'm calling my pest control company."

"Don't."

"Why?"

My mother thrust her hands into her skirt pockets. "Because that's not your pest control company."

I counted to ten. "I know that, but—"

"It's mine."

"Yours," I said. "You mean, he's here to remove the you-know-what?"

"Well he's not here for the squirrels."

I would hope not. Bailey might not like the squirrels, but I thought they were cute.

"That's... great," I said. And about time. "Thank you."

"We can hardly sell the B&B with a body in it."

My hand tightened on the phone. "I'm not selling the B&B."

"Of course you are. I don't know when you got so obstreperous. You didn't get it from your father."

"I'm not selling, and I'm not moving back to San Francisco. The only place I'm going is Iceland, with Arsen."

"Why would you move to Iceland? The lava fields are stunning, but the weather is awful."

"I'm not moving there," I said. "We're taking a vacation."

"The nearest international airport is in San Francisco, so I don't know why—"

"Augh." I grabbed my planner and stormed into the foyer.

Two men laughed loudly in the breakfast room, and I stuck my head inside.

Mr. Baransky and Wolf, the forest ranger from yesterday, lounged around the oval table.

"My theory is sound," Mr. Baransky said.

The ranger caught my eye. "Let's ask the owner."

"Ask me what?" I edged inside the octagonal room.

Mr. Baransky gestured toward the window. Late afternoon sunlight flooded past the blue-patterned curtains. "Man has affected nature, yes?"

"Yes," I said cautiously.

"But nature also affects man, yes?"

It certainly affected me, and for the better. I couldn't imagine living in an urban environment like San Francisco again. "Sure."

"What is happening in Doyle with the squirrels, is, I believe, an example of this."

Arms folded, the ranger leaned back in his chair and grinned. "He thinks people are mistaking squirrels with bubonic plague for alien squirrels."

"It makes sense." Mr. Baransky gestured animatedly. "The squirrels behave oddly when infected. They become more passive, more willing to allow humans to approach. It seems suspicious, but instead of interpreting the squirrels as an infectious danger—"

"They think they're an alien threat," Wolf finished.

"Yes," Mr. Baransky said. "This is a classic example of the unpredictable interaction between humans and wildlife."

Bubonic plague? Was *that* what his visit was about? True, spies had covers. But it didn't seem to make a very *good* cover for espionage. Maybe he really was a specialist in wildlife biology?

The ranger rolled his eyes. "I've been hearing this since college."

"You two went to college together?" I asked.

"Best time of my life." Mr. Baransky beamed. "I love America!"

If Wolf knew him in college... Baransky *could* be a sleeper agent, but what were the odds? "You mean you actually came here to study the squirrels?" I asked.

"Yes," Mr. Baransky said. "I told you this."

"Then," I said, "I may have some bad news. I asked some questions in the, er, UFO community, and I learned the person who made these flyers is a prankster. The flyers aren't based on any squirrel behavior."

Mr. Baransky's face fell. "What? Are you sure?"

I nodded.

He waved a hand, brushing my objection aside. "It does not matter. This prankster got the idea from somewhere. Do you know who he is? Can I speak to him?"

"The person is very private," I said. "But I'll ask. What about your other friend? The one who was missing?"

Wolf rolled his eyes. "He somehow wound up in the *other* Doyle, California."

"Oh…" There were *two* Doyles in the Sierras. People didn't often get them confused. The other Doyle was smaller and in a different county. But it happened.

"But why didn't he answer his phone?" I asked.

"Dropped it in the toilet and broke the damn thing," Wolf said. "He always was a butterfingers. And there was no cell phone store in the other Doyle for him to get a replacement. He had to order one."

"And he couldn't email?" I asked.

"He hates typing," Mr. Baransky said. "Carpel tunnel syndrome."

"But he's definitely okay?" I asked.

Mr. Baransky nodded. "I saw him today."

I sagged, relieved. He wasn't dead. "Oh, boy."

Mr. Baransky chuckled. "He was so angry. He thought I had—how do you say?—ditched him."

"Where is he now?" I asked.

"At the Historic Doyle Hotel." Mr. Baransky checked his watch. "And I believe we will be late to meet him if we do not leave soon."

The two men rose. The ranger collected his hat, and they departed, laughing.

I hurried into the kitchen.

"SURPRISE!"

I jumped backward, my shoulder bashing the door frame.

Dixie, my parents, and Arsen stood around the kitchen table. An enormous birthday cake sat between them. Sparklers shot embers across its pink candy-confetti and white icing.

Bailey sat beneath the table and barked wildly.

I pressed a hand to my thudding heart. "Ah—"

My mother hurried around the table and hugged me. "The exterminators are gone, Susan. They removed the rat your clients smelled."

"That's... all I wanted for my birthday." I shook my head, because it truly was. "Thanks."

She stepped backward and beamed. "Happy birthday, dear."

"Oh," I said, "and it turns out Mr. Baransky is a *real* wildlife biologist."

"What does that have to do with your birthday?" Dixie asked.

"Nothing. But he'd like to talk to you about the flyers."

My cousin's green eyes widened. "You didn't tell him—"

"No," I said. "I didn't tell him who posted the flyers. Talking to him would be purely voluntary. A gesture of goodwill."

A smile played about her face. It was strangely disturbing. "I'll think about it," she said.

Arsen pulled me into his arms and kissed me. And even though the kiss was chaste, it almost made me forget Dixie's creepy smile.

Almost.

Involuntarily, my gaze drifted from Arsen to my cousin. Why *was* she smiling? She almost never smiled unless she was up to something or had just done something.

"Happy birthday," Arsen said. "You told your parents about Iceland. I'm glad."

"I didn't see any reason to hide it," I said.

He gave me a knowing look, and my face heated. My reluctance had been about more than Iceland. In spite of everything, this really was the best birthday ever.

My father cleared his throat and raised a champagne flute. "I think we should clear the air. About San Francisco—"

The kitchen door slammed open. Jacob Parker strode inside brandishing a gun. "Susan—" His eyes widened.

He scanned the gun across the room, pausing on my parents, Dixie, me and Arsen, and he rubbed his goatee. "Oh, hell."

CHAPTER THIRTY-ONE

WORST. BIRTHDAY. EVER.

"Jacob?" My heart banged unevenly against my ribs. "Did you, er, want something?" *Take the hint. Pretend this was a mistake, a joke, anything but what it really is.*

He aimed the gun at my chest. "Get over there." Jacob nodded to the sink.

The cake's sparklers crackled, and Jacob started.

Arsen grasped my wrist. He tugged me behind him, against the counter. "You don't want to do this, Jacob," he said. "You haven't done anything yet. Put down the gun."

"Susan should have let this go," Jacob said, his voice high and fast. "But she kept pushing and pushing and pushing."

Dixie pressed against my other side, and I realized Arsen had her wrist as well.

Breath rasping, I edged slightly sideways.

The barrel of Jacob's gun wavered toward my parents, who hadn't moved from their positions beside the kitchen table. The barrel shifted in turn to Arsen, to Dixie and to me.

A phone rang, vibrating in my pocket.

"Who's phone is that?" Jacob demanded.

"Mine," I squeaked.

"Show it to me."

I slid it free and checked the number. *Sheriff McCourt.* "It's the sheriff," I said, thrusting the phone out from behind Arsen. "If I don't answer, she'll know something's wrong. I always answer."

The phone rang again. The sparklers burned lower, shooting ash onto the cake's white frosting.

"Put it on speaker," he said. "And don't say anything about me."

I answered the phone. "Hi, Donna. How's it going?"

"Don—? Is your internet out?"

Dixie made a small, choking sound.

"I don't know," I said. "I haven't checked."

"Well, check, will you? Something's going on. I'm getting complaints from all over Doyle, as if they expect *me* to fix it. I'm not an internet repairwoman."

I checked my phone. No internet. "No, I don't have internet, *Donna*. Something *is* going on."

"Dammit." She hung up.

Oh, come on. Why hadn't she gotten the hint? I *never* called her Donna.

The phone rang again, and my heart jumped. Sheriff McCourt *had* taken the hint. I glanced at the screen. It was a number I didn't recognize.

"Who is it?" Jacob asked.

"A telemarketer."

"Put the phone on the table," Jacob snarled.

I sidled from behind Arsen, and Arsen moved forward with me.

"Not you, Arsen. Just Susan."

Arsen's muscles tensed. "Jacob—"

I touched his hand. "It's okay." I stepped forward and laid the phone on the kitchen table. "I'll just let it go to voicemail."

Looking confused, Bailey sat up in his dog bed.

I smiled and nodded at the beagle. "It's okay, Bailey. Stay."

A sparkler sputtered and extinguished.

"Okay? It's not okay," Jacob said. "Why did you have to keep asking questions? Malcolm's determined to find that manuscript now because of you."

"You mean, the manuscript you *stole*," I said. There were two trained killers in this room. Three, if you included Arsen. All I had to do was distract Jacob. "Did you plan on publishing it as your own?"

He paled. "How did you know?"

"It didn't make sense that Maive didn't care about the manuscript." My voice quavered. "She was covering for you."

"My wife doesn't know anything."

A bead of sweat trickled down my brow. I was pretty sure Maive *did* know. If Jacob knew she knew, would he kill her too? Had I just sold her out?

"Anyway," I said hastily, "if the manuscript was recovered, it would be sold. The proceeds would be split between Maive and Malcolm. There was no reason for them to hide it after Salvatore's death, unless they were trying to keep it from Franklin. But none of you knew Franklin was the heir until too late."

"Franklin influenced Salvatore. He was a conman from start to finish."

My mother edged sideways. The second sparkler fizzled out.

"Maybe," I said. "But there was only one person who could have taken that manuscript and successfully pawned it off as his own. You."

"How?" he scoffed. "As a series knock-off?"

My father shifted slightly to the left. The movement was barely noticeable if you weren't paying attention. But now he was fractionally closer to Jacob.

A third sparkler darkened.

"No," I said. "This book was the beginning of a new series, with a new, female heroine. No one had seen it, not even Salvatore's agent. You could pretend it was yours and finally get the glory. A big publisher, more sales... All you had to do was swap out the titles, and no one would know."

"I wouldn't have just swapped titles. I'd put my own stamp on it, my own style. I would have made it mine. It would have been mine," Jacob said, shrill. "Mine."

"So it's true," I said. "You killed him over the manuscript."

His gun hand trembled. "I deserved that book. I deserved a chance."

"Is that why you were arguing with Salvatore? Because you deserved a chance, and he wouldn't help you?"

"Publishing is about who you know or who you are. Salvatore could have helped me, but he refused." A vein pulsed in his forehead. "He said his daughter's husband should stand on his own two feet. It wasn't fair. Salvatore was privileged, rich, he'd had it all. He should have helped me."

"But he didn't," I said. "And so you killed him."

"I didn't mean to. It was an accident. It wasn't my fault. I lost my temper."

"You hit him with a wine bottle," I said. "What did you think would happen?"

"I *wasn't* thinking. Don't you get it? It was an accident."

"But he died, and you... didn't get the manuscript. What went wrong? Didn't you know where he kept it? Because you left his house without it."

"Franklin," he said. "I hadn't noticed the chainsaw stopping. I was about to search Salvatore's home office when I heard his damn whistling getting close. I barely got out of there before Franklin came in."

While I'd been watching Jacob, my mother had gotten another step closer.

"That's right." I rubbed my chin, drawing Jacob's gaze. "Franklin was nearby when you killed him. But he didn't see any cars in the drive. You must have come the back way, along the hiking trail. That means you were trying not to be seen. You went to the house planning to kill Salvatore. This was no spur-of-the-moment accident."

"You're wrong," he blurted.

"Your wife had been there earlier. Had she gone to plead your case and failed?"

His hand shook. "Salvatore should have been ashamed of himself. Maive was his *daughter*."

I nodded and tried to look understanding. "How frustrating for you."

"Salvatore was old," Jacob said. "He'd had his time. What did he need that manuscript for? His life was over anyway."

Two more sparklers winked out.

"I doubt Salvatore felt that way," I said unevenly. "And then Franklin found the manuscript. What happened next? Did he offer to sell it to you?"

"To Maive." He pointed with the gun for emphasis. "She knew what it could do for my career. But Franklin wanted a cut of the royalties. I could see he'd be bleeding us forever."

Then Maive *did* know about the book, and she knew Jacob wanted it badly.

"Why didn't you go with her to meet Franklin?" I asked.

"How do you know I didn't?"

"Because Arsen and I saw them together at that hotel. We assumed they were having an affair."

Jacob blinked. "An affair? She'd never to do that to me."

"Then why'd you let her go alone?"

"Because I didn't know about it. She didn't tell me about Franklin's proposal until afterward." His voice rose. "If I'd gone, things would have been different."

Of that I had no doubt. He'd have killed Franklin then and there.

I shoved aside the question of why Maive had kept the meeting secret. "So after Maive got home and told you the bad news, you went after Franklin. You took your car, parked in the garage, and exited out the rear of your condo complex." I nodded. "Once again, you drove alone to the trailhead. Then you walked to the mansion, killed Franklin, and took the manuscript. Was it on a thumb drive at that point?"

The last sparkler fizzed on, refusing to give up the ghost.

"Malcolm didn't need that book," Jacob said. "He had enough money from the estate. Half the value of that book was meaningless to him."

"But it meant something to you," I stalled. My father had edged another six inches closer to Jacob, and that was all he needed.

Jacob aimed the gun at my mother. "Back off."

Her mouth pressed tighter.

He jerked his head toward my father. "You too."

My father raised his hands and smiled. "I wouldn't dream of interfering."

"Step back," Jacob said. "Both of you."

My parents did, and my hopes of rescue evaporated. Jacob was on to my parents.

They couldn't save us.

We were on our own.

The final sparkler sputtered and died.

CHAPTER THIRTY-TWO

My stomach hardened. You'd think having spies for parents would give you *some* advantage over the bad guys.

My gaze darted about the kitchen. The knife block beside Arsen—useless. I couldn't throw knives.

The wooden chairs around the table? I wouldn't be able to club Jacob with one before he got a shot off.

Bailey beneath the table... Even on his best days, he'd never been an attack dog.

How was I supposed to save everyone? I was an amateur detective, not an assassin.

It's really unfair for people to expect you to excel at *everything*.

I exhaled slowly. *Okay. Calm.* In absence of a better plan, I'd just keep on with what I'd been doing. Delaying.

"Arsen and I were actually sitting outside your condo the evening you went to kill Franklin," I said. "But we were in the front lot. We'd watched Maive go inside. We didn't realize there was a rear exit."

Sweat beaded the thin strip of flesh above Jacob's goatee. "Now you're just stalling."

So is he. Hope rose in my chest. Jacob thought he'd catch me alone, and now he had a roomful of people to deal with. He didn't know what to do.

"I don't need to stall," I said. "You can't kill all of us."

"Why not?"

My insides turned to jelly. *Good question.* If he had a full magazine, he had at least seven rounds. He actually *could* shoot us all.

"Because... the other guests will hear you." Did Mr. Baransky's ranger friend carry a gun? Even if he did, they'd left the B&B and were probably out of earshot.

"Your guests will cower in their rooms until I'm gone," Jacob said, his goatee quivering.

"Take me as a hostage," I blurted.

Arsen growled low in his throat and grasped my hand. "No."

"It makes sense," I continued. "No one here will call the police as long as you have me. You can get away to Mexico, change your name, publish the book. It will all work out," I gabbled.

"Jacob can take me," Arsen said.

Jacob tilted his head. "No. I think Susan has the better plan. She's less likely to cause trouble. Susan, get over here. And move slowly."

Arsen's grip tightened on my wrist.

"It's okay," I whispered. "I know what I'm doing."

But I *didn't* know what I was doing. I had no clue. No idea. No plan. I didn't know how to improvise. All I knew was I needed to get Jacob out of here and away from the people I loved.

Arsen's grip loosened. He met my gaze and nodded slightly. And in spite of the situation, my heart lurched. Arsen believed in me, and that was all that mattered.

At least, I hoped that nod meant he believed in me, and not that he thought he'd figured out my mythical plan. That could make things complicated.

"Wait," Dixie said. "Take me."

"No," I said. "Shut up, Dixie."

"You shut up," she said.

"Don't take Dixie," I said. "She once stole a police car. You can't trust her."

"That is so unfair," she said. "I was an underprivileged, misunderstood youth. Plus, there were extenuating circumstances."

"And she's a hacker," I said. "She took down the Doyle internet."

Dixie's eyes widened. "How'd you know?"

Holy cow. She *had*? "You, um, looked too pleased when the sheriff called," I said, disbelieving. My cousin knew how to wreck the internet? I knew she was good with computers, but... Wow.

"Wait," Jacob said. "You really did that?"

"Why on earth would you shut down the local internet?" my mother asked.

"Because the internet's spinning everyone up," Dixie burst out, her pink-tipped hair quivering. "People found some innocent, joke flyers, which never meant to hurt anyone, and once they started talking about them online, it made everyone angry and scared and suspicious."

"I never liked the internet," my father said.

"I just wanted to give Doyle a break from thinking their neighbors might be evil aliens in disguise," Dixie grumbled. "I wanted them to think a little more critically about what they hear about UAPs."

"UAPs?" Jacob's brows slashed downward.

"That's the new acronym for UFOs," I said. "It stands for—"

"I *could* use someone who knows computers," Jacob said. "Dixie. Come here."

Dixie stepped from behind Arsen.

"She knows martial arts," I said quickly.

Dixie glared.

"Well," I said. "It's true. She has a brown belt in... something."

"Hapkido," Dixie snarled.

"That can't be a real thing," Jacob said.

"I know," I said, "right? But honestly, I'm the weak link here. Plus it's my birthday."

Jacob's brow drew downward. "What does that have to do with being taken hostage?"

"I didn't mean that as a birthday wish, just..." What had I meant? "Never mind. Don't take her, take me."

"Take me," my mother said. "I'm no threat."

"Oh, for Pete's sake," I stomped my foot.

Bailey started beneath the table and lumbered to standing.

"Will you all stop being so damned noble?" How was I supposed to formulate a plan with everyone confusing things?

"She's right," Jacob said. "This is taking too much time. Susan, get over here."

"*Thank* you." I edged toward the kitchen table. Because I finally had an idea. I had two trained spies, an ex-Navy SEAL, and Dixie, who was no dummy. They'd figure it out. They had to.

"Susan," my father said. "This is a bad idea."

"It could be worse," I said. "After all, the kitchen could be infested with *squirrels*."

Bailey howled and bolted for the kitchen door.

Jacob jerked backward, his gun arm swiveling.

Everything happened at once. An object bulleted past my left shoulder. My parents pounced, leaping toward Jacob. Dixie flung herself at my knees, and we went down in a heap.

There was a crash, a pained shout, a shot. Glass shattered. Bailey barked frantically.

"Everybody down," Sheriff McCourt roared.

I looked up.

My mother had pinned Jacob to the floor. One of her legs wrapped around his ankle in a lock that I knew from experience hurt like crazy.

My father kicked Jacob's gun across the linoleum toward the sheriff. Bailey bolted through the slowly closing porch door. Blood pooled beneath Jacob's shoulder.

Sheriff McCourt holstered her gun and pulled out a pair of cuffs. She glared at me. "Don't ever call me Donna again." The sheriff strode to Jacob.

"There's a knife under him," Arsen warned.

The sheriff grabbed Jacob's wrists and cuffed him. She lifted his shoulder slightly, withdrawing my bloodied paring knife.

"A knife?" That was what had zipped past me? I looked past Arsen to the butcher block counter.

My knife block had been pulled close to its edge, where we'd been standing. Arsen must have been working on getting the knife the whole time I'd been distracting Jacob.

Dixie untangled herself from my legs.

Helping me to my feet, Arsen pulled me into his arms.

I sank into his comforting embrace. Spent adrenaline cascaded through my system. I leaned against Arsen harder and blinked rapidly.

My father grasped my mother's hand and pulled her to standing. "Nice job, Susan, keeping him distracted."

"Getting in the way always was her strong suit," my mother agreed.

Ignoring the jab, I closed my eyes, hot with repressed tears. I could have lost everything tonight.

Arsen rubbed my back, and I focused on the gentle pressure of his palm. *Strange.* The shadow hadn't shown up in this, the worst of moments. I wasn't sure what that meant. But we were alive, and that was enough.

I blinked rapidly. And I wasn't going to cry.

Outside, Bailey loosed a low howl.

I stepped from Arsen's arms and forced a smile. "I'd better get Bailey before he actually finds a squirrel."

Arsen stretched his hand toward me. "Susan—"

"It's okay." I hurried outside.

Bailey braced his front paws on the wooden post holding Gran's spirit house and howled again.

I picked up the dog and studied the miniature house in the dusky evening light.

The beagle stretched his neck toward a nearby rose bush, sniffing.

I blew ash from the incense I'd burned that day off its tiny porch. A fallen pink petal fluttered into the air. The breeze caught it, and it floated over the picket fence.

Bailey sighed, and the petal vanished in the growing darkness.

Heart squeezing, I turned and carried the beagle toward the Victorian.

CHAPTER THIRTY-THREE

"HELLO?" A WOMAN CALLED from behind me.

Beagle in my arms, I turned.

My new neighbor stood on the other side of the picket fence. Her long blond hair was bound in a braid, and she wore a simple t-shirt and jeans. She was of Amazonian proportions, tall and fit.

She smiled at Bailey, fine lines crinkling the skin around her eyes. "Oh, hey there. You must be the dog mine is so terrified of."

"Your dog is afraid of Bailey?" I asked, incredulous.

"My dog is afraid of everything," she said, wry. "I heard a gunshot. Anyone hurt?"

"No. I mean, yes, there was a gunshot, and no one was hurt."

"Good. Can I assume the local cops have everything in hand?" She nodded toward my driveway, and Sheriff McCourt's SUV.

"They do," I said.

"Then next question: have you got internet?"

I winced. *Dixie!* "Um, no. There seems to be an outage."

"Rats. My phone's no good either for going online."

"Reception in the mountains can be spotty," I agreed.

She extended her hand. "I'm Rocky. Rocky Bridges."

"Susan Witsend." I shifted the beagle, and we shook.

"This is just a weekend cabin for me." She turned and motioned toward the A-frame. "I needed a getaway." She paused. "I don't usually volunteer this much info to someone I've just met. But since we're neighbors, it makes sense for you to know." She rubbed the back of her head. "And I can't seem to stop talking." She laughed lightly. "I blame not having internet service."

"The internet can be addicting," I agreed.

"If the internet's not working here," she said, "maybe I'll try that coffeeshop on Main Street."

"Sorry, I heard it's off all over Doyle."

"Then I guess I'll take the evening off." She grinned and wandered into her shingled cabin.

A woman's laughter carried from the court, and I ambled to the front yard. The couple who lived on my left stood in the street chatting with the stoners across the road.

Another couple wandered into the road to join them. A second Sheriff's SUV pulled into my driveway.

"Everything okay?" one of my neighbors asked me. She motioned to the sheriff's car.

"Yes," I said.

"I thought I heard a shot," she continued.

"Yes, you did, but no one was hurt. It's my birthday," I said, apropos of nothing, and heat raced to my face.

"Happy birthday," she said.

One of the stoners scratched his bare belly. "Hey, Susan. You got internet?"

"No," I called back. "It's out all over town, I hear."

"Bummer." He turned to the others, and they laughed.

Bemused, I wandered into the B&B. Of course Dixie had to turn the internet back on. But I'd never seen so many people outside and just talking.

It was... nice.

Guests converged on me in the foyer.

"What's going on?" an elderly man with coke-bottle glasses asked. "We heard a shot, and there's a police car in the driveway."

I stiffened. "I'm afraid there'll be more cars soon." There was no use hiding what had happened. This would make the news. "There was an arrest in the Van Der Woodsen murder case."

The other guests looked at each other, eyes widening with excitement.

The old man gaped. "An arrest? Here?"

"Yes," I said. "I'm sorry if the noise startled you."

"A killer? At Wits' End? This is the best B&B ever," a woman said loudly.

"That's..." I love UFO *people*. "Thank you."

"Is that why the internet's not working?" another woman asked.

"No," I said. "I hear it's out all over town. You know, you can get a good view of the action from the turret room upstairs. It should be unlocked since it's empty."

They bustled up the stairs and out of the way.

I blew out my breath, and Bailey and I walked into the kitchen.

Jacob sat, sullen, in one of the wooden chairs, his hands cuffed behind his back. "I'm not your problem," he said to the sheriff. "Dixie's the one who shut down the internet. You've got a terrorist in Doyle. She's probably the one who killed my father. I only came here to get her to confess."

"Shut down the internet?" My mother arched a brow. "Where did you come up with that fiction?"

Jacob's eyes bulged. "She admitted it, right here."

My parents looked at each other.

"I have no idea what he's talking about," my father said.

"All I heard was you telling us how much you hated your father-in-law," Arsen said.

Dixie folded her arms. "Lame."

"Plus," I said, "he tried to run me down with his bike."

A blond detective named Owen grasped Jacob's arm and hauled him to his feet. "You can tell us all about it at the station." He rolled his eyes and looked toward Dixie. "Sorry, Dix," Owen mouthed.

"Everyone blames me for everything," she said. "You steal one police car—There were extenuating circumstances, I tell you. But does anyone want to hear about that? No—"

"Susan?" the sheriff asked. "You know anything about this internet business?"

The others in the kitchen looked to me. But I couldn't lie to the sheriff. We were a team.

"Jacob's a liar and a killer," I said. "He threatened to shoot us all. What else do I need to know?"

"All right," the sheriff said. "I overheard enough before the shooting started. Since it's Susan's birthday, we'll take the rest of your statements tomorrow." She folded her notepad shut and slipped it into the breast pocket of her uniform shirt.

The sheriff and deputy strode from the kitchen, the deputy pushing Jacob ahead of him onto the porch. Their footsteps thunked on the stairs outside.

"Thanks," Dixie said to my mother. "For not narcing on me about the internet."

My mother shrugged. "You *are* my niece. And it seemed the least we could do after you knocked Susan out of the way of that bullet."

Arsen frowned at the broken window above the sink. "I'll get some plywood." He winked. "We wouldn't want to let any squirrels in."

Bailey bounced on his forelegs and barked. Arsen ruffled the beagle's fur and strode into the side yard.

"About the internet," I said. "You've got to fix it, Dixie. People and businesses depend on it."

"It's Thursday night," Dixie said. "Can't I just leave it off for the weekend?"

"I imagine the internet companies will be working on repairing it before then," my mother said.

My cousin smirked. "They can try."

My mother tapped her chin. "There's more to you than meets the eye," she told Dixie. "Have you ever considered a career in—"

"No," I said quickly. The last thing the world needed was Dixie in the spy industry. "No, she doesn't. Fine, keep the internet off until tomorrow."

"Whatever," Dixie said.

My father removed his glasses and polished them on the white tablecloth. "It seems we've underestimated you too, Susan."

"We have?" my mother asked.

"She did an excellent job diverting that Jacob fellow, talking his ear off. And then she set off Bailey." He chuckled. "I should have thought of it myself. We all knew his feelings about squirrels."

Short, vertical lines appeared between my mother's brows. "Well—"

"And we underestimated how tied in you are to this town," my father continued. "You, Arsen, and Dixie worked like a well-oiled team. I almost felt like your mother and I were in the way."

I shifted my weight. "I was sort of counting on you to take Jacob out. Not literally," I quickly added.

"We're proud of you," my father said. "You've made a home here and a thriving business. But now, we really need to go. We'll see you on your next birthday."

"You..." I stammered. "Next birthday?"

"You wouldn't be happy returning to San Francisco," he said. "Who needs an office job? I always hated that part of our work.

Here you've got fresh air, alien wildlife, and the occasional murder or two to solve. It's idyllic."

My mother's mouth puckered. She exhaled slowly through her nose. "Your father... is right. As usual," she said sourly. "Are our bags in the car?"

"Of course," my father said.

"Then we'll see you next year," she said.

"Wait," I said. "You're going now? What about the cake? What about the sheriff? She'll want to talk to you tomorrow."

"Oh," my mother said, "I doubt that. And we really do need to leave."

"But why?" I asked. "You're retired."

"Yes," she said, "but our old company insisted we be back in San Francisco in roughly three hours. If we leave now and I drive, we should be able to make it."

Three hours was tight, but my mother always had been the speedster in the family. "But—"

Arsen returned inside, a sheet of plywood beneath one arm. "There's a regular block party going on outside."

"Where'd you get the plywood so fast?" I asked.

"Got it from your new neighbor next door," he said. "Did you know she's in security?"

"No," I said, distracted.

My mother kissed my cheek. "Happy birthday, Susan. Goodbye, Arsen. Take good care of our daughter."

"She can take pretty good care of herself," Arsen said.

My mother drifted from the kitchen, and my father followed.

"Cool," Dixie said. "More cake for me."

"Not if I get to it first." Arsen pulled the plate closer.

I remembered the phone call. The telemarketer had left a message. I pressed play.

"Susan, it's Lupita. I just wanted to apologize for... You must have thought I was awful this morning at Alchemy. But Malcolm's writing again. Really writing. He says he's going to finish this time, and I'm damn well going to make sure he does. No more nice Lupita. Fierce Lupita seems to be more inspiring. So... All's well that ends well?" She hung up.

"Everything okay?" Arsen held a long knife poised above the cake.

"I think so," I said. "But... what about Jacob? What about Maive? She must have been covering for him, don't you think?"

"Oh, totally," Arsen said. "She had to have known Jacob had something to do with Franklin's death."

"Do you think the sheriff will arrest her?" I asked.

"It depends on whether she thinks Maive was in on it," Dixie said, "or just not wanting to face the facts."

Arsen studied me. "Part of the problem is your reputation. Jacob thought you were a threat from the get-go. I'd be willing to bet there were plenty of vacancies at the Historic Doyle Hotel."

"Jacob admitted the real reason they came to Wits' End was it was cheaper," I said.

"Or maybe he came because you were here. By staying at Wits' End, he could keep tabs on you."

I glanced at the plywood stapled over my kitchen window. Had I brought a killer to the B&B?

"I'd be willing to bet he was the one who threw that Jai Alai ball," Arsen growled. "He probably took one of Maive's."

"That does make sense." And if he wanted to frame Maive later...

"Your dad was right about solving murders though," he said. "It sure beats giving diving lessons."

Dixie made a face. "Ugh."

He sliced into the cake. Hastily, I plucked free the remains of the sparklers, now thin, gray sticks. The cake looked like strawberry—my favorite.

"I'm sorry about your friends," I said.

"Jacob wasn't a friend," he said. "And Maive was always the kind of person to look away from unpleasantness. It was one of her least attractive qualities. She looked away from the way her father treated her husband. And she looked away from the way it festered inside Jacob. And she looked away when her husband committed murder."

I gasped. "The stairs."

Dixie stabbed her cake with a fork. "What about the stairs?"

"Maive's fall," I said.

Bailey growled and raced through the doggie door. His howl echoed through the kitchen.

"She didn't even say *squirrel*," Dixie shouted after him and rolled her eyes. "I'll get him." She strode outside.

"You were saying about the stairs?" Arsen asked.

"I couldn't find anything that would have caused Maive to fall, but she was standing right next to Jacob. He must have tripped her up. She might have been looking away from the truth, but deep down she knew, and Jacob knew it. He must have planned on getting rid of her before publishing."

"Maybe." He caught my gaze. "You don't look away from anything."

I hesitated.

"What?" he asked.

"You said something earlier..."

"About Maive?"

"No, about me." I felt myself blushing. "You started to say something about the way I looked at you, and then you stopped. What were you going to say?"

Arsen's ears reddened. He reached across the table and took my hand. "I was going to say, that when you look at me, I see the past and the future. I see the man I want to be. I see everything that's good about Doyle and our lives, and I want to hold onto that. Because none of the craziness matters. You matter, and Dixie and my aunts and Mrs. Steinberg and the people at Antoine's and Ground..." He shook his head. "Sorry. I'm not making much sense."

"No. You do make sense." We were together, now, and that was what counted, and we sat in silence, content to hold hands.

The porch door opened, and our hands jerked apart.

Dixie stomped into the kitchen, Bailey in her arms. "Crisis averted."

"I should call the sheriff about Maive." I reached for my phone on the kitchen table.

"Sheriff McCourt's got Jacob in custody," Arsen said. "It can wait."

I wasn't so sure, because I didn't want to jeopardize my relationship with the Sheriff. We might not *exactly* be partners in crime solving, but we were partners of a sort. "I'll just make a quick call—"

Arsen took the phone from my hand and replaced it with a plate full of cake. "Cake first. Crime second."

Or I could just send her a text.

<<<<>>>>

Note from Kirsten

Though the title of this book comes from HG Wells's *War of the Worlds*, the story was inspired by the screwball comedies of the thirties and forties, and particularly by *Arsenic and Old Lace*.

As to the squirrel subplot, it was inspired by REAL EVENTS. While I was wandering around a small town in Colorado, I came across a flyer about trained squirrel spies. I hope whoever created the flyers posts more, because the world needs more ridiculous fun. Hopefully, this book has added a bit.

And there will be more! Susan and Arsen will be back for more UFO shenanigans in *Gnome Alone*, a holiday-themed mystery.

But while you're waiting, why not check out my quirky Tea & Tarot mystery series? Abigail Beanblossom dreams of opening a tearoom in her home town of San Borromeo (patron saint of heartburn). But a pesky body gets in the way...

Click here to get your copy of *Steeped in Murder* and start reading this cozy mystery series today!

A picture containing text, cup, coffee, drink

Description automatically generated

Tea, tarot, and trouble.

Abigail Beanblossom's dream of owning a tea room in her California beach town is about to come true. She's got the lease, the start-up funds, and the recipes. But Abigail's out of a tearoom and into hot water when her realtor turns out to be a conman... and then turns up dead.

But not even death puts an end to the conman's mischief. He rented the same space to a tarot reader, Hyperion Night. Convinced his tarot room is in the cards, Night's not letting go of the building without a fight.

But the two must work together, steeping themselves in the murky waters of the sham realtor's double dealings, in order to unearth the truth – before murder boils over again.

Steeped in Murder is the first book in the Tea and Tarot cozy mystery series. Recipes in the back of the book!

Click here to get your copy of *Steeped in Murder* so you can start reading this series today!

Turn the page to find a sample chapter of Steeped in Murder.

SNEAK PEEK OF STEEPED IN MURDER

IN MY DEFENSE, THE day didn't *seem* that murdery.

The scent of salt air mingled with my herbal teas – mint and rosemary and roses. Whimsical stalls for the farmer's market lined each side of the broad pier. The scene was cheerful, colorful, and felony-free.

I couldn't wait to escape.

My first-of-the-morning customer adjusted the glasses on her nose and peered at the tin. Her graying hair tossed in the warm breeze. "The leaves look so beautiful. I'd think you'd keep them in glass jars."

A teenager in a black maxi-skirt and thick eyeliner drifted across the pier to stand beside her.

"Tea keeps better out of the light and heat." I glanced longingly toward the end of the pier, and the labyrinth of low, pastel buildings that climbed the hills encircling the bay.

My customer opened the tin and sniffed. "Mm. Olallieberry. This tea won't be around long enough for me to worry about storage."

The teen grunted and pointed at the bundles of dried herbs, dangling from the black canvas awning. "Do any of your herbs have, you know, magical properties?"

The woman rolled her eyes. "Beryl, you and your ideas."

Magic? I smiled. "Magic is as magic does."

"What's that supposed to mean?" the goth asked.

It had been a saying of my grandmother's. It meant we make our own magic, that dreams come true when you work toward them. But instead, I said, "When prepared and drunk mindfully, a good tea transports you to another world of peace and tranquility. If that's not magic, I don't know what is."

"No, you don't." Beryl slouched across the pier toward a Tarot reader who'd set up across from my stand. A giant tabby cat sat in a miniature throne beside his table, covered in a purple velvet cloth.

"Ouch." I laughed. Fifteen years ago, I'd *been* that girl. "Tough crowd."

"Beryl's going through a phase." My customer stuffed the tea tin into her carrying bag. "It's hard to believe she was such an adorable toddler."

"Have a great morning," I called to her departing figure. Because in that moment, I was certain it *was* going to be great. I'd learned not to trust my intuition long ago, but who can blame me for being buffaloed? I lived in an adorable California beach town. The sun was shining. And I was about to start my new and improved life and open an actual tearoom. Things couldn't be better.

A voice in my head chirruped that I'd just jinxed everything, I didn't deserve perfection.

I told the voice to shut up. This was my fairytale, dammit.

I rearranged tins on the shelves and surveyed my tiny kingdom of tea. Tea blends mounded in antique copper bowls lined the front table display. A pallet sign – *Abigail's Teas! Hand blended!* – leaned against the metal pole that held up my black awning.

An elderly accordion player wandered down the pier. He waved to my grandfather, seated on a folding metal chair behind my table.

"Go and bother Tomas!" My grandfather shouted and pointed to the black canvas wall on his left. They normally shared a table – Gramps selling his horseradish and Tomas his salsa. The two men had an informal competition over which of their wares could make more grown men cry.

Gramps popped a blueberry into his mouth and laced his fingers over the stomach of his beige sweater vest. It strained against his brown-checked shirt.

The accordion player paused in front of the Tarot reader and blatted out a tune.

The fortune teller, a slender, Eurasian man about my age, narrowed his eyes and shooed away the accordionist. The giant tabby stared at me from its throne.

Unnerved by the cat's unwavering gaze, I shifted my own to a vegetable seller with Alice-in-Wonderland-sized purple cabbages and reddish carrots. Beside her stall, a little girl and her father sold ducklings and baby chicks from an apple crate.

I wiped my hands on the front of my apron and checked the clock on my phone.

My grandfather chuckled and adjusted the brown plaid cap on his head. "You know you want to see your new building." His blue eyes twinkled. "Just go. I can manage your stall."

"You're supposed to be managing ours, Frank," a wheezy masculine voice drifted through the black canvas wall.

"What's the matter? You think I don't know how to make change?" Gramps lifted an untamed gray brow.

Maybe I *could* sneak away. "Are you sure you don't mind?" The market wouldn't get busy for another hour or so.

"I mind!" Tomas laughed. "If you expect me to flog your horseradish, Beanblossom, you've got another think coming."

A duckling the color of Amish butter escaped the apple crate. It waddled toward my tea stand, and Gramps tossed a blueberry the duckling's way. The berry bounced along the rough wooden pier.

"See?" Gramps motioned toward the black canvas. "Tomas is okay with it."

Tomas poked his head around the canvas. Tall, lanky and olive skinned, he was the Abbott to my grandfather's Costello. They'd been best friends for decades. "I'm just giving you a hard time, Abigail." He straightened his plaid bowtie.

The duckling beelined for the berry and snapped up the treat. The tiny bird tilted its head and gazed at Gramps adoringly.

On its throne, the tabby hunched its shoulders and eyed the tiny puff of down.

I scooted around the table and swooped up the duck. "I think this is yours." I handed the warm fluff of down to its owner.

The duckling peeped.

"Thanks." The man strode to the apple crate. Shaking his head, he said something to his pigtailed daughter, and she pinked.

I wiped my hands on my apron. "If you're sure you don't mind."

"I once killed a man with a bottlecap," Tomas said. "I can sell my salsa and your grandfather's horseradish without breaking a sweat."

Gramps snorted and rolled his eyes.

Ignoring the invitation to rehash Tomas's old war story, I glanced toward the Tarot reader. He spoke to a woman draped in filmy scarves and hooked a leash on the tabby.

The woman dropped into his chair and riffled a deck of Tarot cards.

I fingered the key in the pocket of my jeans. I'd been plotting and planning my tearoom since I was a little girl. A room that would be elegant, cozy and fun, filled with warmth and genteel laughter.

The building of my dreams had been vacant for decades. I'd been certain someone would snatch it up before I could afford to. But the building had waited for me, like it was meant to be.

Whipping off my apron, I snatched up my purse filled with swatches and business plans. "Thanks. For everything." I kissed my grandfather's rough cheek, and my heart swelled with love. If it wasn't for him, none of this would be happening.

"Get out of here," he said.

Giddy, I strode down the pier, past stands of brilliant flowers and stalls flogging jam and honey, past stenciled signs proclaiming NO OVERHEAD CASTING to the fishermen who lined the railings.

My blouse's billowy blue-and-white sleeves rustled, tickling my arms. I swiped a curl of brown hair, streaked with gold highlights, out of my face.

To my left, a movement caught my attention. I glanced over my shoulder.

The Tarot reader paced me on the opposite side of the pier. He was handsome, with a straight nose, chiseled jaw, high cheek-bones, and almond-shaped eyes. His shock of black hair was fashionably tousled. In spite of the morning's warmth, he wore a gray turtleneck above his elegant slacks.

The tabby tugged sulkily on its rhinestone leash and pulled back toward the pier.

California. Grinning, I strode down the pier's sloping deck to the cement walk. The spring air smelled of suntan oil and ice cream cones. Surfers plied the Pacific's low waves. But the beach was mostly empty at this early hour, as were the narrow streets.

And my new building was just around the corner.

Footsteps sounded behind me, and the skin between my shoulder blades prickled. I shot another quick look over my shoulder.

The Tarot reader was there, close, his expression intent. He crossed to the opposite side of the narrow road, and my muscles released. *Ridiculous.* He wasn't following me. There was only one way off the pier, and the town of San Borromeo was small. I was being paranoid.

I clasped my big portfolio bag to my chest and resumed daydreaming. My menu had been planned to the last scone. I'd drawn up sketches of the interior. But I needed to spend time inside to see if my dreams would fit the reality of a sixty-year-old structure that hadn't been occupied for thirty-plus years.

The kitchen would need new equipment. I'd have to strip the walls. New floors – wooden, of course, for warmth. Would green florals be too cutesy? Because they'd match my potted ferns perfectly and the drying herbs I intended to hang over the counter. Shelves behind it, where I'd sell tins of loose tea...

I glanced to my left.

The Tarot reader strolled past a shop selling beachwear. The tabby sneered.

I did a doubletake.

Yes, the cat was definitely sneering.

Lengthening my strides, I passed a restaurant and glanced in its broad, picture window. It was packed to the gills with diners eating leisurely breakfasts. In the reflection, the Tarot reader fell slightly behind me.

My new tearoom, a faded purple stucco building, stood on the corner of a pedestrian shopping area opposite. Art galleries and shops selling whirligigs and seashells lined the brick walkway. The owner of the t-shirt shop next door waved from his doorway. "Glad you got the place, Abigail!"

"Thanks!" Heart pounding with excitement, I fingered the key in the pocket of my jeans and jogged across the street. The building wasn't much to look at now, not with brown paper lining its dusty windows. But once I'd painted the stucco white, cleaned the windows and added flower boxes, the exterior would be perfect.

It was the sky-blue door that had captured my heart. Intricate molding. Tall, narrow windows at the top. A gorgeous doorknob with a poppy inset. Its siren song had been calling me for years, hinting at treasures hidden within.

The Tarot reader's footsteps padded behind me, and I dared another look over my shoulder. The enormous cat bounded forward. Its tawny eyes focused on my ankle.

Clutching my purse, I nodded to the man and promptly stumbled over a loose brick.

He nodded back as he caught up with me.

In awkward silence we walked side by side, weaving around potted plants. He pulled a key from the pocket of his gray slacks.

We reached the blue door at the same time and grabbed for the intricate knob.

"Hey!" We said in unison, twin keys extended.

"What are you doing?" he asked.

"What are *you* doing?"

"That's my building."

I blinked. "No, it's my building. I rented it starting today."

"I rented it starting today."

We eyed each other.

My stomach plummeted to the tips of my sandals. It was a mistake, that was all. A mistake. Something silly I'd laugh about with Gramps and Tomas later.

"My realtor," I said, "is Reince—"

"Briggs," he whispered.

"Oh, no." Something was seriously wrong, and my heart clenched. "I rented this building from Reince Briggs for a tearoom."

His skin turned a shade lighter. "I rented it for a Tarot parlor."

In a major earthquake, the ground is not your friend. The solidity of something beneath one's feet is so taken for granted that the shock of it confuses, disorients, terrifies. I felt that shock now, and the image of tiny white shoes floated into my mind.

A nearby whirligig rattled loudly.

"But… it's my new tearoom!" I bleated. "I have swatches!"

He glanced at the green and white fabrics spilling from my ginormous purse. "They're lovely swatches."

"You don't think… It has to be… Could it be a mistake?"

"Check your key."

I slid it into the lock, turned it. The blue door clicked open. Dust billowed from the opening on a draft of stale air. "Now yours."

He tried his key. It turned smoothly. His Adam's apple bobbed. "You didn't, er, pay up front, did you?"

"Six months' rent." My voice cracked. At California prices, it had been a lot of money. "I paid yesterday."

"I paid for three months yesterday too."

"How could Reince have rented it to us both?" I raked my fingers through my hair. Saint Borromeo *was* the patron saint of indigestion. Maybe I should have taken that as an omen before trying to start a tearoom here.

"Obviously, there's some mistake." A muscle pulsed in his jaw. "I should have known when I drew the five of swords. It's always trouble for me."

The cat stood on its hind legs and pressed its front paws to my knee.

"Ignore Bastet." The man's face cleared. "But I also drew the World card, and that means my Tarot room can't go wrong." He snapped his long fingers. "Who put you up to this? One of the gals at the Ren Faire? It was Winifred, wasn't it?"

"I'm not joking. This isn't a joke."

Oblivious to the drama, a family of three ambled past us in shorts and tees.

"No." I shook my head and stepped backward. The Tarot reader was right. It was a mistake, that was all. It had taken me years to save up the money for the tearoom, and in the end, I'd had to borrow some from Gramps, the man who'd raised me like his own daughter. But the image of those childish shoes rose again to my mind. I pushed the vision away. "There's got to be a rational explanation. I'll find out what."

"Good for you," he said briskly. "Let me know what you learn." He pushed open the door and stepped inside.

"Wait. What are you doing?"

"Going inside of course. World card!" He hauled the resisting feline inside.

"But I rented that building too."

"Look, you seem like a sincere sort of schmuck, so I say this with heartfelt sincerity, goodwill, peace on earth, and all that jazz. It ain't happening. You've made a mistake. This is my building."

"But—"

"The cards don't lie. I even consulted an astrologer, though I find that form of prognostication wooly at best, but she gave me a discount. And she assured me that today was my day. The stars are aligned. This is my tarot room, all's fair in love and Tarot, and you, dear lady, are SOL, even if you do look like an elf." He patted my head. "Buck up. You'll get through this." He shut the door in my face.

My hands clenched. "Oooh!" I blew out my breath. There was no sense in getting mad, even if he totally deserved it. And I might be height-challenged, but I do *not* look like an elf.

I'd just sort things out myself.

Forcing down my panic, I walked down the brick walk and around the corner to the parking lot. Parking was tight in the tiny beach town, and I'd figured now that I was a renter, I could use the building's rear lot.

My throat tightened. It was a little ridiculous how excited I'd been parking my car here this morning.

Unlocking my blue Mazda, I dumped the fabric swatches in the hatchback.

I leaned against the warm car door and called the realtor. Maybe the Tarot reader had taken the wrong key or... something.

The phone rang twice before I noticed an answering echo nearby.

Brow furrowed, I scanned the lot, still near-empty at this early hour.

The ringing seemed to come from a dumpster near the bank's rear entrance.

Wary, I followed the sound, my head cocked, my phone loose at my side. "Hello?"

I passed the ATM and the glass door to the bank. A faint, unpleasant odor wafted from the dumpster, and I wrinkled my nose.

The ringing stopped.

I checked my phone. It had gone to voice mail.

I hung up and dialed again. An answering ring echoed off the concrete wall. Hand tightening on my phone, I walked around the dumpster. Reince's red sports car sat parked on the opposite side.

I sucked in my breath.

The realtor lay on his back beside the dumpster. His head rested against a concrete parking curb, stained brown-red with blood.

Click here to get your copy of *Steeped in Murder* so you can start reading this hilarious cozy mystery series today.

Join the Society

Escape with Fortune Favors *the Grave*, a free novella in the Tea and Tarot series, by joining .

Plus, society members will get other free short stories and exclusive reads. Sign up and become a member today!

If you have trouble with the image above, click here:

Here's a bit from Abigail about *Fortune Favors the Grave*:

Some people have the cockeyed idea running a tearoom is an elegant and genteel profession. I'd thought it would be elegant and genteel.

Some people haven't met my business partner, Hyperion Night.

In fairness, I can't entirely blame Hyperion for embroiling our tea and tarot room in a murder. After all, he was chained to the San Borromeo pier when California's most famous psychic, Trevor Amalfi, was killed.

And yet, here I am. And here we are. Embroiled.

Fortune Favors the Grave is an exclusive *Tea and Tarot* novella only for Raven(ous) Society Members!

More Kirsten Weiss

THE PERFECTLY PROPER PARANORMAL Museum Mysteries

When highflying Maddie Kosloski is railroaded into managing her small-town's paranormal museum, she tells herself it's only temporary… until a corpse in the museum embroils her in murders past and present.

If you love quirky characters and cats with attitude, you'll love this laugh-out-loud cozy mystery series with a light paranormal twist. It's perfect for fans of Jana DeLeon, Laura Childs, and Juliet Blackwell. Start with book 1, *The Perfectly Proper Paranormal Museum*, and experience these charming wine-country whodunits today.

The Tea & Tarot Cozy Mysteries

Welcome to Beanblossom's Tea and Tarot, where each and every cozy mystery brews up hilarious trouble.

Abigail Beanblossom's dream of owning a tearoom is about to come true. She's got the lease, the start-up funds, and the recipes. But Abigail's out of a tearoom and into hot water when her realtor turns out to be a conman… and then turns up dead.

Take a whimsical journey with Abigail and her partner Hyperion through the seaside town of San Borromeo (patron saint of heartburn sufferers). And be sure to check out the easy tearoom recipes in the back of each book! Start the adventure with book 1, *Steeped in Murder*.

The Wits' End Cozy Mysteries

Cozy mysteries that are out of this world...

Running the best little UFO-themed B&B in the Sierras takes organization, breakfasting chops, and a talent for turning up trouble.

The truth is out there... Way out there in these hilarious whodunits. Start the series and beam up book 1, *At Wits' End*, today!

Pie Town Cozy Mysteries

When Val followed her fiancé to coastal San Nicholas, she had ambitions of starting a new life and a pie shop. One broken engagement later, at least her dream of opening a pie shop has come true.... Until one of her regulars keels over at the counter.

Welcome to Pie Town, where Val and pie-crust specialist Charlene are baking up hilarious trouble. Start this laugh-out-loud cozy mystery series with book 1, *The Quiche and the Dead.*

A Big Murder Mystery Series

Small Town. Big Murder.

The number one secret to my success as a bodyguard? Staying under the radar. But when a wildly public disaster blew up my career and reputation, it turned my perfect, solitary life upside down.

I thought my tiny hometown of Nowhere would be the ideal out-of-the-way refuge to wait out the media storm.

It wasn't.

My little brother had moved into a treehouse. The obscure mountain town had decided to attract tourists with the world's largest collection of big things... Yes, Nowhere now has the world's largest pizza cutter. And lawn flamingo. And ball of yarn...

And then I stumbled over a dead body.

All the evidence points to my brother being the bad guy. I may have been out of his life for a while—okay, five years—but I know he's no killer. Can I clear my brother before he becomes Nowhere's next Big Fatality?

A fast-paced and funny cozy mystery series, start with Big Shot.

The Doyle Witch Mysteries

In a mountain town where magic lies hidden in its foundations and forests, three witchy sisters must master their powers and shatter a curse before it destroys them and the home they love.

This thrilling witch mystery series is perfect for fans of Annabel Chase, Adele Abbot, and Amanda Lee. If you love stories rich with packed with magic, mystery, and murder, you'll love the Witches of Doyle. Follow the magic with the Doyle Witch trilogy, starting with book 1, *Bound*.

The Riga Hayworth Paranormal Mysteries

Her gargoyle's got an attitude.

Her magic's on the blink.

Alchemy might be the cure... if Riga can survive long enough to puzzle out its mysteries.

All Riga wants is to solve her own personal mystery—how to rebuild her magical life. But her new talent for unearthing murder keeps getting in the way...

If you're looking for a magical page-turner with a complicated, 40-something heroine, read the paranormal mystery series that fans of Patricia Briggs and Ilona Andrews call AMAZING! Start your next adventure with book 1, *The Alchemical Detective*.

Sensibility Grey Steampunk Suspense

California Territory, 1848.

Steam-powered technology is still in its infancy.

Gold has been discovered, emptying the village of San Francisco of its male population.

And newly arrived immigrant, Englishwoman Sensibility Grey, is alone.

The territory may hold more dangers than Sensibility can manage. Pursued by government agents and a secret society, Sensibility must decipher her father's clockwork secrets, before time runs out.

If you love over-the-top characters, twisty mysteries, and complicated heroines, you'll love the Sensibility Grey series of steampunk suspense. Start this steampunk adventure with book 1, *Steam and Sensibility*.

Get Kirsten's Mobile App

Keep up with the latest book news, and get free short stories,
scone recipes and more by downloading Kirsten's mobile app.
Just click HERE to get started or use the QR code below.
Or make sure you're on Kirsten's email list to get your free copy of
the Tea & Tarot mystery, *Fortune Favors the Grave*.
You can do that here: KirstenWeiss.com or use the QR code below:

Connect with Kirsten

You can download my free app here:

https://kirstenweissbooks.beezer.com

Or sign up for my newsletter and get a special digital prize pack for joining, including an exclusive Tea & Tarot novella, *Fortune Favors the Grave.*

https://kirstenweiss.com

Or maybe you'd like to chat with other whimsical mystery fans? Come join Kirsten's reader page on Facebook:

https://www.facebook.com/kirsten.weiss

Or... sign up for my read and review team on Booksprout:

https://booksprout.co/author/8142/kirsten-weiss

Other misterio press books

Please check out these other great *misterio press* series:

Karma's A Bitch: Pet Psychic Mysteries

by Shannon Esposito

Multiple Motives: Kate Huntington Mysteries

by Kassandra Lamb

The Metaphysical Detective: Riga Hayworth Paranormal

Mysteries

by Kirsten Weiss

Dangerous

and Unseemly: Concordia Wells Historical Mysteries

by K.B. Owen

Murder, Honey: Carol Sabala Mysteries

by Vinnie Hansen

Payback: Unintended Consequences Romantic Suspense

by Jessica Dale

Buried in the Dark: Frankie O'Farrell Mysteries

by Shannon Esposito

To Kill A Labrador: Marcia Banks and Buddy Cozy Mysteries

by Kassandra Lamb

Lethal Assumptions: C.o.P. on the Scene Mysteries

by Kassandra Lamb

Never

Sleep: Chronicles of a Lady Detective Historical Mysteries

by K.B. Owen

Bound: Witches of Doyle Cozy Mysteries

by Kirsten Weiss

At Wits' End Doyle Cozy Mysteries

by Kirsten Weiss

Steeped In Murder: Tea and Tarot Mysteries

by Kirsten Weiss

The Perfectly Proper Paranormal Museum Mysteries

by Kirsten Weiss

Big

Shot: The Big Murder Mysteries

by Kirsten Weiss

Steam and Sensibility: Sensibility Grey Steampunk Mysteries

by Kirsten Weiss

Full

Mortality: Nikki Latrelle Mysteries

by Sasscer Hill

ChainLinked: Moccasin Cove Mysteries

by Liz Boeger

Maui Widow Waltz: Islands of Aloha Mysteries

by JoAnn Bassett

Plus even more great mysteries/thrillers in the *misterio press*

bookstore